About the author

Hedley Harrison graduated from London University and joined a major oil company, progressing to senior management and seeing service in the UK, Nigeria, Australia and the North Sea. He has published four other novels with The Book Guild: *Coup* in 2011, *Disunited States* in 2013, *China Wife* in 2015 and *Sorak's Redemption* in 2016.

Sorak Returns

Hedley Harrison

The Book Guild Ltd

First published in Great Britain in 2018 by
The Book Guild Ltd
9 Priory Business Park
Wistow Road, Kibworth
Leicestershire, LE8 0RX
Freephone: 0800 999 2982
www.bookguild.co.uk
Email: info@bookguild.co.uk
Twitter: @bookguild

Typeset in Sabon MT

Printed and bound in Great Britain by CPI Group (UK) Ltd, Croydon, CR0 4YY

ISBN 978 1912362 684

British Library Cataloguing in Publication Data.
A catalogue record for this book is available from the British Library.

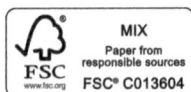

FSC
www.fsc.org

MIX
Paper from
responsible sources
FSC® C013604

*How can we know that what's out there
is any different from ourselves?*

CITY MAP

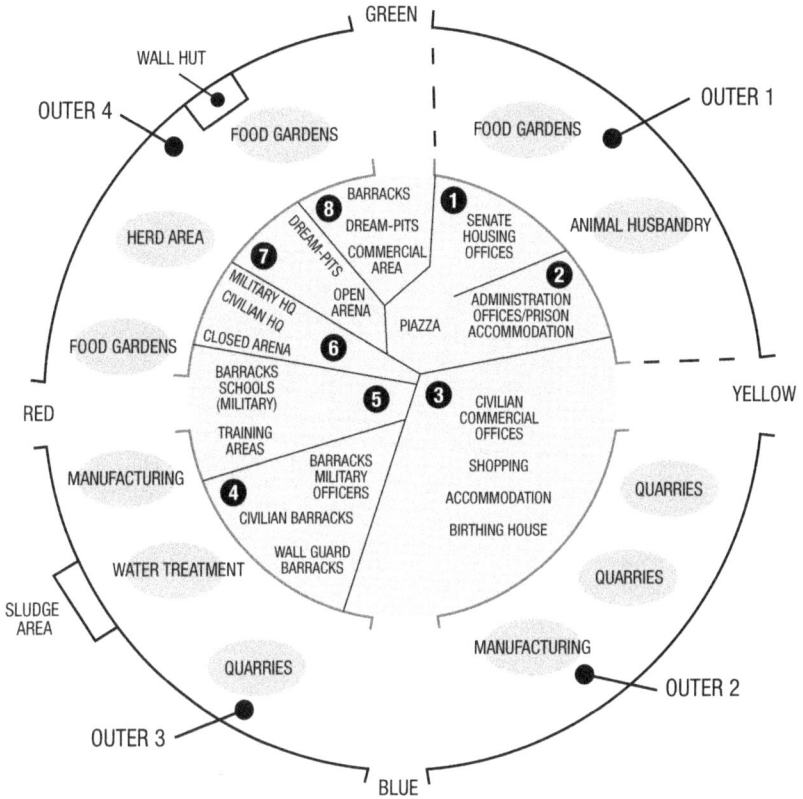

GREEN

WALL HUT

OUTER 4

OUTER 1

FOOD GARDENS

FOOD GARDENS

HERD AREA

❽ BARRACKS

DREAM-PITS

❶ SENATE HOUSING OFFICES

ANIMAL HUSBANDRY

❼ MILITARY HQ CIVILIAN HQ

DREAM-PITS

COMMERCIAL AREA

OPEN ARENA

❷ ADMINISTRATION OFFICES/PRISON ACCOMMODATION

FOOD GARDENS

CLOSED ARENA

❻

PIAZZA

RED

BARRACKS SCHOOLS (MILITARY)

❺

❸ CIVILIAN COMMERCIAL OFFICES

YELLOW

TRAINING AREAS

SHOPPING

MANUFACTURING

❹

BARRACKS MILITARY OFFICERS

ACCOMMODATION

QUARRIES

CIVILIAN BARRACKS

BIRTHING HOUSE

WATER TREATMENT

WALL GUARD BARRACKS

QUARRIES

SLUDGE AREA

QUARRIES

MANUFACTURING

OUTER 3

OUTER 2

QUARRIES

BLUE

SECTOR **❶** – **❽**

PART ONE

1

The sudden cries, the thuds of crossbow fire, only lasted what seemed like no more than the passage of a few breaths. The silence that followed was ominous.

Later as a night patrol hurried into the square in front of the burned-out Senate House the carnage was obvious. The bodies of three men, their clothes identifying them as administrators, lay in a tangled mess as if they had been killed separately and then dumped together in a heap. The patrol tenant immediately recognised what had taken place. Nervous, new to the job of soldiering and all too familiar with the inter-gender warfare going on, all he wanted to do was pass responsibility for dealing with the situation on to someone else.

"Call the capan," he told himself, "it's happening again."

The capan, an older man with marginally more experience, arrived with a second patrol as escort, a mark of the fearfulness that had seeped into the city when night fell.

"Women," he muttered. Who else could it have been?

What he was witnessing was the aftermath of yet another incident in the escalating violence between the male city authorities who had replaced the women of previous times, and one of the increasing numbers of dissident female groups. Such killings were an almost nightly occurrence.

At first capable of only imitating the administration that they had taken over from the women, the successive male Senates had failed to establish an authority comparable to that of the past, and the expectations from the revolution after seventeen cycles of the distant star had become lost in petty squabbles and increasingly violent gender rivalries. The men had proved incapable of establishing a more equitable society for the benefit of everybody. And it was far from clear that ultimate equality was what the men who had risen to the top of the city structure over the cycles truly wanted. Throughout the city's history they had known only domination and subjugation, either directly or through the tales from the past of the older men. Thinking of anything other than domination and subjugation had now become beyond the capabilities of most of the inhabitants of the city, irrespective of gender.

With no other experience to draw on other than the imperfect past, and a jaundiced view even of that, the male Senates, as the cycles passed, had slowly become more repressive and increasingly dominated by small cliques of younger men whose violence and arbitrary behaviour over the years had steadily alienated both the women and many of the men. In place of the restrictive but rigidly structured society that had once existed, the baser instincts of a few aggressive, under-educated, but power hungry younger men, who had known no slavery, increasingly prevailed. There seemed to be no obvious body of men to challenge this perception. With the passing of the original women's administration survival in the present had replaced any thoughts of the future.

* * *

As the second passing of the second moon faded and the light from the distant star began to filter down the valley the two of them returned dispiritedly to the homestead. It was the end of the cold season, but the crisp, clear air of morning passed unnoticed.

Father and son trudged silently side by side. The son, now after seventeen cycles of the distant star stood taller than his father; the product of a healthier diet in his formative years than had been available to the older man. It had been a tense and stressful night. The only high point had been the son making his first kill using his throwing spear. But even this was a hollow triumph.

It was only one of the pack of the savage hunting dogs, and it wasn't the spear that had killed the animal but the pack turning on its injured member. But it was a good throw at a small, rapidly moving target. Never fully inured to the savagery of the dogs, the spectacle that followed the throw took the gloss off the boy's achievement.

But there was other news to counterbalance this killing of the dog.

"Another three," the man reported to the woman as they dragged themselves wearily into the warmth of the kitchen.

The valley had been the refuge, the provider of their food, and indeed the supplier of most of their wants during the seventeen cycles that they had lived there, but for Sorak and Nasa it had slowly become a nightmare. The arrival of their son, almost as they had discovered the valley after leaving the city, and having converted it to their needs, had been a time of such joy that any thoughts of what the future in the long term might hold had never been formulated. But, slowly, they were being forced to look ahead; the future could no longer be ignored.

The son, called Lenar by Sorak, was fully grown and had effectively reached manhood. His future needed to be considered and his life was going to be totally different from that of his parents. Lenar was content with his life but disturbing thoughts were beginning to emerge in his brain. Knowing no restrictions on his condition or on his thinking, Lenar was aware that there had to be a world outside their valley; after all, his parents had come from such a world, and his curiosity was growing.

Coming then from this world where men had simply been numbered slaves, Nasa, himself named by Sorak, had had no idea what to call his son. Lenar was a corruption of Lenen, a woman from Sorak's past, whom she still mourned after her untimely and horrifying death. And as Lenar grew and thrived, loved and cared for by both his parents, he had no knowledge of the concepts of slavery, or of the unique nature of his upbringing.

Life on the planet, as far as Sorak and Nasa had experienced it, had been dominated by women. Nasa had started life as Sorak's slave 1562, far away in the city from which they had escaped and fled to their valley haven. Things had changed, inspired to a significant extent by Sorak's rebellion against the established order and, unbeknown to the two of them, the domination of women was over. In consequence, the domination of black and brown women, the defying of whom had been an underlying cause of Sorak's rebellion, had also ended. Sorak's blonde hair and blue eyes, albeit unknowingly inherited from the only white general the city had ever had, in combination with both her independent streak and her supposed unnatural attraction to 1562/Nasa had been the cause of her downfall. Coupled with the antagonism between Sorak and her unacknowledged half-sister Mareck, and Lenen's infatuation with her, escape from the city with her erstwhile slave had been her only option.

Sorak and Mareck had been soldiers – officers, but nonetheless lowly in the women's pecking order – but Lenen had been a brown-skinned mangeneer, a much higher category of individual, which had complicated things immeasurably.

Both Sorak and 1562/Nasa had become folk heroes in

the city, after their escape, both to the slaves and to the more independently-minded women who chafed under the mindless restrictions that had been a part of the rigid order of the city. Not, of course, that, as they settled into their life in their valley, they had any idea of their notoriety.

But, equally, Sorak and Nasa had no idea that the domination of the women had been replaced by a series of short-lived male administrations that followed often in violent succession. The establishment of a supposedly more equal society had just never happened.

All of this was in the seventeen cycles of the distant star of the past, and was rarely referred to by either Sorak or Nasa. Some of their adventures during their escape they did sometimes talk about, but more as fairy tales to enthral their growing son in the long dark nights of the cold season. They assiduously avoided schooling Lenar in the world that they had left behind and he was innocent of much of the worldly knowledge of his parents.

"Three more!"

Nasa reported the loss of beasts to Sorak as they settled with the bowl of broth that was their usual breakfast.

It was a morning ritual.

When they had first come to the lush valley it was grazed by a herd of animals of such surprising docility that they had allowed Nasa to fence them into a paddock and manage them for both milk and meat production. The herd had multiplied, but it had also attracted a range of the savage creatures that Sorak and Nasa had encountered on their journey to the valley. Unable to roam freely and escape the predators, as they had previously been able to do, the toll of the animals of the herd over the years had slowly increased.

Armed with the rifles that they had removed from the metallic object embedded in the cleft of the mountain that had provided the two of them with a refuge in their travels to the valley, Nasa and, eventually, his son had protected the herd by shooting the creatures seeking to pray on them. But the supply of projectiles for the rifles had run out and the only weapons left with which to attack the predators were spears and a bow and arrows that Nasa had modelled on Sorak's lost military crossbow.

But they were fighting a losing battle.

The depredations had increased. With easy pickings, the creatures got bolder, the carnage greater and in the last few cycles of the distant star, first one and then two packs of the hunting dogs had arrived. Scavengers, they inevitably followed the more powerful predators, who had already begun to frequent the valley.

"The animals are in fear," Nasa said, "they produce no milk."

"And they have trampled down our growing garden again in their efforts to find safety from the 'leopards'."

Way back in her early life, Sorak had been allowed to browse in the Senate Library in the city. She had seen many pictures of different wild animals and had remembered many of the names, which she had then accorded to the savage creatures that inhabited the nights in the valley and in the plains and mountains that had to be crossed to reach it. The creatures that so ferociously now nightly attacked the herd animals Sorak had called 'leopards'. Coupled with the easily recognisable dogs that scavenged the carcasses and preyed on each other, Nasa had observed that they were now attracting the larger predators that they had been aware of but hadn't clearly seen on their journey to the valley. It was these last that Nasa and Lenar where increasingly unable to deal with. And it was these that threatened not just the herd animals. Nasa knew that they would attack him and his son given the opportunity.

As the days lengthened and warmed, the herd animals

would start to give birth, providing an even more attractive feast for the predators, and exposing even further Nasa's impotence.

"We won't be able to produce enough food to provide for the next cold season if we lose many more beasts."

Sorak was voicing the thought that was constantly in Nasa's mind. Life was only possible in the valley in the cold period if they had built up enough food stocks, fuel and material to make clothes, all of which depended on the herd animals. With the declining herd, it was the dung stocks, dried and used as fuel that was their greatest exposure. Without heat, life would be impossible. Nasa's ability to cut timber had also become severely limited. The axes rescued from the mysterious wreck embedded in the mountain were both beyond repair.

Nasa knew what they had to do. But even after seventeen cycles of their shared life he was reluctant to take the lead. Time and again he had proved that he was capable and willing to take the decisions that were necessary for normal living, but the situation that was now confronting them was very different. Something hidden deep in Nasa's brain was telling him that he should seek Sorak's support for what to do.

The Sorak that Nasa was used to dealing with was a totally different person from the one who had left the city those seventeen cycles ago. Yet, he knew that she could be commanding, and if he didn't take the lead in the decision that had to be made, then she would. It was always a wonder to Nasa that Sorak had accepted his change of role, had even engineered it at the beginning, and had settled into her new role as a partner and mother as if she had never been a military officer at all. But he knew that she had, and just as he had clear memories of their relationship before their escape from the city, he supposed that she did too. But something had to be decided.

The decision to leave the valley affected all three of them, but as males the consequences were much more far reaching for Nasa and Lenar. Knowing nothing of the changes that had taken place and were still taking place in the city, they only had their past experience to guide them. This said that a return to the city was certain death for Nasa and slavery, if not death, for Lenar. Sorak could expect some sort of trial, but death was probably just as certain for her.

Nonetheless they had to find somewhere else to live, somewhere where their primitive weapons would provide for their protection and for them to successfully meet their food and other daily wants.

The following night, only two animals were killed, but both were pregnant females.

Lenar killed another hunting dog with the same horrifying consequence, but he also speared one of the leopards, not killing it, but again making it prey for the dogs. Nasa and his son were forced to watch the savagery. The prospect of ever more violent competition with the predators finally forced Nasa to make up his mind.

"We have to leave the valley!"

He knew that they had to go, despite his misgivings.

In his anxiety over making the announcement, he almost shouted it at Sorak. It was in their bedroom and out of Lenar's hearing that they were at their most intimate. A feeling of relief swept over Nasa as he made his statement.

Taller than Nasa, Sorak for once stood over him and tried to meet his gaze. The valley was her home, the only place where she had ever known certainty and peace; she had, many times, told herself that she would never leave it. But the pain in Nasa's eyes told her that he was equally devastated by what they had to do.

"I know," she said quietly in agreement.

Somewhere buried in her brain, something of the old order of things stirred. She knew that Nasa was right. She hadn't wanted to make the decision for them, even if she had known that Nasa would have been happier if she had. And her instinct told her that that was the case. That worried her. She had become too used to Nasa taking the lead, to him making the day-to-day decisions in their lives, and setting off on another journey into the unknown had too many memories. But they really had no choice.

"Maybe we can find another valley, another place like this."

Nasa took the statement as agreement to the need to leave. They indeed had to find another valley so that they could recreate the lifestyle that they had established in the current one. That it wouldn't be easy, Nasa had no doubt. What it represented as a future for Lenar was as yet a thought too far, but not one that might remain unformed for too much longer.

* * *

In the plain that Nasa knew they would have to search for their next haven, the noises at night were no longer just the hunting cries and death throes of the animal life. The city was no longer isolated. Unbeknown to Sorak and Nasa, their journey to the edge of the plain in which the city stood and beyond had punctured all the myths about what was out there. Myths largely created and sustained by the women dominating the city in the past to prevent very much what had now happened. Very much like the night patrols of Sorak's military days, it was all about keeping the people in the city and managing their lives.

In the memories of many of the older women and the ex-soldiers were the tales of the soldier and the slave who returned from the hunt for Sorak and the slave 1562, and of what was over the mountains that, on the best of the clear days, they could see from the towers of the city walls. The tales had been suppressed at the time, the soldier and the slave had been sent to the quarries in the hope that the knowledge would die.

And as the situation of the women deteriorated after

the revolution that Sorak and Nasa had inspired but had no knowledge of, bands of women had left the city and roamed the plains and mountains, and the wilderness that surrounded it in all directions. Parties of male soldiers were often sent to try to bring the women back, but lessons from the past seemed never to be learned and they rarely returned.

Stories of women bandit groups abounded, groups made up from the old senate guard, from civilian engineers, but no one knew for sure how much was truth and how much was fantasy. And in their ignorance, Sorak and Nasa knew nothing of these stories at all.

2

The decision to leave their valley home seemed to Sorak at first to have been too easily taken. Her instinct was to fight back, to confront the savage animals. Nasa understood this and he made no effort to rehearse the arguments for going, or for staying; he just stated that they had to leave. With so much of their lives, and that of their son, invested in the valley, Sorak found this inevitably hard to accept. But, she knew that she didn't think like Nasa, he only dealt with practical realities, whereas she thought more tactically, about risks, about the hazards on the journey that they were going to undertake, what was possible and what was not.

She also knew that this reflected their backgrounds and origins. She was educated, she could read and write; Nasa had learnt alongside their son as she taught him using books and writing materials brought back from the wreck in the cleft of the mountain. Even then, the skill in both men, for want of opportunity, was only rudimentary.

As she lay beside her man, the decision having been made, whilst he snored gently, she did rehearse the arguments. At least she rehearsed the personal arguments.

But the risk for him is much greater than for me. We can

never go back to the city. He would immediately be killed. I at least would get a hearing.

But Sorak knew that even this was wishful thinking. She could never go back to the city, given a hearing by the generals or not, the fact that she had rebelled against the system meant certain death. The senators would never tolerate such a challenge to their authority.

And why should Nasa be so acquiescent in the face of their determination to leave the valley, it was almost like the old days.

Can I really remember the old days when I had a slave?

She wasn't sure that she could!

We must find another valley.

When he was told of the decision, Lenar only had one question. "Why?"

His father responded.

"Our animals are being killed every night. We can't defend them. Our weapons are useless against the 'leopards'. We can't always rely on the dogs to finish off the ones that we do manage to wound."

Nasa knew that it seemed like a rather weak response, but Lenar was old enough to understand that they couldn't maintain their lifestyle if the herd couldn't be maintained at a much larger size than to which it had recently been reduced. And they had no means of doing this.

The issue for both Sorak and Nasa of Lenar's future was something that neither was keen to discuss with their son, since they couldn't visualise what that future might be. If they couldn't go back to the city, what then?

"So where will we go?"

It was the inevitable question.

Lenar knew that there was a world outside of the valley. Nasa had taken him more than once to the mysterious metal object jammed into the cleft in the mountains. They had spent many hours removing everything from the wreck that they might find useful. They had also buried the bodies that Sorak and he had found at the site. Kept ignorant of the city, Lenar took the existence of males and females as equals for granted. But they knew that their son had begun to questions things in his mind, and it wouldn't be long before he would be thinking about a woman for himself.

"Over the mountain and down into the flat land beyond."

It was Sorak who provided the answer to her son's question. In her logic it was better to go back to an area that they had some familiarity with than to head over the mountains further beyond the valley to an area about which they knew nothing. She and Nasa had explored beyond their valley when they had first arrived, but the terrain beyond the next mountain range was rough and largely barren.

Nasa recognised this logic, but anything that took him closer to the city made him unhappy. The fact that he instinctively accepted Sorak's decision was a subconscious reversion to their old relationship. It was something that Nasa was aware happened from time to time.

But the lapse was only momentary. When the practicalities of organising their departure, what to take, what to do about the remnants of the herd, what to do about the homestead, Nasa took the lead as powerfully as ever.

It was to be Sorak's first trip away from their valley home. She had always refused to accompany Nasa, even when they had first arrived and were removing anything and everything of use from the battered wreck. Since she found the wreck and all that they had discovered in it reminded her so much of her life in the city, and particularly the times that she had spent browsing in the Senate library, something that she had tried to erase from her mind, she preferred to concentrate her whole life on the valley. She knew that she owed it to herself and Nasa to reject all vestiges of their previous life.

For Sorak, even though she realised as readily as Nasa had done that they had no long-term future there, leaving the valley still felt like cutting off one of her limbs. It was the only place that she had ever known true happiness. But this didn't alter the increasingly dire circumstances of their lives.

For Lenar's sake, we have to find a better life.

The thing that troubled her most, however, was that she couldn't visualise where and what that better life might be.

But Sorak was a natural optimist, at least in her own assessment of herself.

It was the day of departure. Nasa and Lenar had broken down the fences that retained the herd and set fire to anything that they cherished but couldn't take with them. Sorak couldn't understand why Nasa had done this; it was if he wanted to deny that they had ever been there. Nasa couldn't understand either, but some deep instinct told him that they should leave no evidence of their identity. It was one of many things deep in his brain that were emerging that seemed to have linkages to his past and his old relationship with Sorak.

"I'm ready," Sorak said as she shouldered one of the packs that she and Nasa had made for the journey.

It was like an order for Nasa and, as Sorak headed down the valley, he automatically fell in behind her.

Lenar, notwithstanding his heavy pack, skipped alongside his mother in a way that brought tears to Nasa's eyes.

He has no idea what's in store for us!

Nasa acknowledged that neither had he any more idea than his son, but he had a whole swathe of memories of the trials and tribulations of their outward journey to the valley that kept pushing to the surface of his mind. They were experiences on which he expected he would have to draw.

But first we must get passed the wreck and down the hillside.

The climb up the mountain was slow and easy. They were in

no hurry and they didn't hurry. As they had progressed, Sorak had fallen back and the three of them walked side by side whenever possible. But, as they approached the top of mountain, Nasa took the lead, since he was more familiar with the route.

When they came to the cave where they had taken final refuge from their pursuers, Sorak paused at the entrance. Nasa wondered whether she would want to go in, but she just stood for a brief moment deep in thought and then moved carefully around the track to where the wreck was. Sorak was surprised that the memories that pushed to the surface were the happy ones of her working out her new relationship with Nasa.

Much of the area was overgrown. Over cycles of the distant star much of the metal had collapsed. There was evidence of wild animals now using the body of the wreck for shelter. Thanks to Nasa's and Lenar's efforts there were no longer any signs of there having been any survivors or habitation.

This time Sorak made no effort to stop, but headed on around the rock overhang and onto the top of the downward hillside.

As they started down the first part of the slope, the uncertain surface covered with loose scree and boulders of all sizes, Nasa led the way cautiously. Sorak held Lenar back with a gesture. Adventurous and with the confidence of youth he was keen to get after his father and even to go on in front of him. But, as they breasted one of the many rocky outcrops, Sorak's heart leapt into her mouth. This time the memories weren't so joyful.

"Nasa!"

But Nasa had seen. He had been looking for the sandy areas, knowing that they could be treacherous. There in front of them was the sand trap that had swallowed Lenen up as she pleaded with Sorak all those cycles ago.

Instinctively they moved over to the edge of the slope and into the rough area of trees and undergrowth. Lenar followed without wondering why they had chosen to take such a difficult route when the main slope seemed easier. Nasa was concentrating on his navigation, but Sorak was lost in her grief.

Sorak's relationship with Lenen had been a complex mixture of stimulating company, arrogant contempt and physical manifestations of love that she had found hard to deal with. Her growing attraction to her slave 1562/Nasa made it impossible for her to respond to Lenen's caresses and her other expressions of her infatuation with the blonde and blue-eyed military officer. But, nonetheless, she knew that Lenen had had a place in her heart, albeit well hidden.

Only with hindsight did Sorak understand the extent of Lenen's love for her. A brown-skinned mangeneer destined for a high level management role in the city, she risked her entire life's prospects by seeking Sorak's intimate company. Even when attached to the party charged with bringing Sorak back to the city for punishment, as one who understood the way she thought, and disillusioned by her rejection of her, in the end she still craved Sorak's love in the depths of her mind.

And over the cycles of the distant star Sorak had come to recognise Lenen's devotion and increasingly her memories of her were more and more painful as the petty irritations faded.

To have to walk around the very sand trap where she had met her death was almost unbearable for Sorak. Only the need to keep a check on Lenar and to follow Nasa's lead forced her thoughts away from the horrors and onto the practical.

Nasa saw the tears rolling down Sorak's cheeks, understood the cause, but kept his peace.

Again, to Lenar's confusion, Nasa eventually brought them back onto the slope and the footing got easier. Since he and Sorak on their original journey had entered onto the slope from the forest halfway up, they were now entering unfamiliar ground.

Once again, Lenar forged ahead, keen to get to the tree line at the bottom of the slope.

But Sorak's thoughts were still elsewhere. Lenen wasn't the only person killed on the slope; there was Lerick, a fellow officer, the soldiers, and the slaves, Mareck, all sacrificed. They had all died for nothing. Not to maintain the Senate's authority, and to allow their escape to set an example, the expedition to bring her back to the city, Sorak had long ago concluded, was never intended to succeed.

Unaware of the rebellion, the revolution, that her actions to escape had prompted, Sorak could never understand why this should be.

"Sorak!"

The agitation in Nasa's voice brought her instantly back from her memory trip.

She could see Nasa scurrying down the slope and throwing himself over another rocky outcrop. Where was Lenar?

She quickly followed. As she scrambled over the outcrop it was clear where Lenar was. He was up to his waist in another sand trap that sat immediately under the outcrop and was completely invisible from the slope above.

It was only by good fortune that Nasa hadn't followed him directly, otherwise he would have dropped into the sand trap too. Sorak had followed Nasa's scramble over the outcrop to find herself, like Nasa, struggling to get their footing on the friable edge of the quicksand.

But Sorak didn't have time to panic. Her half-buried military training switched on instantly.

Moving downhill to firmer ground Nasa had shrugged off his backpack and was searching in it for the old harness that he had worn in his slave days. Strong and serviceable, the leather was as good as when Nasa had worn it and had had many uses during their time in the valley. And just as she was reverting to her former persona, Sorak recognised that this was the old resourceful 1562/Nasa spurred on by the peril of their son.

Lenar had quickly realised that with the added weight of his backpack the more that he struggled to get out, the deeper into the sand trap he was sinking. He raised his arms above his head and froze, his pleading look to his father burning into Nasa's soul.

Holding one end firmly, Nasa tossed the harness to Lenar. It only just reached, and it took a couple of pitches before the boy was able to grasp it. Nasa lay down on the edge of the trap inching forward on his elbows to get a good hold on the harness and then braced himself to pull. Sorak immediately realised that she would somehow have to pull on the harness too if Lenar's weight and the suction of the quicksand weren't to defeat them.

Watching Nasa and testing the ground beside him she took a few deep breaths and dropped gently down at his side.

She lay close to Nasa leaning over him and like him digging her knees in to create purchase as she prepared to pull. Being taller than Nasa she was able to reach over him to grasp the harness. She could feel the tension in his body, mirrored by the tightness of her own. Only later did she recognise the calm determination of his actions; a determination that she had instinctively felt in herself.

No words were necessary and the horrors of Lenen's death had to be relegated to the depths of her brain if she was to concentrate. Both understood what they had to do and began to heave together on the harness whilst levering themselves backwards with their elbows and knees. Once Lenar had moved sufficiently towards them they would be able to move from their prone position and increase the strength of their pull.

Everything seemed to go into slow motion.

But, firstly, they needed to prevent Lenar from sinking any further. Then, as he bent towards them, he began to slowly flex his legs to try to release the suction. Sorak couldn't believe the sensible way that her son was behaving. Surely he must be terrified.

How did he know to keep still? Lenen had effectively buried herself in her frenzied efforts to try to free herself.

But so concentrated was she on coordinating her pulling in unison with Nasa's that she didn't hear the father to son conversation that both kept Lenar calm and told him what to do.

It seemed like an age before anything tangible happened.

Then, slowly, Lenar moved towards them; slowly, they both began to adjust their bodies into a crouch and, slowly, as they were able to increase their leverage, his movement became more pronounced. But they still had to be careful; the edge of the sand trap was so ill-defined that they couldn't be sure when he would be free of the suction. To relax too soon might have resulted in him being pulled back into the quicksand.

With sweat pouring from them, with agony in their eyes, with muscles taut with the strain, little by little, Lenar was pulled out. They were unaware at first, but the pulling eventually got easier and the movement quicker and harness slacker as Lenar seemed to get a foothold and to be able to propel himself forward.

Taking up the slack, Sorak was eventually able to reach out and take hold of Lenar's outstretched arm and to pull him directly until Nasa too could grasp him. And then, like a cork out of a bottle, he came free and landed in a panting heap beside them.

Still conscious of the risk, Nasa hurriedly dragged his son away from the soft edge of the quicksand and the three of them collapsed against yet another rocky outcrop further down the slope where Nasa had deposited the backpacks.

Too exhausted to speak, they laid side by side, gasping and panting, with Sorak crying uncontrollably in relief.

3

"They were three of our best administrators. Why were there no bodyguards?"

The chairman of the Senate was furious.

The attack and the killing of the three men late at night was one of many such incidents that had plagued the city in the recent passages of the distant star. And the attackers were growing more confident and more daring. The Senate, largely self-appointed henchmen of the chairman, were in a dilemma. They needed to clamp down on the groups of women who seemed to inhabit the streets of the city at night, yet they didn't have the resources to do so without some sort of enforced recruitment of more soldiers.

Uncertain of the depth of support that they had, the Senate were reluctant to force any man to do something against his will.

It was seventeen cycles since the rebellion that had swept away the women's powerful administration, and the old Senate-controlled breeding programmes were anathema to many of the men in the city; anything that harked back to the old days of servitude was resented. Breeding between the women and former slaves, as a consequence, had been very limited, and the Senate's efforts to encourage it rather than enforce it had taken some cycles to produce results. Increasing numbers of youngsters were being born, but it would be some cycles yet before they could contribute to city life. But there were significant numbers of men born before the rebellion who, as a result of it, hadn't become slaves. Now in their early years of manhood, these were the people of whom the Senate was most fearful. With the male administration largely a copy of the old female one, there being no other model, these young and ill-disciplined men were a problem.

Managing and controlling the free citizens of the city was inevitably a major issue.

After the overthrow of the original women's Senate and the imprisonment of the bulk of the top echelons of the city's society, there had been a disorganised interregnum. Following an initial rather fearful calm, a whole range of activities had begun to emerge, some for the benefit of the more equal society that both the small numbers of women and men idealists were trying to create, some anything but.

The biggest problem during this period was food. The former slaves who cultivated the vegetable gardens, for example, like the quarry slaves, only wanted to be free of the drudgery of their lives. They stopped work and very soon, with nothing to do and nothing to eat, they began to form gangs and to prey on other citizens, first targeting the women, and then anyone who had something that they wanted. With many unemployed but still armed women soldiers, violence soon erupted as they began to fight back.

It was during this period that several atrocities were perpetrated that began to polarise the city inhabitants back into the women versus men mentality. With falling food stocks, the ex-slaves guarding the former Senate and several hundred black and brown-skinned administrators massacred their prisoners at the Edge on the opposite side of the city from where Sorak and 1562/Nasa had escaped.

Former soldiers from the red and blue platoons, some of whom were from Sorak's former command, then reacted by slaughtering as many ex-slaves that they could before a cycler, a violent rain storm, inundated the city, flooding many districts and destroying yet more of the vegetable gardens. Many of the women soldiers then disappeared from the city to take up residence in the forest at the other side of the Edge, but this only provided limited relief.

Throughout this mayhem, individual acts of revenge or just gratuitous violence occurred almost every night. The city's population was significantly reduced and both the remaining civilian women and soldiers and the more intelligent of the former slaves realised that there would soon be nothing left of the city for them to inhabit if something wasn't done.

"But it will take time."

Order eventually started to come out of the chaos when a group of former personal slaves to the now-dead former administrators began to copy the actions of their ex-mistresses and to get an essential administration going. Former women soldiers were recruited to train the menial ex-slaves in arms and to rebuild the armed guard system to keep order. Initially, units were officered by women, but, as competent candidates became available, men began to take over as officers. Eventually, as the character of the subsequent male administrations emerged, very few women were willing to work for the men. After around four cycles of the distant star the uneasy calm that had prevailed allowed food production and animal husbandry to be increased to try to meet demand. Breeding between the women and former slaves slowly became acceptable, but still on a limited scale.

"But there are many people that we can't count."

Marcan, a former office slave who had worked for Alsan, a key former administrator and friend of Lenen, Sorak's would-be lover, had been intelligent enough to understand what his former mistress did and to see how some of her activities were still needed.

"We don't know how many women are living over the Edge."

He was voicing the concerns of the more thoughtful men who were beginning to come forward to run the city. Alsan had been killed in the rebellion but others, like Kragar, the former tenant of the Senate Guard, hadn't been captured, but had left the city inspired by Sorak. Marcan knew that until all the escapees were reconciled to the new order, there was always going to be trouble. How this was to be achieved, he had no idea.

Living outside the city was no longer a feared option. The original female Senate had defined the edge of the plain in which the city had been built as the edge of civilisation and had created many myths to keep the women under control, the horrors awaiting outside of the city and beyond the Edge being one of them. The scale of banditry that developed was small, but as an all-male Senate, small in numbers but ambitious, was formed, armed patrols were sent out from the city to hunt down the renegade women. Many patrols returned without success, others didn't return at all.

After about ten cycles of the distant star a far more stable society had been achieved with many of the lower grade women and ex-soldiers now fulfilling the menial roles carried out by the former slaves. Marcan had risen to head the Senate but, as much of the form of the old way of life returned, he was still troubled by a feeling of some terrible, impending catastrophe.

With the dream-pits re-established but no longer segregated, Marcan made it his business to meet both men and women to try and gauge feelings in the city. One elderly brown-skinned man was a useful source of information. A former slave to an administrator who had favoured him, he was in touch with many of those with a similar background. He was contemptuous of the low-grade ex-slaves who seemed to be forcing their way to prominence. Only when the more intelligent men, as he considered himself to be, took charge did he see the possibility of lasting stability.

"What's it all for?" he asked Marcan, in an effort to understand what the current Senate leader thought the future might look like.

It wasn't the amber liquid, the favourite drink of the dream-pits, talking, the old man avoided it, but against the pulsating background music and heaving mass of dancers lost in the drugged world that they were allowed to sample again, it was a question that kept emerging.

"In the old days," the man said, "we all had a purpose. We all had a job to do that we were bred for, there was something to achieve at the end of each day. The Senate regulated everything, but everything worked, everything carried on, both men and women in their separate ways were a part of it, we knew what was in the future. But now…?"

It was a dilemma that Marcan recognised, but he had no answer for. Did the city now have a purpose? The man was right; when the old Senate ran things they were ordered in a way that ensured a self-perpetuating society even if only very few people knew what the objectives of that society were. The Senate was the fount of all knowledge and the controller of everything. And society had been like that for so long that only an exceptional few thought to challenge it.

But it wasn't like that now. Marcan was troubled. He knew that the other members of the male Senate wouldn't understand his concern that the city no longer had a reason to exist. That it existed in the first place as a result of a long-range space probe from far away in another galaxy becoming stranded was unknown to him, and since the burning down of the Senate library he would never know.

But forces that he knew nothing about were gathering

momentum. There was a vacuum and, although Marcan didn't have the knowledge to recognise the concept, he recognised its existence, and inevitably it was going to be filled.

In the wreck of the Senate library a group of shadows coalesced. It was the meeting place of a body of former quarry slaves, aging but long in memory of such women as Mesrick, who sowed the first seeds of revolt. Seventeen cycles on she was not forgotten, nor was her inspiration, the rebellious military officer who escaped the city because she wanted to have relations with her slave. And, during those seventeen cycles, the memories of what had happened had become myths, myths that had now lost touch with reality. Idealism was lost to ambition and to the more basic instincts of the less intelligent of the ex-slaves.

Plans had been laid. Action was imminent. Whether Mesrick or Sorak would have approved of what was being planned was seriously doubtful.

"One more passage of the two moons," the broken down old quarryman with deep, shining eyes said. "The young men are set."

An unlikely leader with little time to live, the old man had only one instinct: revenge.

The next day Marcan and the senators were all killed. Armed groups of men, male soldiers, with the occasional dissident woman, sealed off the sections of the city that they still controlled. Anyone thought to be likely to be a centre of resistance, man or woman, was killed.

This rebellion was every bit as brutal as the previous one. But it had a different purpose. Mesrick and Sorak would most definitely not have approved of this purpose. It was focused on gaining power for the small group of middle-aged former quarry slaves and their adherents; absolute power, not power to be shared or dissipated, and certainly not to be shared with any women.

Marcan was replaced by a young quarryman who called himself Soran, a boy when Sorak left the city, a man of overpowering arrogance and self-interest, and only marginally more intelligence than his peers, who had gathered a group of equally ruthless individuals around him. Nurtured on hate, oblivious to any finer feelings, his time in the quarries as a youth had been brief but had left an indelible mark on his warped mind.

The city had its first dictator.

"So why were the three of them out at night without a bodyguard?" Soran repeated.

The anger of the new chairman of the self-appointed Senate was directed at the sour-looking brown-skinned man in an impressive uniform, the commander of the Senate Guard.

But Soran's anger was also fed by the sense that beneath the enforced calm in the city something was still brewing. His anger also covered fear. His hold on power was, as yet, not completely established. His instinct told him that it only needed some small spark and the whole city would be in revolt.

And it wouldn't just be men against women next time.

Soran had inherited some of the buried fear of the women; his nightmare was an organised campaign against the male administration and he knew that that would have male participants. Much of what he set in place was designed to head off such an eventuality.

4

Neither Sorak, Nasa, nor Lenar moved for some time after collapsing against the rocky outcrop. All were gasping for breath and trying to relax their overstrained muscles. It took time. Eventually the panting subsided, muscles did relax, sweat dried and brains started working again. And each desperately tried to shut out the horror of what had just almost happened from their minds.

But it was Lenar who was the first one to move. Frantically cleaning the sand from his body he shuffled so that he had his back to his parents. It was almost the movement of a defiant child.

Nasa, who was closest to him, reached out and rested his hand on his son's shoulder. The gentle, rhythmic movement that he felt told him that Lenar was crying and hadn't wanted his distress to be observed. The horror of the experience had overcome his growing sense of his manhood. His father understood. Nasa withdrew his hand and reached out to touch Sorak instead.

"My mother's heart, that was…!"

But she couldn't articulate what they had just been a part of and what they had just prevented; it was too traumatic.

Nasa did a shuffle of his own that brought him right up against Sorak and pulled her close to him. There was a long moment of silence, no words were necessary between them, so familiar with each other's thoughts were they. Needless to say, the reality of Lenar's escape for Sorak, as a result of Lenen's death, was the most vivid and would take a long time to dissipate. As the days went by and she tried to force the horror from her mind, she sometimes wondered if it would ever leave her.

The rare smile that played across Nasa's face was as much about Sorak's reversion to language that he had almost forgotten, as it was about his own feelings. No one in the city, on the planet, knew who their mother was, with the exception of Lenar, so swearing by her mother's heart was as powerful an indication of Sorak's relief as he could imagine. Needless to say, his own relief was as great, although he was never likely to express it in such a way.

But time was moving on and Nasa knew that he had to take charge of the situation again.

The beginnings of shadows were forming as the distant star began to sink below the mountain from which they had just descended and the loss of heat that followed alerted Nasa to the need to find a safe place for them to sleep.

"We must head into the trees and find somewhere for the night."

Since they weren't following the route that they had taken to get up the mountain and then eventually to their valley seventeen cycles ago, neither Sorak nor Nasa had much idea what the immediate terrain in front of them would be like. Nasa probably had a better idea than Sorak and he began to scour his memory for any insights.

"We can't be far from the plain," Sorak said.

Nasa agreed, but as he tried to recall what he could remember of the landscape from all those cycles ago, all he could visualise was water.

He'd made an expedition across a part of the plain then, but he couldn't be certain that he would have recognised anything of it again now. Why would he? It was a long time in the past and, as he readily admitted to himself, he was terrified, and consequently not as observant as he should have been. They were both terrified, but he had felt that he had to hide his fears for Sorak's sake, a novel thought for someone who was supposed, then, to have been an unthinking slave. She had been injured, and in the added confusion at the time, in her mind, over her relationship with her slave, her memories were even less clear than Nasa's.

But the thing that Nasa did remember, nonetheless, was that this relationship with Sorak had definitely changed when he returned from his exploratory trip. He felt that he had somehow become more equal to his then mistress, but it took him some time before he understood why. The idea that a military officer was happy when her slave had returned to her safely was beyond his comprehension at the time. The idea that the military officer was just as terrified as he was took some time to establish itself in his mind as well. The idea that that military officer was struggling with her intense feelings for her slave had then as yet to percolate into 1562/Nasa's consciousness. But the seeds had been sown.

The only common feature of the plain that remained in his memory was a succession of lakes of various sizes, some fed by streams and rivers, some seemingly not fed by anything. Large areas of ground were boggy and impassable and he had had to make many detours before he was able to find his way back to Sorak. But at least by then he had charted a route to the mountain that all these cycles later they had just come down. However, the broader details of the landscape were beyond his recall.

But that very plain of Nasa's exploration was their objective now.

Nasa stood up and readied himself, shouldering his backpack and helping Sorak with hers.

"Lenar, we must move on. We need to find a safe place to sleep."

Whatever feelings that Lenar harboured over his recent experience he was now sufficiently in control of himself to hide them from his parents. He checked that the contents of his own backpack had safely survived their being dragged through the sand trap and announced himself as ready.

They set off, Nasa leading, Lenar following, with Sorak in the rear. Lenar's youthful exuberance had abated. His experience in the sand trap had chastened him, even if he wouldn't have understood what that meant. Neither of his parents made any comment about his narrow escape, Nasa because he had seen how upset his son had been, and Sorak because, being his mother, she knew that she had to hide her anxieties from him. To do otherwise would have undermined his confidence.

He's a grown man now. In the city, as a slave, he would have had to face all manner of challenges.

But Sorak, in her ignorance of the changes that had taken place, was sure that she would never allow Lenar to go to the city. She was unable to see him in any other guise than as a slave there, and that was something that she knew she would never countenance.

They trudged on.

The trees began to thin out. The slope was increasingly covered first with small bushes and long, grass-like vegetation, and then as the ground levelled out with a sodden mass of dead and decaying leaves. Top-heavy with their backpacks, they all struggled to maintain their footing, Lenar most of all.

"Ah!!"

It was he who let out a grunt of surprise. As he stopped and pointed and readied his spear, something foul-smelling slithered out of the thick layers of rotting vegetation and then disappeared again further into the developing gloom under the trees.

"It's more frightened of us than we need to be of it," Nasa said confidently.

Sorak shuddered. It was an unexpected memory from the past for her too.

They needed to find some firm ground and a large tree. Unspoken, both Nasa and Sorak increased their pace. There were fewer trees, but so far they hadn't seen any that were large enough for them to climb into as a safe place of refuge. If they couldn't find suitable trees they would have to sleep on the ground, which meant that one of them would have to stay awake all night. More memories were stirred.

At last they came to an open area of firm ground, but with no trees. There was a small lake. They were in one of the clearings that they had come upon on their outward journey. This one had an area of sloping rock to one side.

"We'll have to camp here," Nasa decided. "Lenar, we need to start collecting as much firewood as we can. Dry wood. We will have to keep a fire going all night."

It was only as he unshipped his backpack and set about gathering three or four small boulders to make a hearth that he realised that Sorak wasn't with them. He called to Lenar to be silent and listened. The shuffling and snuffling sound that was immediately audible proved to be a small foraging animal that hurriedly disappeared into the tall vegetation on the other side of the lake in fright at the strange animals that had invaded its territory.

"Mother?"

Lenar had now also realised that Sorak hadn't followed them into the clearing.

Nasa was in a dilemma. It didn't make sense for both to go and search for Sorak, leaving no sign of where he intended to camp. But he was reluctant to leave the boy and search on his own. There were too many risks. Dusk was when the bulk of the animal life became active, and Nasa knew that his son's only experience, gathered in their late home valley, was with the smaller varieties of predator. And, of course, they had no idea how many of the predators might be around.

Instinctively, the last thing that Nasa wanted was attract attention by calling out to Sorak.

Confident in Sorak's ability to look after herself, the most immediate priority seemed to be to start a fire. Lenar had gathered a large pile of fallen timber surprisingly quickly considering the paucity of trees and the general dampness; enough to build and keep a substantial fire going. They just needed to get it started.

Sorak's ancient military flintlocks had long since been worn out, so in their valley they had become used to keeping a fire always burning even in the hottest weather as the easiest way to provide for cooking as well as heating. But Nasa knew how to start a fire with the materials that they had gathered, so he set to work to whittle a stick and dig a small pit in a piece of flat tree branch. He then squatted over the hearth that he had made.

"Collect some of the dry vegetation and small twigs as kindling," he told his son.

Sorak had read in the old books in the Senate library how people before the oldest mothers had made fire. It was the sort of thing that the practical Nasa had remembered.

Watched by a fascinated Lenar, he pushed the whittled stick into the pit he had made along with a few small pieces of dried vegetation, and began to rotate the stick between the flat of his hands rapidly working up a speed. As Nasa panted and gasped for breath from trying to keep up the rotation, a wisp of smoke appeared in the hole. Lenar, who by now understood what his father was doing, pushed a few more pieces of dried vegetation into the hole. It didn't catch fire.

"I will," Lenar said.

Taking the whittled stick from his father he copied what he had seen Nasa doing. By now it was pitch black and both had to peer closely at the hole to detect the wisp of smoke. The smoke eventually came but, before Nasa could apply the dried vegetation, a piece of orange twig was dropped onto the smouldering shavings. There was an instant burst of flame.

"Mother!"

The light from the small flame exposed the grinning face of Sorak. Nasa quickly fed the flame with more dry vegetation and kindling, before reaching out and touching Sorak on the face. In the dark, his relief, the joy on Lenar's face and the amusement on Sorak's went unobserved.

In the gathering gloom as she had trailed behind Nasa and Lenar, Sorak had seen one of the orange twig trees just off the route that they were taking. Impelled by the need to find a suitable camping place, Nasa was pushing on so fast that Sorak simply decided that the most sensible thing for her to do was to pause and collect a bundle of the twigs. And finding them raised Sorak's spirits; they had so many useful properties.

If Nasa had given any thought to it he might have concluded that she had been a rather longer time than ought to have been necessary to gather the quantity of twigs that she deposited with her backpack. She had. But Sorak wasn't going to report that their journey had for some time been spooked for her by a pair of large, bright eyes that never quite materialised into an animal that she could see. Nasa knew that there were fierce animals about; he didn't need telling that they were close by. And there was no need to alarm Lenar.

As the fire was steadily built up, a sleepy Lenar crept up beside his mother and forgot that he was now a grown man ready to face any challenge. Sorak gave him a gentle hug, more man to man than mother to son.

Nasa had chosen a place for the fire at the base of a gently sloping bank covered with soft vegetation, with a small rocky upwards incline behind it, enough to give them the best protection that was possible in such an exposed area.

"I will watch," Nasa said as the first moon began to cast its vermillion light over the landscape.

Sorak accepted the decision, knowing that she would wake up sometime before the second moon appeared and be able to relieve him. It was a trained-in mechanism from her far off military past that had never left her. If Lenar thought that he ought to take a turn on watch he was sensible enough not to suggest it. He was all too conscious of his lack of experience in forest living.

With Sorak and Lenar wrapped in the animal skins from their backpacks and quickly asleep, Nasa built up the fire and settled to watch. Wrapped up in his own skins, he positioned himself some way from the fire so that he could scan the entire area around the lake without the obstruction of the firelight. It was the sort of tactic that he had instinctively picked up from Sorak, from her military days, and that had stayed with him.

It was cold, but not so cold that the lake might freeze. He grinned to himself when he recalled his introduction to a frozen lake and Sorak's amusement at his ignorance. It was the sort of memory that he cherished because, by then in their original journey, Sorak had begun to unbend from her military reserve and share thoughts and then feelings with him. It was then that he began to understand the concept of equality.

How different things are now.

Such knowledge that he had acquired, as a successful breeding slave, before he was allocated to Sorak by a sympathetic administrator, told him that the events of that bitterly cold night had indeed been fruitful. He couldn't see Lenar from where he was sitting, but he didn't need to to feel his pride in his son. It was another feeling that he knew to be unique; Lenar was the only one of his several progeny that he knew to be his own.

But practical thoughts were never far away in Nasa's mind.

Once we reach the plain we must decide in which direction we must go.

It was a thought that assumed much more importance in the dark of the night between passages of the two moons. It was a thought that had been worrying him for some time. They needed a plan.

During their original journey of escape from the city they hadn't had any clear idea where they were going beyond evading the pursuing party. They had followed the line of the distant star, which had taken them to the first mountains, to river crossings and then down to the plain. They had been aware of vast swathes of forest and plain disappearing into the distance each side of their route. For their present journey, once they reached the plain, the only direction that Nasa was sure that they shouldn't follow was the reverse of the way that they had come all those cycles ago. That way would lead them to the Edge opposite the city. If, in the intervening cycles of the distant star, the women of the city had lost their fear of the Edge, that direction could only lead them into trouble.

The city and the plain that surrounds it are only a tiny proportion of the area that we have seen. We must head down to the plain; if we keep the distant star alongside us that will keep us away from the city.

Nasa knew that his advice to himself was sensible; however, it didn't satisfy him. But his vision of what they would be looking for was ill-formed and not much more than a replicate of the valley that they had just left. He had no idea how realistic this was.

He had a sense that Sorak might have a yearning for the city. She would know that it was an irrational feeling, but it was something that had to be confronted before they settled down again. So far, they had given no more thought to what that settling down might entail, not just for them, but much more importantly for Lenar.

"What sort of life can he have?"

Seeing things perhaps with more clarity in the calm

and coldness of the night, Nasa wondered whether Sorak's attraction back to the city was her way of envisaging a future life for her son. But what life could that be? Nasa's perceptions of what the city would still be like told him that the last place that he would want Lenar to be was there. Even if he survived the return, he had no concept of servitude, nothing to prepare him for city life.

"Nasa!"

The faint glow through the trees at the other side of the lake announced the rise of the second moon and, as he became aware of it, Sorak crept quietly to his side and nestled against him.

He knew that he must now sleep, but with her closeness and warmth he was reluctant. His whole world was within arm's length of him and he had never felt happier.

5

The small body of women dressed in rather tattered military uniforms had entered the city in the darkness between the two moons. Entirely against the male Senate's strict edit they were fully armed with crossbows and swords. But then the Senate's writ didn't run too far with the rebellious women.

They had entered the city from an area of the Edge probably furthest away from and in the almost opposite direction by which Sorak and Nasa had originally left the city. It was an area close to where the elite women of the city had been massacred in the early days of the rebellion and was forbidden to both men and women.

Moving quickly through the deserted quarries they worked their way into the overgrown food gardens and into Sector One behind the burned-out Senate House. It was in the area where three male administrators had been killed recently.

"They will have increased the guard patrols," the leader of the party said.

But since there were far fewer male soldiers than there had been female ones in the old days, guard patrols had to be concentrated on specific activities like protecting the food production areas. This gave the marauding groups of renegade women greater opportunities.

"The patrol isn't due back until the second moon rises," the leader continued.

The women had gained this information on the patrol schedules from an elderly ex-slave who was opposed to a benign dictatorship, female, being replaced by a vicious dictatorship, male. He was one of a small number of men who supported the opposition to the current male Senate, just as there were a small number of women who were prepared to work with the current male administration. Mostly civilians, these women would have been totally destitute without employment.

The party of six experienced ex-soldiers crept towards their final destination, the private residence of the top administrator under the Senate. Although the Senate House and Library had long since been destroyed, most of the living accommodation from former times had been preserved and enhanced. This administrator, who called himself Kragan, had once been the slave of the Senate Guard Commander, Kragar, in the final days of women's rule. Black, highly intelligent, much as 1562/Nasa had been, his influence over the male Senate was powerful, and baleful. Kragan was determined to subjugate the women much as the men had been previously subjugated. For him there was no compromise, no living together, no future amity.

"Until Kragan is dead there will be no peace."

This was the view of the women who had escaped the city and who formed the most potent resistance groups.

The low thud of a crossbow bolt signalled the beginning of the action. The male soldier guarding the surrounding wall of Kragan's house pitched forward, shot in the heart.

"There should be two guards inside the house, possibly three," the leader said, "we have to get to them first."

Again, they had received accurate information from their spy.

Four of the six ex-soldiers were quickly through the gate, up the short path, and standing ready at the front door as the remaining two ran around the side of the house to the back to prevent escape from the rear. They made not a sound.

The next actions had been rehearsed many times to ensure success. The door was kicked down by the leader and the four rushed in. Taken by surprise, the two guards were quickly despatched.

Kragan, attempting to escape by the back door walked into the arms of the two waiting women ex-soldiers.

The action was momentary. Kragan's hands were tied behind him and a roll of dirty cloth stuffed into his mouth. His whimpering brought only contempt from the ex-soldiers.

"Quickly, we have to go before the patrol returns!"

They began to retrace their steps. The action had taken almost no time at all.

The leader had been given specific instructions on how to deal with the captured official.

* * *

Sorak carefully moved away from Nasa when she sensed that he was falling asleep; he needed to sleep.

The second moon passed and the first light from the distant star began to percolate into the clearing where they had settled. As the range of her vision expanded, Sorak's attention was immediately drawn to her son, curled up into a ball under the animal skins that were keeping him warm. He was being warily watched by one of the fierce hunting dogs that had crept into the encampment. Nasa, who seemed totally dead to the world, was laying on his spear, and Sorak's weapons were over by Lenar. On the opposite side of the small lake by which they were camped, in the still, dim light, multiple pairs of eyes darted about. Sorak knew that there were very few benign animals out on the plain where they were and, if there was one dog, there would be a pack.

Don't do anything in a hurry.

She had moved away from Nasa earlier to let him sleep; now she was too far away to rouse him. She couldn't rely on him waking up without making a noise and making a noise could either frighten the dog away from Lenar or make it attack him. Pitching a rock at Nasa to wake him wasn't an option either.

Past experience told Sorak that the dogs were always dangerous and never predictable.

A shaft of light suddenly emerged from the trees opposite and fell onto the marauding dog. Startled, the animal sat back on its haunches and let out a whine. The pack the other side of the lake set up a responding whine, slowly at first, but then getting louder. They were beginning to edge their way around the lake. Sorak hadn't the time to wonder why the dog hadn't attacked Lenar, or to be thankful that it hadn't.

Keep still, Lenar!

For her son to move without knowing the peril he was in could prove fatal.

During this small passage of uncertainty, Sorak had shuffled her way soundlessly towards the sleeping figure. If she stretched out she could now just reach hold of her bow. Nasa had always laughed at her because she insisted on carrying her arrows tied to the bow rather than in a holder on her back. He wouldn't laugh now!

Still moving imperceptibly slowly, she carefully strung the bow, fitted an arrow, and took aim at the dog, still upright on its haunches. She still couldn't understand why the dog hadn't leapt onto Lenar. The arrow struck the animal in the breast, killing it instantly. It didn't make a sound.

On her feet in one movement, Sorak ran to the dog, grasped it by it still quivering hind legs and ran partly around the lake. Finally, she flung the dead beast into the undergrowth, close enough to the pack for them to sense that it was dead meat. The cacophony of snarls, yelps and whines immediately woke Nasa and Lenar. Arming themselves, they joined Sorak and watched and waited. The pack of dogs, fighting amongst themselves as they always did, disappeared out onto the plain the other side of the band of trees from which they had emerged.

"We won't be going that way," Nasa said, as much in relief as anything.

Lenar, pale and thoughtful, had seen such spectacles before in the valley as the dogs slowly encroached on their living space – it was one of the reasons why they were leaving – but was always horrified by the uncontrolled violence of the dogs' behaviour.

As Sorak began to unwrap a portion of their food supply and Nasa tested the water in the lake to see if it was drinkable, Lenar began to gather his scattered belongings and repack his backpack. The mystery of the non-attacking dog was revealed as he gathered up a scattered handful of the orange sticks that Sorak had found. Nasa had laid them on the ground by Lenar's exposed head as he slept, they having discovered on their outward journey that, amongst others things, the sticks were not only good for lighting fires but they gave off an odour that the dogs found offensive and which deterred them from approaching the area where the sticks were. Once again, Nasa's forethought had saved the day.

Chastened, they ate their modest meal in silence.

"We will have to decide which way to go once we get to the edge of the plain and the beginnings of the next mountains," Nasa said as they set off from their overnight camp.

From experience from their outward journey, Sorak and Nasa knew that there was a mountain range between them and the forested area opposite the city. They had passed over it, crossing fast-flowing rivers and avoiding other hazards, which included the pursuing party. Nasa had at that time also explored the area that they were passing through, but they had little idea what was beyond the plain if they followed it around the base of the mountains rather than went up and over them.

I would like to see the city again.

Sorak was walking along behind Nasa and Lenar in their well-established trail order, relaxed and happy, when the thought leapt out at her. It wasn't the first time.

See? What is there to see? You have no idea how the city might have changed!

Practical, and from common sense, Sorak knew this to be right, but she acknowledged an indefinable yearning, a desire to know what the last seventeen cycles of the distant star would have brought for her. Change there had been, unbeknown to Sorak, of course, but, in her ignorance of that, her common sense also told her that in reality she would have had no life at all in the city had she remained. And if she went back?

A fight to the death in the closed arena!

Sorak had left the city a fugitive. Recapture would have meant punishment and death. Of course, she knew that in her conscious mind, but yet she couldn't explain the yearning.

They marched on until the distant star was overhead and they had escaped from the waterlogged plain onto the firmer ground that skirted around the base of the mountain range. Nasa edged around until the distant star was over his left shoulder and set off to follow the contour of the base of the range. This was new territory to him, but a weird sense of familiarity began to invade Sorak's mind.

Injured on their outward journey by one of the savage dogs, she had taken refuge in a tree when Nasa had gone exploring the wetlands that they had just traversed. It was there that she first met the 'leopard'-like creature that had followed her into the tree, and killed it. She soon realised that it was the different shapes of the trees that was familiar to her. As they moved away from the wetter areas the trees were taller, broader and the branches wide and almost flat; the perfect place to hide, to sleep and to be safe.

"Father?"

Nasa had stopped and waited for Sorak to join him. Lenar could see no reason to stop.

It was as if Nasa had understood what Sorak was thinking. There was no chance that their earlier encampment, the fireplace, the area of cutback timber from which Nasa made spears, would still be visible, but he shared Sorak's sense of the proximity of it.

Lenar knew the story of his parents' escape by heart, at least a sanitised version of it, so he knew about hiding in trees and keeping quiet to disguise their presence from the pursuers. And, as Nasa approached one of the tall trees as if to climb it, he also understood why they had stopped.

"Can you tell which tree you hid in?" asked Lenar.

Nasa shook his head.

"It was one like this."

Sorak could no more tell either, but she wasn't sentimental, so she very soon indicated that they should move on by heading off towards a wooded area in the distance on a lower slope of the mountain range.

"The distant star will disappear over the mountains soon; we should not be out in the open."

Nasa and Lenar fell in behind. A flash of Sorak the young officer flickered in and out of Nasa's mind. Not for the first time on this journey did he get the sense of her being in charge again.

Dusk was falling fast as they finally entered the wooded area. As they did so, Lenar hesitated, cocking his head to one side. Unlike the plain, the wood wasn't silent. But if Lenar didn't know what the muffled rumble in the background was, Nasa did. Amongst the most prominent of his memories of their former journey were the river crossings. It was in crossing rivers that they had come closest to disaster. What he knew they were hearing was the sound of a fast-flowing river nearby. Whether they needed to cross it he decided was a decision for the next day.

Where they had hesitated seemed like a good place to spend the night.

Nasa and Lenar soon got a fire going as Sorak, recognising some of the edible berries that they had eaten on their outward journey, foraged again. Noting that the vegetation had been trodden down into what looked like a path, she headed deeper into the wooded area until she saw a group of the deer-like creatures that she also remembered from the past. Selecting a juvenile, she shot it as the herd made off. Wary of the animal's mother, she collected the corpse and took it back to Nasa. Lenar was most impressed.

She and Nasa set about preparing the meat.

"Nasa, if we were to climb up and over, do you think that we would be able to see the city?"

They had finished their meal, one of the best since they had left the valley, and Sorak and Nasa were leaning side by side against a tree. Lenar was out of hearing, fashioning more arrows from branches that he had cut. Sorak broke into the companionable silence between them.

The question had just leapt out before she was aware enough of it to stop it.

Nasa didn't respond, but Sorak could feel the tension in his body as she rested against him.

"Nasa?"

"Why would you want to see the city? The city brought only trouble for you, for us. You would be killed if you went back there. We both would."

"Not back there, I just want to see it. Just in the distance."

This was beyond Nasa's comprehension. The city to him was

bondage, pain, hopelessness, things that their life in the valley had banished. In the city, there would be no intimacy possible between them, no Lenar; surely Sorak didn't regret their son. She had seemed happy in the valley. The only regret she ought to have had was being forced out of it. But the conversation was unsettling. This was something new for Nasa.

Sorak didn't regret leaving the city, how could she have done? As she felt, as well as heard, Nasa's resistance she knew that she would never be able to explain her yearning to the straightforward, uncomplicated Nasa. It was an unsentimental desire simply to know what her life would otherwise have been. Equally, although over the years she had acquired a greater understanding of Nasa, she still found it hard to envisage his position as a slave, what that would really have felt like. Since she had always had her own free will she couldn't imagine a world where she had none and everything she did was at the behest of someone else, even if it was her.

Nasa didn't respond. She said no more.

Later, as the darkness enveloped them and Lenar again settled under his animal skins, Nasa felt the gentle rhythm of Sorak's breathing as they settled side by side on the ground. He pulled her bedding over her. His quiet smile was of pleasure and affection, but the question of "just wanting to see it" he knew had not been resolved. Eventually, he slid away from her and set himself to watch.

Nasa found Sorak awake as the second moon arose, casting a gloomy, diffused light onto the wooded area where they had camped, and settled under his own animal skins as she took over the watch.

After the previous night's experience Sorak kept her bow and arrows immediately to hand. The long-toothed creature that cautiously approached the group, sniffing the air, threw Sorak instantly back into her past, and her night injured in the tree. But her movement to fit an arrow to her bow seemed to spook the animal and it turned and loped off into the trees again. For Sorak, this was unexpected, knowing how savage these beasts could be. She supposed that even these fierce creatures had a fear of the unknown.

She didn't mention their visitor to Nasa and Lenar.

As they ate the remainder of the food from the previous day and packed up their belongings, neither Sorak nor Nasa referred to their previous conversation. But Nasa realised that Sorak had some unspoken feeling that he couldn't understand that was behind her rather wistful desire to have sight of her birthplace and the city where she spent her childhood. That he had no such nostalgia he also realised was reflected by their original disparate positions in city society.

All of their thoughts and speculations were in ignorance. Certainly Nasa, if not Sorak, realised that. That life in the city might be almost unrecognisable to them with all the time that had passed was a thought too far.

6

In the short time that they had been camping in the wooded area, the three of them, in their separate ways, had become used to the rumble of the nearby river. Lenar was conscious of the sound and was keen to see the phenomena that his father had described to him, but Sorak and Nasa had blanked the noise from their minds.

But fed and watered and packed ready to depart, the issue of the river had to be brought back into their conscious minds. River crossings had figured significantly in their original outward journey. Was this going to be another epic crossing that they had to make?

However, Nasa was confused. His original plan was to work his way up into the mountains, as far away from the route that they had taken all those cycles ago, to get enough elevation to see back out over the new areas of plain that they had come to, then to return to the plain and seek out another valley, or secure place for them to settle again. That would inevitably mean crossing the river that was so obviously close by. And from his past experience he knew that there would be other rivers whichever route they took.

Nonetheless, Sorak's desire to physically see the city again had unsettled him.

He himself had no such desire. But there was something in Sorak's demeanour and attitude, or so he imagined, that was different. Things had changed. The flashes of Sorak, military officer, the leader rather than companion, came more frequently to him; and that was what was confusing him.

Surely she doesn't want to be a soldier again? Nonsense! Of course she doesn't, why should she?

But, in this unfamiliar confusion, Nasa really didn't know what to think. And he couldn't remember when he was last so uncertain.

"So which way?"

Then it was back to the Sorak of the valley, the mother and soulmate again. No military officer, leader, here, just his companion seeking guidance.

"We need to find the river, it clearly can't be that far away, and we need to see if we can cross it."

"Will we need to cross it?" Sorak asked.

"I don't know. But even if we were to just carry on along the edge of the plain, we would probably have to cross rivers, they all flow onto the plain this side of the mountains."

"But if we head up into the mountains we will be able to see much more of the plain."

Nasa acknowledged that this was his plan.

Sorak nodded and set off towards the direction of the rumbling river noise. Nasa quickly followed, urging Lenar with him.

They arrived at the river bank together. Or rather, they arrived at the edge of the gorge through which the river was pouring in a frothing turbulent torrent. The river was way below them. The noise was painfully loud; conversation was going to be impossible.

The gorge ran as far as they could see in the uphill direction and obviously further. The going was easier as the edge of the gorge was mainly flat rock without vegetation. They walked until the distant star was over head and then stopped to rest. They still couldn't see the end of the gorge.

"We will have to get down to the river somehow," Nasa said, "we need water to drink."

Sorak grinned. They both realised that they were talking to each other again; the noise of the river had diminished, which meant that they couldn't now be far from the end of the gorge.

They moved on. With the path clear, Lenar went on ahead with his parents following. The ground eventually levelled off, which meant that the walls of the gorge were getting lower and acting less like a sounding box. As the distant star's shadows began to lengthen they caught up with Lenar as they found themselves almost at water level and approaching a curve in the river. The inside of the curve on the other side of the river had formed a sandy beach. Lenar was pointing.

"Mother's heart!" Sorak muttered.

Laid out on the beach were four of the scaled creatures that she remembered from their outward journey that had devoured several of the soldiers pursuing them when they fell into a river that they were trying to cross. Sorak shuddered as Nasa focused on what his son was pointing at.

Since all three of them could swim and had done so regularly in the lake near their home in the valley, Nasa had had no doubt that they would be able to get across the river when they found a suitable point. But this was not it. They would clearly have to move further up the mountain to find what they were looking for.

"Father?" Lenar, of course, had never seen anything like this.

"River creatures. We can't cross here, they would attack us, and our weapons would be useless against their tough skins."

"At least we can get water," Sorak said.

The river bank was still about a third of a man's height above the water, but there was nowhere where the creatures could leave the water on their side. With Lenar and Sorak holding on to him Nasa reached down and filled all of the water containers that they had, providing enough to last several days.

"It will soon be dark, we'll have to camp in those trees ahead."

Gathering his backpack, Nasa followed his own suggestion and headed for the trees. A wave of familiarity came over both him and Sorak. Two of the broad-limbed trees that they had slept in on their previous journey overhung a small clearing with a narrow stream that flowed on into the river. It was dry and seemingly free of any signs of wild animals. It was an ideal place to camp.

Nasa and Lenar again started a fire and they ate more of the flesh from Sorak's kill. They would soon have to find more flesh, but Sorak had no doubt that they would. Then, after securing their backpacks each to their chosen broad branch and Nasa had showed Lenar how to secure himself, wrapped in their animals skins, in their exhausted state, Lenar and Sorak were soon asleep. As before, Sorak took over the watch as the second moon rose. It was almost a peaceful night, the animal noises were distant and nothing entered the clearing that either Nasa or Sorak saw.

The first part of the next day was very much as the one just passed. They continued to walk along the river bank, sometimes having to detour to get around impenetrable areas of trees and bushes; they rested when the distant star was overhead and then continued.

Whenever they stopped to check whether they could cross the river they found either turbulent cataracts or un-scalable embankments on the other side. They also became aware of an increase in the noise from the river again.

"It's not the same noise," Lenar said, his young hearing probably more acute than that of Sorak or Nasa.

He proved correct. As the trees thinned out again and the climb became much steeper, they could see a cloud of mist and then the waterfall that was making the sound. The footing deteriorated as the mist condensed and made the undergrowth a wet, slimy mess that their feet could not grip. Sorak removed her shoes. Their homemade footwear had no tread, but by digging in her toes Sorak was able to make progress. Nasa and Lenar followed her lead and took off their shoes too, but made better progress by levering themselves up with their spears.

"Mother's heart, that was hard."

As they threw themselves down on a dry patch of vegetation alongside the lake at the top of the waterfall, Sorak couldn't be sure whether Nasa was laughing at her for using the ancient curse again, or in relief that they had made it safely.

But Nasa didn't rest for long. They needed to camp again, and he headed around the lake to find another clearing and another set of suitable sleeping trees. It didn't take long.

The mechanics of eating and settling for the night were soon accomplished.

Next morning, from the vantage point of her sleeping tree, Sorak could see that the river that fed the lake was broader, flowed more slowly, and the trees on the other side were sparser and more mixed, as they had been on their outwards journey. It again seemed like familiar territory. She also envisaged that they would be able to get a good view back over the plain so that they could plan their downwards journey. But clearly they had to cross over the river to do so.

As they organised themselves, none of them were in much of a hurry to get started on the next phase of their journey.

Walking around the lake and then crossing the river proved even easier than they had expected. Only a few paces from where the river gently flowed into the lake, Nasa probed his way into the water to find that at no point was it deeper than his waist. They were soon shaking the water off themselves on the other side.

"I was expecting a better view."

Sorak was conscious of several feelings all jumbled up in her mind. She was disappointed that there were too many trees to allow them to immediately look back out over the plain and identify an area to head for, yet the yearning to see the city was still there, but now accompanied by an anxiety over what Nasa might be thinking over her desire to do so.

"We will have to climb higher."

Nasa wasn't so much disappointed that their expectation that they could look out over the plain hadn't been fulfilled, more that it was going to take them still longer to be able to start down again.

They had no choice but to move on uphill.

As they did so, the light from the distant star was increasingly excluded by the increasingly densely-packed trees. This was something that they hadn't encountered before, except on the verge of the Edge when they had first left the city. Nasa instinctively followed an animal track, again leading with Lenar behind him and Sorak in the rear. He knew from experience, and from what he had been able to see already, that the wooded area couldn't last forever. Keeping alert for the animals who used the track, all they could do was push on as quickly as they could. They needed to be out of the woods by the time the light failed.

Eventually, the gloom disappeared and quite suddenly they were out of the trees.

The track had led to a small, flat, rocky area with a shallow lake fed by a spring somewhere in the rocks further up the mountain. The area that they had entered seemed to be linked to a series of much larger rocky plateaus, but Nasa couldn't get a clear view of them. It was a good place to camp.

"No. Lenar!"

Nasa was jerked back from his pondering by a sharp exclamation from Sorak as he saw her violently dash Lenar's hand away from his face. Water spilled over both of them.

Lenar looked shocked and then puzzled. He had never ever been struck by his mother before.

"Look, Lenar, look."

Settled on the bottom of the shallow lake were the bodies of two animals. Around the far edge of the lake was a mass of animal droppings both in the water and out of it.

This was yet something more beyond her son's experience.

"Lenar, the water is unfit to drink. There are dead bodies in it and animal…" She pointed at the droppings.

Lenar understood and hurriedly wiped his hand down his jerkin.

Nasa quietly handed Lenar one of their water bottles. His son now realised why his parents were always so keen to carry so much water. Chastened, he wandered off whilst Sorak and Nasa prepared to camp. This time it would have to be on the ground again with all the necessary precautions that that entailed. Neither immediately noticed that Lenar had disappeared.

At least they didn't until he reappeared looking anxious.

"Lenar?"

Nasa was quick to sense that something was wrong.

"Come!"

Puzzled in their turn Sorak and Nasa followed their son in the direction of the next rocky plateau adjoining the area where they had stopped. Lenar had gone on ahead. When they joined him he pointed silently at the ground.

What they were looking at were the remains of a fire that gave every appearance of being recent.

7

Nasa felt the ashes of the fire. He could hardly have expected them to have been warm, but they certainly seemed fresh. The area around where the fire had been was trampled down and scorched, but there were no signs of fresh growth in the vegetation.

"This is recent," Sorak said, stating the obvious in her surprise and incomprehension.

"Who could have been here?"

It was Lenar who asked the question, his confusion and anxiety stemming from his ignorance of any world but the one created by his parents. Of course he knew that there were other people on the planet, but he had been taught to believe that they were far away in the mysterious city. Yet here was evidence that that was not necessarily the case.

But neither Sorak nor Nasa had an answer for him. They were as surprised and bemused as he was.

"Keep still," Nasa said abruptly.

He was looking for other signs of occupation of the site. If someone had started a fire then clearly someone had to have been there and Nasa didn't want their trampling around to destroy anything that might tell them who that might have been.

Sorak, recognising what Nasa was thinking, stood still

where she was at the edge of the open area. Lenar had held back when they had arrived, letting his parents inspect the fireplace that he had discovered.

"Footmarks," Sorak said, "look for footmarks where the ground isn't rocky."

Lenar walked carefully over to his mother; he was mystified by his parents' sudden intense interest in the area away from the fireplace. Being youthfully impatient he walked around the very edge of the rocky area and went further into the trees that ran up the mountainside. He had no idea what his parents were looking for and was happy to leave them to it.

His attention was soon diverted.

There was another much smaller rocky clearing in the trees just out of sight of the one that they had discovered. He walked into it. This time it wasn't a fire that he found.

"Father!"

Lenar came running back to Nasa.

"Lenar?"

The boy mutely gestured to the path into the trees. His agitation quickly attracted Sorak, and whilst Nasa tried to understand what was upsetting his son, she set off immediately, her spear at the ready, in the direction that Lenar had indicated. It was only a short distance.

What she found were two dead soldiers in familiar uniforms, both lying face down. It was only when she bent down to check that the bodies were cold did she realise that they were male. It took some time for this fact to register with her since she had never ever seen such a sight in the city.

"Men soldiers!"

Nasa and Lenar had followed Sorak. What the youngster's agitation had been about was now obvious.

Unsurprisingly, Nasa was quicker to recognise that the bodies were male, but his face expressed the same puzzlement that was now showing on Sorak's.

"They can't have been dead long," Sorak said, "there's no decay, no signs that the animals have got to them."

It was true. The two men almost looked as if they were asleep. It wasn't immediately obvious how they had died until Nasa pulled back the collar of one of them. The bruises told him that they had been strangled, the standard way of slave killing slave in the city. The knowledge did nothing to allay the puzzlement of either of them. It also told them that there were more males potentially in the area. Both Nasa and Sorak went on to heightened alert.

Lenar had retreated in horror. He'd seen plenty of dead animals, but he had never before seen another person, alive or dead. He even knew that his mother had been a soldier, whatever that was, but it was never clear to him what Nasa might have been, or whether he too had been a soldier. The concept of slavery wasn't something that they would have wanted him to know about. The idea of a person killing a person was totally new to him. His experience was only of killing as a means of obtaining food.

Maybe we should strip them of their uniforms. Leaving them for the animals to tear apart when Nasa and Lenar could use them would be a waste.

Sorak was astonished that such a thought should have crept into her mind.

"We can't bury them here," Nasa said, "in the rock. We need soft ground."

"We can't bury them at all," Sorak replied, "we don't have anything to dig a hole with."

She wasn't sure that Nasa was really serious about burying the bodies, it seemed like a reflex reaction in his uncertainty over what was going on. But certainly they ought to do something with them, in all decency.

Were these the people who made the fire?

But Sorak's thoughts had instinctively moved on. Nasa

dragged a few fallen branches that still had leaves on them from within the trees to cover the bodies. Lenar saw what he was doing and started to help. Since there were very few fallen branches where they were he moved further up the hill to yet another rocky clearing in search of them.

"Ahhr!"

"Lenar?"

Nasa and Sorak could hear him, but not see him. Then an ashen-faced Lenar came back to his parents. Nasa and Sorak, on full alert, retraced their son's steps for a second time. It was obvious what had happened. Dragging a leafy branch to cover the bodies from what he clearly thought was a pile, Lenar had revealed yet another body.

"A woman," Nasa muttered.

But this time the body was naked. Lying on her back there was a ragged entry wound over her heart.

A crossbow bolt!

Her soldiering memory coming back to her aid, Sorak could see no other explanation for the wound other than a bolt striking the woman and it being retrieved.

The three stood together beside the dead woman. They had no explanation for the dead male soldiers, and now they were confronted with what was most likely a dead female soldier. What did all this mean?

The obvious interpretation was that there had been a fateful encounter, but between whom? Men soldiers were unknown to Sorak and Nasa. But why was this encounter so far from the city? And why had the woman's body been stripped naked, but not the men's? Questions, there were only questions. And they seemed to have no chance of any answers.

The distant star was overhead. Their journey had been interrupted in a most unexpected way. Both Nasa and Sorak knew that they had to move on, to ignore what they had found, to seek a new haven for themselves, but they were both transfixed by the situation that they had uncovered and seemingly unable to walk away from it, at least not without some semblance of an explanation.

Neither of them could make any sense of what had appeared to have happened. Nothing in their experience in the city or in their valley had prepared them for the situation that confronted them. They were both strangely impelled to stay until they could explain the dead bodies, the male soldiers, and how they came to die. Equally, neither had any idea how they might achieve enlightenment.

As they pondered, they both noticed that Lenar had frozen on his tip-toes. With his acute hearing he had heard something that they hadn't at first.

"Lenar?"

But then they heard it too.

There was movement in the trees; it appeared to be coming from the area somewhere behind the clearing where they had found the fireplace. There was no stealth about the movement. In concert they retreated to that area, no longer mindful of footmarks.

The noise of movement increased. Sorak and Nasa both instinctively knew that whatever was moving about wasn't an animal or group of animals. The most dangerous creatures were nocturnal, the dog packs kept up a continuous yelping, but there was no such sound accompanying this movement. And as the sounds clarified, it was clear that it was a group of people. But what people?

Both Nasa and Sorak immediately concluded that the bodies that they had discovered had to have something to do with this new manifestation. But they didn't really have time to imagine what the connection might have been; they were about to find out.

"Mother's heart!"

As Nasa and Lenar raised their spears in defence and Sorak

fitted an arrow to her bow, a group of five women soldiers in well-worn uniforms emerged into the clearing, weapons raised at the ready. It was a tense moment.

Behind the soldiers, remaining in the trees but largely visible, was another body of young women and girls dressed in a variety of equally well-worn clothes. It wasn't at first clear how many of these women and girls that there were. Who they were, and why they were with the soldiers, was a thought way too far for any of the three of them.

The soldiers cautiously moved forward into the clearing and formed a tight group, seemingly to shield their civilian companions.

Neither Sorak, Nasa nor Lenar could at first see who was in charge of the soldiers who nonetheless conducted themselves in an orderly and disciplined manner.

Then it became clear.

A black woman with a tenant's markings on her uniform then stepped forward, her crossbow raised and aimed at Sorak.

"Kragar!" Sorak muttered.

Then there was total silence.

8

Soran, the self-appointed chairman of the Senate knew that something was wrong. Not sufficiently intellectually endowed to actually worry too much, he nonetheless disliked any unexpected changes to the highly controlled management of the city, or at least the part of it that was within his remit, that he had set up. He was well aware that his minions had been unable to suppress the renewed fighting between his men and the bands of women who lived outside the city but who also seemed to enter with impunity.

His efforts to track down and eliminate Kragar, the arrogant tenant of the Senate guard in the old days, the most prominent of the dissident women's leaders, had so far proved unsuccessful. And the return of his latest punitive expedition into the hinterland beyond the Edge was now well overdue. It wouldn't be the first such expedition not to return.

His arrival at the Senate administration building and his carefully guarded office before Kragan was unprecedented. Kragan was always there before him; something must have happened to him. Something had.

"Soranmam, Kragan's house has been broken into. His guards are all dead."

The current commander of the Senate guard, having no idea what a male form of respect might be, persisted with the old form, even though he knew Soran hated it. Soran had the vague feeling that he was being laughed at.

"And Kragan, where is Kragan?"

"We have no idea. His woman was in another part of the house and only found out that something had happened when the patrol found the dead guards and roused her."

Soran was immediately suspicious.

"In another part of the house: how convenient. Torture her, she will know more."

The guard commander, knowing Soran's limited patience, didn't think it prudent to tell him that the woman had disappeared as soon as the guard patrol had alerted him. But Soran would not have been surprised. By quietly unlocking doors, it was the woman who had facilitated the capture of her tyrannical companion. She was now in a safe house in Sector Four awaiting the opportunity to leave the city.

The small crowd of both men and women that had congregated in front of the outer city gate adjacent to Sector Four stared at the figure hanging from the top battlement with varying degrees of interest. Most of the women seemed content to see that it was a man. The men were angry. The man's clothes suggested that he was someone of importance, but it was the obvious signs of mutilation that was causing the anger.

Then the mood changed.

"Kragan!"

The body had at last been recognised. The fury of the men, mostly ex-workers from the vegetable gardens and water plants, focused on the women present, but they were outnumbered and unarmed and unable to vent their anger.

Once they knew who the dead man was, the women, however, began to hurriedly disperse. No one as important as

Kragan had been killed in the now almost perpetual warfare, at least not since the original rebellion, and the reaction of the Senate was expected to be ferocious.

* * *

"Kragar!"

As Lenar looked totally perplexed but unafraid, and Nasa watched his son anxiously, Sorak spoke the name of the guard commander aloud. The first live person that their boy had met couldn't have been more different from his parents.

There was an almost comic frozen moment whilst Kragar digested the fact that apparently in the middle of nowhere, a woman dressed in clothes made of animal skins actually knew her name.

"Sorak?"

The question came slowly and in disbelief. Both Kragar and Sorak, like Nasa, were in their middle years, both had become leaner, tougher, but older in the face. Recognition took Kragar longer than Sorak.

Kragar threw down her crossbow, gestured to the other soldiers to lower theirs, and advanced on Sorak with open arms. With what little memory that she could conjure up, Sorak could only recall Kragar's arrogant contempt for her and her toleration of her simply for Lenen's benefit. This was not what she would have expected Kragar's reaction to be.

The black woman grasped Sorak by the shoulders and held her at arms' length, her eyes meeting the white woman's as they never had before.

"Sorak," she almost whispered, still not quite believing what she was seeing.

Sorak gently pulled back, not because she resented the contact but because Lenar had moved towards his mother as Kragar held her and Nasa had had to restrain him.

Poor Lenar, it was one shock after another in a very short space of time. Just as he was becoming reconciled to the dead bodies he was confronted with someone, who was obviously a woman, but being black was once again beyond his experience.

"Nasa, you will remember him," Sorak gestured at her partner. She was determined not to introduce him by his slave number.

"And this is Lenar, our son."

Kragar held out her hand to Nasa. He took it in surprise, but of course he had no idea about the changed status of men. As Kragar turned to Lenar he retreated, but when she smiled, something that Sorak had never seen her do before, her face lit up and Lenar tentatively reached out his hand.

"I can't believe it," was all that Kragar was able to say.

Then the movement behind her brought Kragar back to the realities of the moment.

The group of young women and girls gathered with the soldiers began to push forward. Sensing nothing hostile they seemed anxious to be a part of what was now going on.

At a signal from Kragar the soldiers divided and the group, three young women and four girls, moved into the clearing and as a body stood around Sorak, Nasa and Lenar, and stared. All, that is, but one of the older girls who hung back and agitatedly shook her head and wrung her hands.

"We must deal with the bodies," Kragar said, the officer in charge again.

The soldiers began to strip the uniforms from the bodies of the two men. When they had finished they carried them off into the trees beside the lake. They returned without them; Sorak presumed that they had thrown them into the lake.

None of the three knew what had happened to the body of the woman, but Sorak didn't suppose that she too had been thrown into the lake.

"We must camp here for the night," Kragar said once the bodies had been dealt with.

Camping for the group was obviously a familiar routine. Everybody seemed to know what to do and in no time a sleeping area had been established for the unexplained young women and girls, with the soldiers billeting themselves around the edge of the clearing. Under Kragar's instructions a separate area was reserved for Sorak, Nasa and Lenar.

The same fireplace was used.

As things settled down, groups formed amongst the young women and girls, but Sorak noticed that the older girl, who was probably Lenar's age, had held back again and kept herself to herself.

There's something odd about that one.

There was a vacant look in the girl's eyes that Sorak found disturbing.

"We rescued her from a group of men."

It was Kragar who had seen Sorak, and also Lenar, looking at the girl. Kragar didn't say that the men were soldiers and that they were now all dead.

"They misused her," Kragar continued. "She's terrified of men."

Both women by instinct looked over at Lenar. He had clearly sensed the girl's terror and, although he was smiling at her, he made no attempt to approach her.

"Desak, she was administrative category despite being so white."

Sorak looked at Kragar as she said this, but she saw no signs of the contempt that such a statement would have been accompanied with in the past. Kragar appeared to have changed and, for Sorak, very much for the better.

Desak was aware that Lenar was looking at her. But, unlike the violent men soldiers that she had only met, she felt no terror of him. But in her tortured mind she wasn't able to grasp the significance of this lack of fear.

Again, to Sorak's surprise the initiative later came from Kragar.

"We need to talk," she said to Sorak.

Sorak and Nasa were sitting together away from Kragar's party. Lenar was asleep, just visible as a heap of animal skins.

Nasa made as if to move away, uncertain whether he was included within the invitation or not.

Yet more surprise for Sorak; Kragar drew Nasa back by gently pulling his arm.

"Things are very different in the city."

Remembering the Sorak of old, Kragar knew that her best approach was to be direct.

"Soon after Mareck and Lenen left the city to chase after you, the quarry slaves rebelled."

"Mesrick," Sorak muttered.

Why doesn't this surprise me?

"Yes, but she was killed soon after things got going."

Kragar's description of the rebellion was sanitised largely because she was prominent in resisting the slaves' uprising. The overthrow of the Senate, the take-over by the generals and their defeat by the slaves and dissident women, Kragar equally skipped over, giving little detail. Both Sorak and Nasa recognised that they weren't being told everything.

"You were the hero, Sorak, the inspiration. You had broken free, taken control of your life, so had 15... Nasa, and for a few cycles men and women worked together to make the administration of the city work."

Sorak's attributed role didn't register with her, so surprised was she at what she was hearing. She found the idea of rebellion hard to grasp.

"The Senate?" asked Nasa.

"The Senate, the administrators, the black and brown women were no longer in charge. They were retired, at least for the first few cycles. Eventually they were imprisoned in a camp on the Edge."

Both Sorak and Nasa found themselves struggling with what Kragar was telling them. There was nothing in their experience to aid their understanding.

"It was an uneasy relationship. The change came when the old senators and administrators were all killed by what you might call a new generation of men."

"Born as slaves but brought up as free men," Nasa said.

There was a distant look in his eyes that Sorak had never seen before. It was as if he could relate to this new generation of men.

"And free from any concept of restraint," the black tenant added.

Kragar realised that her narrative raised more questions with Sorak and Nasa than it was providing answers for. She decided to hurry on to the current situation.

"After about ten cycles or so, the young men formed a small Senate and the self-appointed leader of the Senate, Soran, in effect ran the city. Anybody, men or women, who resisted his rule were killed, if they didn't escape into the area beyond the Edge.

"The women of the city were increasingly being forced into servitude. It's become a version of the old administration, except that there are increasing numbers of resistance groups."

Nasa waved his hand at the lazing women soldiers. Kragar nodded without admitting that she was seen as the leader of the most notorious resistance group, or bandits as they were known to Soran.

"So, what happened to the soldiers here?"

Sorak, direct as ever, needed time to digest what she had been told, but couldn't prevent her curiosity from getting the better of her.

"The male Senate sends out parties of soldiers to hunt down the resistance groups. We are a resistance group; that must be obvious. On this occasion we weren't being hunted, but we came across a group of women and girls guarded by two soldiers, where the rest of the party were we didn't know at the time. We killed the guards and headed for the mountains with the women and girls. Our trail was picked up by the other male soldiers. They followed us. There were running battles, then, as we came down the mountain, they sent a couple of their men to try to get in front of us and cut us off. They killed Aslak, but we captured them and dealt with them as you saw."

"And," said Sorak.

"We ambushed the main party and killed them all."

The finality in Kragar's voice said that there was nothing more to tell about the incident. But still there were questions unanswered.

On this occasion, and at no other time, did Kragar explain where the rescued women and girls had come from, and why they were so far from the city.

Nasa was increasingly uncomfortable about the slaughter of so many of the male soldiers, but he recognised that with a strictly limited male population to draw on, the fewer soldiers there were the better it was for the resisting women.

There was another long silence. It was the silence of exhaustion, of utter disbelief, of still-persisting incomprehension. Kragar signified her recognition that Sorak and Nasa needed time to grasp and get familiar with what she had told them. Only then would she know whether they accepted the new world that she had outlined to them and what their reaction to it might be.

9

"What is she not telling us?"

Nasa was suspicious of Kragar's new friendliness. With no experience to draw from but his past, he had never known a black woman even notice the likes of him, let alone shake his hand. But he couldn't see what she could possibly get out of being on terms of equality with him.

"But things are different in the city now," Sorak responded.

Her problem was that she wasn't sure that she fully understood in what ways things were different beyond slavery having ended. Having lived with Nasa on equal terms for so long, Sorak hadn't yet registered that in simple terms all men now had Nasa's status. Simply repeating Kragar's statement didn't help either.

They were finishing their morning meal and packing up. It was about the only stress-free night that they had had for some time. Kragar and the soldiers were already packed and formed up. The young women and girls had nothing to pack up so they were instantly ready. Lenar was distracted again by the sad face of Desak who still kept herself apart from all the other women and girls.

"Why is she so sad?" he asked.

Sorak was surprised that he knew what sadness was, but he had overheard conversations between Desak's companions that he didn't understand. It was they who called her sad; and they, of course, knew why.

"She's had a great shock," his mother replied. He knew what a shock was. "That makes her sad."

There was no way that Sorak was going to explain what had happened to Desak to Lenar. She didn't know the details, nor wanted to, but he definitely would not have understood. Sexual relations were an area of Lenar's education that was lacking, there never having been any need to discuss the topic.

"We have to head back to the city and return the women we have rescued. Rather, we have to return them to a safe place. They can enter the city, we can't."

Nasa realised that there was a question in Kragar's statement. Where were they going to go? But he wasn't sure that he had an answer.

Sorak and Nasa had talked over what Kragar had told them the previous evening, in fact they had talked quietly for half the night. They were still sure that they didn't have the full picture, but they understood well enough how they thought the situation in the city could have changed. As a consequence, both knew that they had a decision to make. Sorak's vague desire to see the city again, physically, if not enter it, took on a new significance in view of what the black woman had said.

Maybe it would be safe to return. With the new male-dominated administration, even if they couldn't visualise it, it meant that the risk to Nasa of returning had disappeared. What it meant for Sorak was less clear.

Nasa was worried. Somewhere inside himself he sensed a change. He couldn't recognise it as the beginnings of a new, different, direction to his life. But somewhere the thought was maturing that there had to be more than just living out his life in remote isolation, achieving nothing but comfortable survival. Something else now had to be possible. It was the uncertainty that this introduced, however, that worried him.

And there's Lenar. What life would that be for him?

This was a question that he and Sorak had pondered over many times, and in their hearts they both knew that leaving the valley was also about trying to envisage a future for their son. But until now there had been no alternative that they could see. Returning to the city now that men were on an equal footing with women would potentially give Lenar the chances that they wanted for him. But whatever way they looked at it there was always still the issue of what returning to the city would mean for Sorak. The one thing that was clear from Kragar's narrative was that women had lost status in the city, but Sorak could get no idea of what the position of women in the new scheme of things now was. And she doubted that Kragar was the best person to give a view on this.

Kragar said that Sorak was a hero. Both the ordinary women and the slaves had been inspired by what she had done.

But having only had a limited involvement with women outside of the military, Sorak had no concept of who 'ordinary women' were, and how they might think.

Equally Nasa was still not sure that it would mean that Sorak would be welcome by the men now running the city, but at least it seemed less likely that he himself would be killed.

Maybe going back to the city is an option now. But how can we be sure?

Nasa's life's experiences told him that they never could be sure. The dilemma was overwhelming for him; a chance for a proper life for Lenar, but still a serious risk of harm to Sorak. What a choice for him to make!

Kragar was keen to depart.

"We must get moving. We don't know how many more

search parties there are, and how far they have spread out from the city.

"We will leave you the uniforms from the dead soldiers. If you were to return to the city, no one would notice you dressed as soldiers, dressed in animal skins..." Kragar didn't need to say any more.

One of the uniforms fitted Nasa, but, because Lenar was taller than his father, the other was less of a fit for him. Kragar simply laughed and said that the men in the city now wore all sorts of odd clothing in place of their slave harnesses. With the crossbow bolt hole in the front, Sorak was less keen on wearing the uniform of the dead Aslak, but she did so anyway. If there was any chance of their meeting a patrol themselves, or of their returning to the city, blending in was going to be important.

"We would only have buried them," Kragar said, "the less we have to carry, the better."

But Kragar also had something private to say to Sorak. She drew her away from Nasa and Lenar this time and, in a few short sentences, told Sorak who and where it would be safe to contact in the city if she chose to follow them, and where it was safe to stay outside the city. Sorak was surprised by the information, it suggested that more of the city than she had imagined was still in the hands of the women.

"But be aware. We are fighting the chairman of the Senate, Soran, because he wants to go back to the old days but in reverse. Not all men agree with him, not all women oppose him. If you do go back to the city, things could well have changed again; they are changing all the time. Be cautious; trust no one until you are really sure of them."

And, without waiting for any response from Sorak, Kragar signalled her soldiers to set off back into the trees and up the mountainside. They herded the young women and girls in front of them. They were soon out of sight and hearing.

Sorak immediately told Nasa what the black tenant had said.

"Maybe what she wasn't telling us was that things in the city are far more dangerous than she had first suggested," she said.

"So, should we carry on with our search for a new homestead?"

Nasa's response to Sorak didn't sound convincing. She had never found him so uncertain, yet, despite the positive intention in his words, there was nothing about his demeanour that said that he was sure that that was what they really should do. She recognised the inherent uncertainty because that was what she felt herself. Somewhere deep in her mind, the thoughts of an idealised life in a hidden valley had faded. Too many thoughts, too many options began to crowd out the purpose of their leaving the valley.

Lenar had wandered off into the trees following the path that Kragar and the soldiers had taken. He could see the track as it came out of the trees and led up to the steep mountainside. He watched as the party emerged and headed up the barren rocky mountain. The figures were indistinct. He wondered if that was the way that they would soon be going.

But his parents didn't seem to be in any hurry to move in any particular direction. This puzzled him. He was so used to their being decisive and knowing what to do that his puzzlement began to turn to concern in his mind. He sensed that something significant had changed in his life, but couldn't visualise what.

"Lenar!"

Nasa was calling him back to the clearing. Maybe they would now set off.

But Nasa simply wanted to know where his son was. There were still hazards in the forested areas around them, particularly wild animals; Nasa had already heard the faint sounds of a dog pack. Lenar had heard that too.

As Lenar returned to the clearing the yelping of the dogs

grew suddenly louder. The excited noise meant that they had located prey, and the increased noise said that it was rapidly getting closer to where they were. All three readied themselves for the arrival of the pack.

The crashing sounds in the undergrowth around the path that the soldiers' party had taken suggested that the pack was about to burst on them from there. But then suddenly it wasn't the pack of dogs that broke cover.

The stumbling figure of a terrified Desak emerged into the clearing with one of the dogs leaping up onto her back. First to react, Lenar speared the dog as the pack snarled and yelped their way into the clearing. With no time to deal with the dead dog, both Nasa and Sorak fired into the seething mass of animals, whilst Lenar scooped Desak up in his arms and carried her to the other side of the clearing.

The mayhem continued as the dogs set upon their dead and injured pack members and finally withdrew back into the forest.

Knowing that the smell of blood would draw other more formidable creatures, Sorak and Nasa gathered up their backpacks, Nasa carrying Lenar's, and immediately headed off away from the clearing and the river, and deeper into the forest. It was the only route possible for them. Lenar carried Desak, who had now fortunately lapsed into unconsciousness. Nasa, with his new-found uncertainties, wasn't clear exactly which way he should be heading, but he knew that, as before, if he kept moving along the base of the mountains they would be heading in the direction that they had first intended to take.

Having put distance between themselves and the dog pack Nasa eventually stopped as they came to the edge of the forest again. They had been climbing steeply up the mountainside; if they were to resume their intended search for a new haven they were going in the wrong direction. They had to decide once and for all which way they were going to go.

Lenar had carried Desak throughout the journey. She seemed to float in and out of consciousness but never uttered a word. It was only as they stopped and Lenar looked for a place to lay her down that he realised that his hand was sticky with her blood.

"She bleeds," Lenar said anxiously.

This was a worry, leaving a trail for the dogs or other animals was not a good idea.

As Lenar laid Desak down, it was obvious from her bloodstained garment that she had been bitten in the back of her right thigh.

"We must hunt for orange sticks. Their juice will help heal the wound."

It was something that Sorak and Nasa had discovered many cycles ago; yet another valuable attribute of the ubiquitous orange sticks. But their previous stock had been exhausted.

Whilst Lenar stayed with Desak, Sorak and Nasa searched. Experience told them that the trees from which the sticks could be taken usually grew near water. So high up the mountainside this looked as if it might be a problem, but a shout from Nasa told the others that he had been successful.

Sorak tore a narrow strip from one of her last remaining undergarments and, crushing the juice into the wound, bound it tightly. Desak let out a plaintive whimper as the juice stung into the exposed flesh. Lenar cradled her in his arms, almost as if she were a favourite animal, and gently rocked her until the pain subsided.

"Will they come looking for her? Shouldn't we have stayed where we were?" Lenar was still anxious.

Sorak exchanged looks with Nasa; they both knew that Kragar wouldn't stop to look for the girl, she would want to get out of the area in case there were more parties of male soldiers.

Kragar would push on. Finding the young women and girls

was a problem for her. If there was one less, there was one less problem.

Sorak knew how the black woman would think. She might seem to have mellowed in the face of the way things had changed in the city, but Kragar was hard and ruthless, and always would be.

Sorak, needless to say, didn't share her thoughts with her son.

The distant star was well below the horizon. Nasa had already located a couple of sleeping trees, but he was concerned about Desak; had she slept in a tree before, did they need to tie her to a branch?

"I will watch over her," Lenar said.

His attention to Desak was noted by both his parents. They were pleased at his obvious desire to help the poor girl, but neither supposed that it was any more than innate kindness. Lenar's upbringing had left him short on the understanding of his emotions; parental love was his limit, love for another person was unknown to him since, until the previous day, he had never known another person. But all manner of unfamiliar and unexpected feelings were washing around his brain and even his body. Something primitive was stirring in Lenar, something that Nasa would have recognised.

Sleeping trees were in abundance on the edge of the forest.

It was a noisy night. The death cries of the hunted filled the air almost continually. Lenar, whilst sitting on the same branch as Desak, had had to fend off one of the 'leopard'-like creatures similar to those that had invaded their old valley with his spear. Clearly there was still enough of a smell of blood about Desak, despite the orange sticks, to attract the sensitive noses of these ferocious animals. And in the way of the planet the injured beast was dragged away from below the tree by something bigger and fiercer that Lenar didn't see.

Desak slept fitfully, but in the morning her skin was no longer burning hot and she was no longer sweating. But still she hadn't said a word.

Nasa drew Sorak away from the tree and their son with his charge. It was obvious what was on his mind.

"So, what are we going to do about her? We know that Kragar will have abandoned her, are we to take her with us to our new home?"

Sorak noted the uncertainty once again in Nasa's voice. Desak was a complication that they didn't need. They had both been pleased by Lenar's compassion towards the girl, but how long would that last once she had recovered? And both Nasa and Sorak knew that she would recover; something was troubling her, as Sorak was aware, but she was a fit and presumably resilient young woman. And soon, when she was fully recovered, she would want to know what was to happen to her herself. Manifestly a city dweller, Sorak had a problem seeing Desak in a bucolic lifestyle.

"What else can we do?"

They both knew that there were options. They could take Desak to the Edge opposite the city and hand her over to one of the resistance groups before finding their new valley. They could take her directly back to the city to the safe house that Kragar had told them about. They could abandon her in the forest, they could even kill her, but these last two options would destroy their relationship with their son.

But the one thing that Sorak now felt that they couldn't do was simply to head for the plain again, hunt for a haven, and integrate Desak into the family. She couldn't see how that would work. Just like Lenar, she needed a future, and Sorak was increasingly realising that keeping them all together in the wilderness really wasn't an option, as it wasn't a future for the youngsters at all. The idea that it wasn't a future for her and Nasa either wasn't very far below the surface.

"We must take her back to the city."

It was what Sorak had started to think, but to hear it straight out from Nasa was a major shock. It was the last thing that she would have expected him to say. She didn't know how to respond. Going back to the city would satisfy her strange yearning, but it would destroy the security of their existence. Sorak knew in her heart that she didn't want that. Only the day before, it was a possibility that she would have rejected outright in her mind because she knew that Nasa didn't want to go anywhere near the city, yet it was him suggesting that they might now do so.

"Nasa, how can we take her back to the city? What if we meet one of Kragan's parties of men soldiers? We have two crossbows now, but…"

The incoherence of Sorak's response told Nasa that she was also uncertain what to do, which, in turn, confused him when it was she who had expressed the desire to see the city again.

So Sorak sought escape in preparing food and checking on Desak.

From long cycles of living together both Sorak and Nasa knew from each other's behaviour that they would be heading back to the city. If they had not been going to do so Sorak would have been more purposeful in her actions and Nasa would have busied himself with preparation for their next day's march. That they were hesitant told them each what the other was feeling: reluctant necessity.

"What's your name?"

The relief felt by all three of them at Desak's question to Lenar was almost palpable.

10

Kragar knew that they had lost Desak and, as Sorak had predicted that she would, she had pressed on up the mountain. Fearful of the black officer, none of the other women and girls dared to question what had happened to their former companion. Kragar's biggest concern now was crossing the fast-flowing river that they had come to.

This is not the way we came.

Kragar was angry with herself at having been forced by their encounter with the patrol of male soldiers to take a different route back towards the city. She realised now that she should have crossed back over the river at the clearing where they had left Sorak and Nasa. But by staying on the side that they were now on she faced a much more difficult crossing further up the mountain. They had no option but to cross.

The possibility of just continuing to climb wasn't open to them as there appeared to be no passage through the mountains at this point, just a line of jagged peaks. If they had taken an even wider diversion, as Nasa and Sorak were about to do, they would have come to a pass, but then they would have had to approach the city from an unfamiliar direction. This, however, was not an option because Kragar knew that the patrols along the Edge had been stepped up by the Senate and the risk of meeting one was too great. These extra patrols were something that Kragar didn't mention to Sorak because, from her conversations with her, she didn't think that she had any intention of going to the city. But, of course, unbeknown to her, rescuing Desak had changed everything!

Nonetheless, what Kragar didn't know was that the patrols had indeed been stepped up both in number and scope, but with a reduced number of soldiers in each patrol. There simply weren't enough male soldiers to meet the demands placed on them by Soran and the Senate. Any patrol that they might have met would have undoubtedly been no match for her and her experienced women soldiers.

But the tumbling, gurgling sound told Kragar that they had reached the river that they needed to cross, forcing her to address the more immediate problem. She ordered a rest whilst she considered how they were going to achieve the crossing.

* * *

With the decision to head for the city made, both Sorak and Nasa relaxed a little. But they needed to give some thought to the problem of how Desak was going to cope with the journey ahead since they had no idea how robust she actually was.

Desak had spoken for the first time and the blank expression had gone from her eyes. That was a good sign. At least it seemed that they would now be able to communicate with her.

Lenar's reaction to Desak's asking his name had been comic. He looked at her in disbelief. Her voice was clearer, higher and sweeter than Sorak's, or Kragar's, the only female voices that he had ever heard. He was captivated. But Lenar, like his parents, was also concerned about her ability to undertake the journey ahead of them.

Having taken the uniforms of the dead soldiers, Sorak,

Nasa and Lenar were well clothed and well shod for the journey. Sorak had given Desak her animal skin jerkin, but her shoes were in no way as good as the military boots that the others were now wearing. But, with nothing else available, they had no choice but to set off and to support Desak as best they could.

As they set off they soon began to wonder why they had worried, as Desak skipped happily alongside Lenar, chattering continually about anything and everything that she was now seeing. Was this the same young woman?

However, there didn't seem to be much point in trying to understand the change in Desak. They were just happy that she looked as if she was going to be less of a burden than they had expected.

With Nasa in the lead, Lenar and Desak behind and Sorak in the rear they were soon making steady progress.

But then they encountered their first obstacle. The familiar yelping of the wild dogs alerted them. As they breasted a small hump in the rocky slope they came to a gully that they would have to cross.

It wasn't a particularly difficult gully to have to cross, but around the rim, oblivious to them, the howling dogs had congregated. They couldn't at first see what was in the gully that was attracting the dogs' interest.

Desak tried to suppress a cry of alarm, her new-found confidence evaporating. But Lenar knew what to do. Now in charge of Sorak's bow, he fitted an arrow and braced himself. He didn't fire at once. Following the seething pack's movements he finally located the alpha male and shot it in the rump.

"How did he know not to kill it outright?" Nasa asked Sorak when they later discussed the incident. She had no idea.

But Lenar had observed the dogs' behaviour sufficiently to realise that when injured they immediately tried to escape the pack. In this case, the alpha male took off down the mountainside as the easiest route. Momentarily confused by their leader being injured, the dogs hesitated, but not for long. The cacophony of noise in pursuit also heralded the new fight for supremacy amongst the pack. As the dogs tumbled down the mountainside they showed no interest in Sorak's party in their frenzy.

Lenar and Nasa carefully approached the gully. What they found was yet another surprise. A family group of the large long-toothed predators that both Sorak and Nasa had encountered lay in a frozen cameo. The female was feeding four young. They then saw what had been exciting the dogs. The male lay on its side, breathing heavily, part of its stomach ripped open. Badly injured in an attack it had clearly crept back to its lair.

"We can't cross here."

But Desak, having quickly recovered her composure, had walked a little way further up the side of the gully to a point where it would be possible for all of them to leap across.

It was the only incident in a long dreary slog up the mountain. The route was clear and obvious with the entrance of the pass visible throughout their climb. It was almost dark when they arrived, but Lenar quickly found a small cave and a trickle of water coming from a spring. The cave showed no signs of having been occupied by any of the fierce creatures of the night. They soon had a fire going and ate a portion of their diminishing food stocks.

Exhausted, they all soon settled down for the night. A grinning nod from Nasa, with a rare show of feeling, revealed Desak and Lenar huddled together under Lenar's animal skins. Nasa set himself to watch.

"Lenar, we are only taking Desak back to safety in the city; then we will come back over the mountain."

There was no conviction in Nasa's voice. He was no longer certain of anything and that worried him. But he felt that Lenar should know what their plans were, even if they did change them later.

As they all stirred after their night in the cave, Nasa's sense of Sorak's feelings told him that she too was uncertain. Now that they were going to see the city again it was as if she no longer wanted to. The reality for her was turning out to be more daunting than the yearning that she had felt, although she was taking her time to recognise this.

And just as Nasa knew that his expectations were changing, so too he sensed were Lenar's. But what his son's expectations now were, he had no idea. The arrival of Desak had seemingly changed everything. Sorak, Nasa knew, lived in the day, so her expectations tended to be fairly straightforward.

"We must find more flesh. We must take every chance to make a kill."

Practical Sorak was packing away the remains of the food supply and alerting Nasa to their growing need.

The journey through the pass was much easier than anything that they had experienced so far. As they left the cave and headed upwards again they very soon entered the high-sided gully that formed the pass. In places the sides were so tall and steep that the light from the distant star, since it was not yet overhead, was almost obscured. On several occasions they had to cross fast-flowing streams that appeared from clefts in the rocks and disappeared again just as suddenly. None of them were very wide and even Desak was able to skip across them with ease. The water was mostly crystal clear and refreshingly cold, but, as Sorak had pointed out, they needed to check each time before drinking as there were plenty of signs that the pass was well used by the animal life.

As the distant star rose to its zenith and was directly overhead, they reached the summit of the pass. The rocky sides had slowly fallen away and at the very top they found themselves in a flat, open area.

Poorly clothed, Desak shivered. They had so far been protected from the wind by being in the gully. At the top they had lost that protection. The wind was bitingly cold.

Nonetheless, Sorak hesitated. Immediately in front of them the rocky area of the renewed gully soon got lost in the forest that stretched out almost as far as they could see. In the haze that accompanied the bright light of the distant star, Sorak could just make out the end of the forest and the Edge. But at that distance the city was far too far away to make out even an outline. She had no doubt that it was there, but it would take more hard marching to reach it. Sorak's feelings were mixed.

"We should move on," Nasa said as Desak shivered again.

They quickly descended into the forest. The quality of the footing got steadily worse. The dank, steamy smells and the foul, decaying mess that they had to walk through brought instant memories to Sorak and Nasa, but revulsion to Desak and concern from Lenar who could see that her footwear was now totally inadequate. Having stopped her from falling into the mess more than once, he knew that something had to be done.

Handing his weapons to his father, Lenar encouraged Desak to climb onto his back, which with giggles that delighted them all, she did.

Progress was painfully slow until the fetid mess underfoot gave way to dryer, firmer ground.

As Lenar let Desak down and they paused to allow him to recover his breath, Sorak gave Nasa a questioning look and moved out of their son's earshot.

"Boot marks!"

Nasa had seen them.

Lenar and Desak chattered away, increasingly content with each other's company. As they all rested, Sorak and Nasa talked quietly. Neither seemed too surprised to find signs of life after what Kragar had said and what she had implied. They had both seen the footprints of military boots in the soft ground.

Patrols made sense if the authorities were trying to capture the women who had escaped from the city. There weren't many prints, partly because of the improving nature of the ground, but also, Sorak assumed, because there weren't many soldiers in the group.

With the reality of their arrival in the area behind the Edge, neither Sorak nor Nasa had a very clear plan on how to proceed. Kragar had only given Sorak limited information on the communities of women in the city, one of which they needed to contact to deliver Desak. Most of what Kragar had told them was about the resistance groups and, as they contemplated their next actions, they were beginning to realise that this information didn't amount to very much, and wasn't a whole lot of use to them. Sorak knew that Kragar only saw things in her own terms, which were narrow and self-interested, so she hadn't really placed much faith in what the black officer had told her. Basically, they were on their own now; that didn't bother Sorak.

After the initial rebellion, the city had lacked a formal administration until some of the more intelligent ex-slaves formed one, essentially by imitation. But, with the upheavals that followed the rebellion and the reaction to the Generals' efforts to run the city, there was no formal military structure.

The forcible takeover of the city by Soran and his supporters provided an administration of its own but only on a limited scale, as there weren't enough capable men willing to get involved. Equally, there weren't enough men drawn from the previous menial areas of activity to form an adequately large military force. Still more fundamental, there wasn't anybody to train male soldiers unless some of the former women troopers could be persuaded to do so. Some were, but in insufficient numbers. But there were still a significant number of men, ex-slaves from the quarries and vegetable gardens, who resisted being forced into the service of the city, or of Soran, to be more precise.

So just as there were renegade women, there were also an indeterminate number of unemployed, and potentially unemployable, men.

None of this was conveyed to Sorak by Kragar, whose inherent arrogance and disdain prevented her from acknowledging anything but the oppressive regime of Soran as being worthy of attention.

So, as Sorak and Nasa contemplated how they were going to enter the city, they really had no idea what to expect from the ordinary women and men. And, more particularly in their immediate situation, they had no idea of the significance of there obviously being a patrol in the area at which they had arrived.

"Men or women? Friendly or hostile?"

Neither had an answer, but Lenar's sudden reaching for his weapons after having heard some movement in the forest suggested that they might be about to find out.

11

Back in the city, Soran's reaction to the death of Kragan was confused and governed by a frustration that he didn't know how to deal with.

He was honest enough to recognise that the dead man was intellectually far more capable than he was, if timid and reluctant to resort to violence. But Soran was beginning to learn that violence wasn't always the best way to deal with the rising resistance to his rule. The obvious fact was that the majority of women were more capable than the majority of the men. Everybody accepted that the breeding programme would eventually relieve this situation, but discouraging the former quarry slaves, vegetable garden workers and other such low-grade men from breeding was causing a major part of his problems. But he could hardly tell these men that they couldn't be allowed to breed because they would produce another generation of intellectually challenged workers whose only role would be the very one that they were actively rejecting. Soran could see no relief from this dilemma.

Kragan would know what to do.

But there was no Kragan anymore.

The Senate were getting restive. None of the five senators had been personal slaves, or had worked in the administration offices. They, like Soran, had relied on Kragan. And, like Soran, their horizons were narrow and their expectations unachievable. It was a combination that also made them dangerous to Soran. Now that at least two of the patrols that they had sent out to hunt down the renegade women had failed to return, one commanded by one of the more obstreperous of the senators, the pressure on Soran had eased somewhat. But the presumed death of a further eight of their precious trained male soldiers was probably just as serious.

"We must punish the women for the loss of our soldiers," one of the senators had proposed.

Soran was wary. Taking reprisals had been something that they had done before, but all it had actually done was provoke yet more violence and the deaths of yet more soldiers. Soran, at least, knew that they could little afford to lose more troopers.

"There's an encampment of ex-garden workers down by the sewage plant, and the old barracks nearby is full of displaced women."

And these women weren't soldiers.

For most of the men, and that included the senators, mangeneers were the most feared of the women. Part engineer, part manager, they had been the hardcore of the old day-to-day administration. Many had escaped with the women soldiers, but many had just faded into the background in the city and Soran and the Senate really had no idea what they were up to, or how many of them there were for that matter. Soran didn't know that the women referred to here were of the old mangeneer category, any more than the senator did, but for him any group of organised women represented a threat.

Soran understood what the senator was implying. The unemployed men were a problem, just as much as the unemployed or dissident women. Set them against each other and no soldiers would be risked.

A plan was agreed.

The senator undertook to provoke the clash. But, for Soran, it was important that the men felt that they were avenging the soldiers killed by the women outside of the city. There was some debate about how that message could be conveyed to the unemployed men when being press-ganged into the military was one of their grievances. Would they care?

The senator solved the problem rather crudely by killing one of the ex-slaves himself and then capturing and attacking one of the women from the barracks. By leaving the dying woman by the man's body in a carefully constructed cameo, the men were immediately incensed and prepared for revenge. The senator, unlike Soran, didn't see the need for a clear justification for the attack that he was fermenting. As far as he was concerned, anything that galvanised the unemployed men to attack the mangeneers was good enough.

The ex-garden workers had retained some of their tools and a body of about thirty of the younger men set off for the barracks in Sector Four. When they arrived at the first barrack block there was no one there. Disappointed, they rampaged through the living quarters, smashing everything that they could lay their hands on and then making an unsuccessful attempt at setting the buildings alight. Having exhausted their energies, the men made no effort to attack the other barrack blocks.

But then, still angry, they eventually returned to where they had camped near the sewage works. Something was wrong. They could find no signs of the older men whom they had left behind. Reluctant to enter the working area of the sewage works, it was only when one of the men climbed the outer city wall did they find out the answer. Pegged out in the detritus of the sewage treatment plant, the ten older men were all still just about alive but bleeding and infested with all manner of the nasty creatures that inhabited the foul smelling mess.

All died before they could be rescued.

But, in a rather perverse way, the incident turned out well for Soran. Recognising their vulnerability if not part of Soran's domain, he acquired thirty new volunteers to be trained as soldiers.

* * *

Kragar's party crossed the river. The women soldiers found a tree that had fallen partially across the water in an open area of wide curves and with beaches inside the curves. Scrambling through the branches, they found that they could drop off the tree and the water only came up to their waists. The young women and girls either waded themselves or were carried by the soldiers. The crossing point seemed tranquil and undisturbed. Unlike Sorak and Nasa, they found no signs of the fearsome scaled creatures to threaten their progress.

The forest and ground-covering vegetation on the side of the river that they had now crossed over to were dense, boggy and, in places, impenetrable. It was almost dark before they could find a place to camp. The remaining young women and girls were fractious and exhausted. Kragar, never a patient person at the best of times, was rapidly becoming intolerant of them.

Why did we have to get burdened with these whining creatures?

"When the distant star rises we will head straight for the Edge. We may then have to go across part of the plain but that should get us to our base camp as quickly as possible."

The soldiers were more tolerant of the civilians, carrying the younger of the girls when necessary, but they understood Kragar's frustration. They would hardly have called their current patrol a success!

The next morning, they set off down through the forest until they approached the edge of the plain in which the city stood. The closer they got to the Edge, the more cautious they became.

"We will keep quiet from now on."

One of the girls was whimpering, a noise that both irritated Kragar but also carried the risk of detection. One of the soldiers took the girl onto her back in much the same way as Lenar had Desak. That solved the problem but reduced the fighting force.

As the plain with the city just about visible in the far distance came into view, the leading soldier hurriedly waved the party back into the shelter of the trees.

"Smoke," she said to Kragar in a careful whisper.

Kragar moved forward to reconnoitre. In a small clearing right at the side of the plain a camp fire was still burning. From the trampled ground and broken-down bushes there was evidence that the clearing had been used as a camp, and the previous night. Kragar assumed that it was one of the new perimeter patrols that had been set up.

But where on my mother's heart are they?

Had the camp been hurriedly abandoned, or were they walking into a trap?

A movement nearby answered her question as she threw herself to the ground. It was simply that the male patrol had been detected and had retreated. A crossbow bolt buried itself in a tree within a hand's width of her head. This was followed by a pause, a scream and then signs of more retreating movements. Kragar just caught a glimpse of a running figure, a male soldier, disappearing into the forest further along the Edge.

Two of her soldiers then re-appeared having also reacted to the movement in the trees and having circled behind the suspected patrol. Knowing that Kragar had been fired at, but knowing not to ask after her wellbeing, they deposited the body of a rather fat, partly-uniformed, male soldier at her feet.

The rest of the party joined them, the young girl no longer being carried.

"Can we be sure that there were only two of them?" Kragar asked.

"We wounded the only other one that we saw. But there was movement behind us as we headed back to you, Kragarmam. So there must have been a third one who, having seen us, retreated." The soldier's contempt was apparent.

This was the case. Soran had increased the patrols around the Edge, but with such a small body of male soldiers he could only do this by reducing the patrols to three troopers each. Kragar now had the first hard evidence of this, but didn't yet appreciate the significance of the move to the resistance groups.

"We must move on. It will take us until the distant star is overhead before we get to our base camp and if we head onto the plain we will be exposed."

Unspoken, the soldiers realised that they would be going in the opposite direction to the way that the male soldiers had retreated, so they had no fear of attack from that patrol, but potentially they were moving into the face of more patrols.

What they couldn't have known was that the retreating male soldiers were heading into the path of Sorak and her party as they approached the Edge.

The rest of Kragar's journey was uneventful. They were aware that they had been detected by another patrol, but this time their superiority in numbers and skill was recognised and the patrol made no attempt to intercept them. The patrol, however, followed them for a while, but retreated when they approached their destination. But whether the detected location of a major resistance group camp would ever find its way back to the city was far from certain.

At their base camp they were received jubilantly. They had returned almost unscathed, one fatality, but had accounted for a good number of 'enemy' soldiers. Since the officers at the base camp didn't know anything about Desak, as they discussed what to do with the rescued young women and girls, Kragar didn't mention her. What could she have said? She had no idea what had become of her.

But she did mention her meeting with Sorak and Nasa. This information was received with incredulity at first and then with delight at what they immediately assumed would be a potentially valuable recruit to their cause. Kragar offered no comment. Again, in ignorance of Desak having been rescued by Sorak's party, Kragar's sense of her intentions didn't include any suggestion of joining the resistance, even if Sorak might have seemed to be a natural resistance fighter.

12

It didn't need Lenar's acute hearing this time to know that something large was moving, albeit cautiously in the trees nearby. The four of them froze.

Sorak loaded one of their few bolts into her crossbow. Kragar had given Sorak and Nasa the crossbows of the two dead male soldiers. Her instinct told her that the movement wasn't that of an animal. Nasa signalled Desak not to make a sound. She anxiously nodded her head.

Suddenly there was crash of vegetation as if something, someone, had collapsed into one of the many bushes that surrounded them. The muffled curse told Sorak and Nasa almost all that they needed to know. They were being approached, without much regard for security, by male soldiers. The only question was how many of them were there, and why were they so incautious?

"Two," mouthed Nasa, as if he had heard the question from Sorak.

But the movement had ceased. The soldiers were no longer making their way through the forest. Why? Had they at last detected Sorak's party?

Gesturing Lenar to stay with Desak, Nasa and Sorak crept into the trees in the direction of the sound.

They very soon came upon the soldiers.

There were indeed two of them; one bleeding heavily from a neck wound lay on his back in the bush that he had collapsed into. The other was bending over his colleague, but they couldn't see what he was doing. However, they could see the armed crossbow slung across his back.

The thud of Sorak's bolt was barely audible. As they peered into the gloom, the crouching soldier fell forward onto his injured companion.

Nasa, who hadn't expected Sorak to fire so suddenly, looked momentarily shocked.

But she's a soldier.

Since they had left their valley it was something that Nasa had been increasingly telling himself

Sorak pulled the bolt from the man's back – they couldn't afford to leave it – and then dragged his body away, as Nasa checked the other soldier. He was dead, presumably that was why he had collapsed into the bush, having obviously somehow escaped an encounter with one of the resistance groups. Sorak wondered if they had met with Kragar's party.

Nasa searched the two bodies before they dragged them into the undergrowth.

They now had three crossbows, but more importantly an additional stock of bolts.

The clothes that the two men were wearing were part uniform and part a mixture of garments that Sorak didn't recognise. She had never seen men, other than Nasa and Lenar, in anything but a slave harness until recently. The garments would not have been a better fit than the ones that Nasa and Lenar were already wearing, but Sorak removed the non-military leather jerkin of the one closest to her son's size. She thought that Lenar might do better if he didn't look so much like a soldier.

Nasa immediately understood Sorak's action, and the quick and decisive way that she had acted once again reminded him that the officer in charge wasn't too far below the surface. But, as they gathered again before moving carefully towards the edge of the plain surrounding the city, Nasa admonished himself for such thoughts, that Sorak, as far as he was concerned, was long gone.

Nonetheless, it was Sorak who led off once they had dealt with the bodies of the male soldiers.

"We must move around the Edge to where the distance across the plain to the city is shortest," Sorak explained to Lenar and Desak.

That would virtually be where they had left the city all those cycles ago.

It was going to be a difficult journey. In places the forest was impenetrable again; in other places they had to scramble up steep, rocky slopes. And Sorak quickly realised that they would probably eventually be following in Kragar's footsteps.

As the distant star disappeared and they began to look for somewhere to camp, they came across a third dead male soldier and all the evidence of the encounter that had clearly taken place. This rather confirmed Sorak's thoughts about the route that Kragar had taken. But Kragar was way ahead of them.

There were good sleeping trees nearby, but it took Lenar some time to persuade Desak that it was a good place to spend the night. After the encounter with the male soldiers and the discovery of the dead bodies, much of her confidence had drained away again.

Mindful of Desak's fragile state, both Nasa and Sorak were reluctant to openly discuss the next stage of their journey. But, as the two youngsters settled down for the night in the same tree, eventually, Sorak and Nasa sat beside the dying fire and waited for the inevitable conversation to get underway. They were about to embark on by far the most challenging part of their enterprise since they had left their valley. Events weren't turning out quite as they would have hoped and were forcing them to behave in ways that they had tried to put behind them.

"I should lead from here on," Sorak said after a long companionable silence.

This certainly made sense to Nasa, but his biggest worry, as much for Lenar as for himself, was still going to be the women's groups. Unlike the male soldiers, the women like Kragar were trained and experienced; how to ensure that any contact with them was peaceable was a serious problem.

Both realised that being the group that they themselves were, they were in jeopardy from both the men and the women, and in both cases from their tendency to shoot first and ask questions afterwards. It was a timeless dilemma.

And there was another worry.

"Kragar doesn't know that Desak is with us, or that we are heading for the city. All she knows is that we were looking for a new home."

Nasa was right of course. But Kragar had by now reached her base camp and reported her meeting with Sorak.

"Knowing Kragar she won't even mention us!"

But Sorak was wrong. Kragar was only too happy to talk about Sorak and her 'family'. Lenar was a wonder to her, someone who not only knew who his parents were, but who was on equal terms with them. Kragar's conditioning and life experiences weren't sufficient to allow her to generalise from what she observed from the Sorak, Nasa and Lenar relationship, but she had already known that Nasa was an exceptional slave. That he had grown into Sorak's equal partner she recognised but didn't understand. The other soldiers, even the officers, accepted what she told them but, since it didn't match their experiences with men in the city, again, they couldn't understand the importance and significance of how the equality of a man and a woman could work.

"But Kragar is only one of the resistance groups, as I

understand it," Sorak said, "we have to be prepared to meet others."

"But we could just head straight across the plain to the city, if we do that we will be less likely to risk meeting more women."

"But we would be more likely to risk meeting more men."

"I know who I'd rather meet," Nasa said.

So did Sorak.

They didn't settle anything. They were in jeopardy from whoever they might meet. The key issue was to be able to identify themselves before any shooting started and to be able to deal with any male soldiers. For Sorak, too, it was the male soldiers who were also the greatest risk.

"We must rest."

Practical Nasa ended the conversation.

Next morning, they prepared to leave with a sense of anticipation and of foreboding.

Desak was crying, silently and with a look of despair on her face. The Desak of the previous days had completely disappeared. Lenar watched her heaving shoulders as she walked behind his mother with anxiety. He couldn't see her tears, but his instinct nonetheless told him that she was definitely crying.

Nasa, who was bringing up the rear, was only aware of his son's discomfort, but not of its cause.

That Desak was distressed as they set off on to the edge of the plain Sorak was fully aware. As she had explained to the young girl where they were going and why, Sorak discovered that Kragar, when she and her soldiers rescued the women and girls from the male soldiers, hadn't told them what was to happen to them. What was apparent was that Desak was frightened to return to the city, but what Sorak couldn't find out from her was why she was frightened.

Progress was initially rapid as they walked along the sandy edge of the plain, keeping as close to the forested verge as they could. Sorak was surprised by the obstacles that they had encountered; three small streams that seemed to flow onto the plain but then just disappear into its surface, two rocky outcrops that were so heavily fouled with animal droppings that they had to skirt around them, and then a deep gulley that forced them to a halt.

They had two options. They could head out onto the plain towards the city and seek to find the end of the gulley, or they could head back into the forest and find a way across there. Neither alternative was very attractive.

Heading out onto the plain exposed them. And they could have no way of knowing who might be watching them. Crossing the gulley back into the forest seemed like the preferred option but, from past experience, Sorak knew that that too might not be so simple.

"If you were to rest in the trees," she said, "I will explore back up the gulley to see if there is an easy way across. If there isn't we should head out onto the plain."

Sorak set off with a feeling of release; she rarely had the opportunity to be on her own and to act independently. It was another feeling that came to her unexpectedly and surprised her.

Tracking the gulley wasn't easy. The trees grew right up to the edge and it was hard to see a way through. When she did finally find an access to the gulley it had widened out into a sunken clearing partially full of water and clearly the home of some unknown wild animals. Crossing the gulley in the forest was not an option. They would have to make the arduous march out onto the plain to find where the gulley ended and then back along the other side.

Sorak rested before heading back, still savouring her small chance of freedom.

Something's wrong.

The thought leapt into her mind as she picked out the landmark trees that she had memorised on her journey upstream. She didn't understand the concept of sixth sense, but an instinct told her that something was definitely wrong and she should be very cautious.

Voices!

She was instantly on the alert. As she listened, she could discern two female voices: one, hysterical and angry, was Desak's, the other more measured and commanding she couldn't recognise.

She loaded a bolt into her crossbow. Then she moved silently forward until she could see through the trees. The cameo in front of her almost made her laugh.

Three armed women, not soldiers from their dress, were menacing Desak as she stood in front of Nasa and Lenar, arms out in a gesture of protection. The postures of the women in front of her suggested that they were training their crossbows onto the group, but Desak was impeding their aim.

"Move aside!"

The voice was nervous. They may have known that Nasa and Lenar were armed, but they were three against two. Four! As Desak shouted "No, no, no", Sorak saw the fourth member of the party standing off in the shadow of the trees a little way from the group. It was she who had spoken.

She's trying to get a clearer shot at Nasa and Lenar!

"Hold!"

As Sorak's order rang out, all four of the women turned to face her.

These aren't soldiers. Soldiers wouldn't have exposed themselves like this.

By the time the women turned their attention back to Nasa and Lenar they were facing two armed crossbows. Caught between Sorak and the two men they were immediately uncertain.

"Lower your weapons. All of you."

The women hesitated.

"Lower your weapons," Sorak ordered again, this time directing her crossbow at the woman standing separately, whom she judged to be the leader.

"Lay them on the ground! Move to the side!"

Desak took this as an order to move from her position in front of Nasa and Lenar, leaving them a clear line of fire.

The four women congregated just out of the trees. The leader stood in front and surveyed Sorak and then the two men. She was a brown woman, again something that appeared to fascinate Lenar, of Sorak's age with the demeanour of someone used to command. The other women were younger. Having grown up in a largely male-dominated world, they were more tentative and now more crestfallen.

"Parlan!"

These are mangeneers. Parlan was one of Lenen's fellow trainees at the water plant.

Recognition was slow, but Sorak knew that she was right. She had met Parlan at Lenen's barracks all those cycles ago. Clearly Parlan didn't recognise her.

Suddenly Desak, who had strayed away from the group to the edge of the gulley, screamed.

Scrambling up the side of the gulley were four male soldiers, crossbows armed. Sorak didn't have time to wonder how they got into the gulley before she shot dead the first man to raise his weapon. Nasa and Lenar both fired. A second solder fell back into the gulley. As Sorak reloaded, Parlan grabbed the nearest crossbow and gestured to her followers to re-arm themselves.

One of the remaining male soldiers leapt back down into the gulley, the other was killed by a volley of crossbow bolts.

Now what?

It wasn't over yet.

Sorak tracked the gulley edge with her crossbow.

There was a momentary silence finally broken by shouting down in the gulley. Cautious hands and then a helmeted head appeared as a woman soldier levered herself out of the gulley. Finally two other women soldiers appeared, roughly dragging the remaining man with them.

"Hold," said Sorak again.

As the women soldiers trained their weapons on Nasa and Lenar, Sorak, as Desak had done, moved in front of them.

"Tenant Pastak," the first of the women soldiers to emerge said.

"These are not 'enemy'," Sorak said gesturing at Nasa and Lenar, who had both lowered their crossbows.

The stand-off held only briefly. Sorak's statement was accepted and Nasa and Lenar were no longer menaced.

As the mangeneers started a fire and brewed hot drinks, Sorak, Pastak and Parlan all explained themselves.

Pastak headed a small resistance group camped a short distance along the Edge. They had heard of the mangeneers fighting their way out of the city and had come in search of them when they detected the male patrol and set out to eliminate it. When the male patrol was attacked they assumed that it was by the mangeneers. To find the stand-off between them and Sorak's group was unexpected and beyond their experience.

Pastak had heard of Sorak, very few people in the city hadn't, so Sorak didn't need to explain more than that they were returning Desak, who had been separated from Kragar's group, to the city. The novelty of a family group was explained by Pastak to the rest of her soldiers who welcomed Nasa and Lenar. Men fighting alongside women wasn't very common, but also wasn't completely unknown.

"News from the city isn't good," Pastak said. "Soran has lost his best man Kragan, not a thug like the rest of them, killed recently in the silent hours. His efforts to make someone pay for

Kragan's death backfired, but he has been urgently recruiting more soldiers. As fast as we kill them off he recruits more from the low-grade ex-slaves, but the numbers are dwindling. The more women that we can get out of the city to fight, or we can harness to resist inside the city, the harder it will become for Soran."

"But to what end?" asked Sorak.

Pastak was puzzled. She knew that Sorak was reputed to be a superhero, but, like most of her kind, she didn't think much beyond the next day; to find that Sorak seemingly did confused her. Yet even Pastak and the other former officers were beginning to realise that there had to be a solution before so many men are killed that the whole future of the city would be at risk.

Men were needed to breed. Breeding had almost stopped.

The three groups headed back to Pastak's encampment. The mangeneers were hoping to stay and find a useful role; Sorak and Nasa still had a duty to fulfil to deliver Desak to the safe house in the city.

13

Quartan was angry. His meeting with Soran had been useless, and the more he thought about it the more he thought that Soran never ever listened to anybody but Billan and Raskan. He certainly didn't listen to him, seemingly. The Senate was down to the three of them and Soran simply wouldn't hear of trying to increase their number again. He saw no need.

"But we have lost control of almost half of the city. There are areas where men dare not go. The old military blocks in Sector Four and Sector Five are completely in the hands of the ex-soldiers who continue to live there and operate from there unhindered. And they are being joined by civilian women and many of the young girls born after the rebellion."

But Soran wasn't listening.

None of the senators, as Quartan would have admitted, were as clever as the women who used to run the city. Soran's response to anything that happened was to slaughter a few more women. And since it was increasingly the younger women whom he was targeting, the women who they needed for breeding, Quartan also recognised that the whole future of the city was at risk. And this was something else that Soran didn't want to hear.

There isn't much point in training more and more soldiers at the expense of workers in food production, if all they do is kill off the next generation. And if we can't make the women work in food production, how will we survive?

Quartan found it all very frustrating.

They needed a new approach, they needed to talk to the women. It was Soran's refusal to even discus this that had made Quartan so angry; that and the decision to reduce personal bodyguards to one per person.

The city was in ferment. The Senate's plan to force the women to work in the vegetable gardens and food production units simply wasn't working. It wasn't that the women weren't actually working in these areas, they were. Platoons of ex-women soldiers had taken over most of the vegetable gardens and the like, and were producing as much as was required of them. They were even opening up new gardens near their Sector Four stronghold. The problem was that insufficient quantities of the food ever found its way into the hands of the Senate's procurement officials. These ex-low grade slaves in the former ministries found it impossible to keep track of the production, most of which ended up in the sectors of the city dominated by the women.

Soran's policy of hanging the occasional woman from the city walls as a punishment appeared to have no impact at all.

But it wasn't just Soran who was frustrated, and who took out his frustration violently on the women. Memories had faded, and the older women were often the first to be targeted, but at least in the days before the rebellion seventeen cycles ago there seemed to be a purpose to everybody's existence. There was a self-perpetuating society, unequal and stratified, but it worked, everybody knew their place and the rules were harsh enough to ensure everybody kept to their place.

This was no longer the case. Men had new expectations;

women had uncertain roles and an uncertain future. Society itself no longer had a definable purpose; it was barely even self-perpetuating any more. Soran and the Senate saw everything in terms of ensuring male dominance where there had once been female dominance, but had no concept of how society might be re-established in a meaningful way for the future.

Those like Quartan, with enough intelligence to realise that the whole structure of the city would implode if something wasn't done, were ignored, ostracised, threatened or even killed.

The commando group of seven women had entered the city by the gate in the old Sector Five. Their mission had two objectives. The first was easily achieved. The Senate's order to reopen the dream-pits in Sectors Seven and Eight had been intended to both ease tensions but also to try to bring some of the recalcitrant women into the open. Identifying who amongst the more amenable women used the dream-pits and fraternised with the men simply meant visiting, watching and noting. Most of the collaborators were ex-administrators, or mangeneers, with the occasional soldier. Motivated only by survival, it was doubtful that the male administration gained much benefit from these women.

After a brief visit, names were ascertained and noted. The leader of the group was amused to note that some of the civilian women still seemed game to stir up fights with the ex-soldiers, as in former times; holding onto a past that had ceased to exist.

The commando group's second objective was equally as simple in concept, but rather more challenging in execution.

Quartan's home was not in Sector One. Unusually, he had preferred not to be too close to the Senate House. But as the situation in the city deteriorated, he realised that he had made a bad decision.

The commandos readily found the apartment block where Quartan lived; they quickly identified the penthouse. Their problem, they assumed, in what had now become an all-male neighbourhood, was how difficult it would be for a team of women commandos to come and go unnoticed. But in reality, the Senate's military resources were stretched so thinly that they had virtual freedom of movement.

Their best time was in the dark period between the transit of the two moons. They had no idea if the apartment block was patrolled; getting such intelligence had become very difficult. The lead commando had already decided that they had to be bold. The seven of them successfully crept into the apartment building and up to the top floor. There appeared to be no guards.

"Two of you guard the stairs. Two stay outside. The rest of us will enter Quartan's apartment and kill him."

They had no option but to break down the door and had come prepared. Entering the apartment was quickly accomplished.

A blow from the leader's sword killed the sole bodyguard as Quartan awoke to the noise of his door being smashed in. He was quickly secured. The leader's orders, as always, were precise.

As the team hurried away from the area they could see the outline of Quartan's body hanging from the balcony of his apartment. Using the same method of execution that Soran deployed was making a point and was a show of contempt for the male Senate.

Soran's fury at Quartan's death was spectacular, but his planned retribution was resisted by the two remaining senators. Not for the first time did those around him think that Soran was insane.

The area of the old women's military barracks in Sector Four, and where Sorak had once lived, was a no go area to the Senate's troops. Several efforts to take control of this area had resulted in considerable loss of life amongst the male soldiers, and Soran's latest instructions to invade the barracks had largely been ignored. At least some of those around him recognised that they needed to be more cautious in risking their soldiers' lives.

Most of the apartments were still occupied by middle-aged women ex-soldiers, ex-officers, many of whom would have known Sorak. The younger women who lived there now that they couldn't be recruited into the military were often much more militant than their elders. For most of them, life was a burden since it had no purpose once the occupation that they had been bred for had been taken away. Combating the Senate and the male soldiers was all that was left to them.

It was to this barrack block that Sorak had been directed by Kragar to deliver Desak to safety, but the young girl was terrified at the thought once Sorak had told her what was planned.

But this was a long way off yet. Sorak's party was resting at the resistance camp at the edge of the plain. They needed feedback from the city before they could set off. Things were changing so quickly that every decision had to be carefully evaluated.

Soran's fury at Quartan's death and the remaining senators' veto on his response was making him impossible to work with. The last thing that they needed was to inflame the women's passions any more. But something had to be done and the two senators knew it.

"We must try to get him to expand the Senate again. With more voices advising him, maybe he would listen more."

It was Billan who made the suggestion, but he didn't hold out too much hope. Soran's behaviour had been getting worse for some time and any criticism of his actions was increasingly risky.

Raskan agreed. No more intellectually capable than Soran, and another former quarry slave, he had always relied on Billan and the other senators to come up with suggestions. Raskan was Soran's personal choice as a senator, a friend from the bad days in the quarries; he had generally been seen as just another reliable vote for the leader. But he had a suggestion.

"Perhaps Pareck could persuade him."

Pareck was Soran's partner. More accurately, she was Soran's sex slave. A young officer sent to the quarries for insubordination she had been a disciple of Mesrick, the inspiration of the original rebellion, who in turn was an admirer of Sorak. A love/hate relationship had grown up with Soran who Pareck had had punished on numerous occasions for the most trivial of offences.

After the quarry slaves had abandoned their workplace and Soran had engineered his installation as the Senate and city leader he had sought Pareck out and taken her to the Senate chairman's residence. Fitted with Soran's old slave collar, she was kept chained up in the food preparation area of the residence until she was needed for bedroom duties. Soran abused her in every way imaginable, but Pareck tolerated her treatment for reasons that the man would have had difficulty in understanding. She knew that her time would come.

Billan and Raskan were often invited to the residence and, in their presence, Soran's behaviour to Pareck was often at its most brutal.

After Soran had stormed out of the Senate House when his two colleagues had vetoed his planned reprisals for Quartan's death he arrived at his residence in the foulest mood that Pareck could remember. Unlocking the chain that held her from the wall he dragged her to the bedroom. This was something that he had never done before. He usually unlocked the chain at Parecks's collar, but he was almost out of control.

Soran's lovemaking was instant and even more brutal than normal. It was only when Pareck realised through the grinding pain in her loins that not only was the chain still attached to her collar but that in the violence of their sex it had become wrapped around Soran's neck, she saw the opportunity.

"Mother's heart," she whispered, "I thank you!"

Stronger than Soran, Pareck jerked the chain sharply and turned him face down on the bed. Kneeling on his back she pulled the chain hard until it strangled him and, with a final jerk, broke his neck.

By the time Billan and Raskan arrived, Pareck was dressed and without the slave collar, something that was immediately noticed.

"Where is Soran?"

Billan knew that something had happened, something had changed Pareck.

She said nothing. She had hoped to have been gone before the two senators arrived, but they had been too quick for her. Raskan called out to Soran and then went looking for him. He found him in the bedroom.

"Pareck, what happened here?"

Billan, when he in turn saw the dead Soran, didn't need to ask. The chain still around Soran's neck made it obvious. Then the hard, mean look that came into Raskan's eyes told Billan that he too had realised.

"You did this."

Statement or question it didn't matter. Raskan knew that Pareck had killed his friend the chairman.

Unsheathing his knife, he plunged it into Pareck's stomach as Billan leapt forward to restrain him. As Pareck slumped to the floor, Raskan slashed at Billan with his blade. Bleeding heavily from the neck he sunk to his knees. Raskan's second blow left himself as the only one alive in the room.

With only Soran as a role model, Raskan knew that he had to get to the Senate House quickly and secure the support of the head of the guards and, just as importantly, of the guards themselves. He knew that two of them would certainly be loyal to him, but if he was to take over from Soran he needed more.

Having reached the Senate House and having told the guards that Soran was dead, it was obvious that the former chairman's increasing random violence had alienated most of his support and Raskan was soon confident that he would be accepted as the new leader.

News of the change spread rapidly around the city. At the military barracks in Sector Four, it was received with dismay. Violence and death were all too common, but this bout of carnage exceeded anything that had happened in the city for many cycles of the distant star.

But other news had reached the barracks with the arrival of a soldier from the resistance groups.

"Sorak, Sorak is alive, and she's coming back to the city!"

All the women knew of the legend of Sorak and her escape with her slave, but what this latest information could mean for the future none of them could imagine.

Raskan's period as leader of the Senate and of the city didn't last the day.

Tucked away in one of the Sector Seven dream-pits, a group of old black and brown men, the former elite slaves of the women's Senate's Administrator Crenan, kept themselves to themselves. They too had quickly heard the news of Raskan's accession to power. However, they had been making plans for some time. Being who they were they had been careful to keep out of the public gaze. A number of the old Senate slaves had been massacred along with the elite women in the early days of the rebellion, and they were still at risk from both the women and the generality of the more menial ex-slaves like Soran and Raskan.

Keeping their old slave numbers rather than inventing names for themselves, 147, 136 and 182 were the leaders of this hidden group. Some of the women from one of the closer old military barracks suspected that the group existed but preferred to ignore the rumours. What could these old administrators do against the likes of Soran?

It seemed plenty.

Arriving at the Senate House quietly and unannounced, ten of the group, fully armed and trained in arms by a renegade woman military officer, they despatched the outer guards and then crowded into the Senate chamber just as Raskan had finally been accepted by Soran's mob of hangers-on. A volley of crossbow bolts quickly reduced the number of Raskan's supporters to five or six and then, along with the man himself, these were also killed. It was as brutal and decisive as anything Soran or Raskan could have devised.

The elite ex-slaves would have had the same problem in consolidating their power as Soran had had and Raskan would have had if it hadn't been for their superior intelligence and their pre-planning. The small squad of heavily-armed male soldiers, who had been carefully chosen, were called to the Senate House and quickly secured the necessary offices and facilities to provide for a new administration. There was no violence, but opposition wasn't tolerated from the men who had tried to run the city under Soran's baleful control.

By the time that the distant star had set, and the first vermillion moon had risen, the city had new rulers. New rulers who were just as determined that the men of the city would have primacy as Soran had been, but who had a vision for the future, something that he was incapable of.

News of the change of leadership was quickly disseminated throughout the city, directly or indirectly, another part of the triumvirate's pre-planning.

It didn't take the women in the military barracks and other parts of the city long to realise that, from their point of view, not much had changed.

Nonetheless, they tacitly declared a truce and awaited events.

14

Lenar was in a quandary, a dilemma; he had no idea what his situation might be called, but he was in a difficulty, and it worried him.

Desak had definitely been crying and, as far as he could tell, she was crying about something that his mother had told her.

That made him angry. As a small boy he had been angry, when he couldn't achieve something he wanted to achieve, when his father had admonished him for wandering off into the forest behind their home without a weapon. But he had known what it was that had made him angry.

But other than the fact that it had to be something that his mother had said to Desak, he didn't know why he was angry now, and he didn't think asking her would tell him. The idea of asking his mother never occurred to him.

This was an entirely new situation for him.

In Pastak's camp, having eaten, he had gone and sat apart to worry at this new feeling because the more he thought about it, it wasn't strictly anger he was feeling, but it did originate with Desak. And it did relate to his wish to do something so that Desak wouldn't cry any more. It was all very confusing.

In the resistance group run by Pastak, a tenant in the

old green platoon that used to be officered by Sorak's friend Lerick, there were twelve women soldiers, including Pastak and another former officer whose name Lenar didn't know. They all seemed to be quite used to living in the forest and were always laughing and joking, but Lenar had noticed that they were wary of him and his father; particularly of Nasa.

Having no concept of slavery or inequality between the sexes, Lenar could not understand this wariness. But this didn't worry him in the same way as Desak's distress did.

All he really knew was that his parent's feelings for each other were totally different from the relations between the women. And his feelings for Desak, he sensed, were like those of his parents.

This was a huge revelation to him.

But Desak was crying again. In the gloom he could hear her.

Lenar walked over to the young girl, sat down beside her and put his arm around her shoulder.

How he came to be lying on his back, staring up at two angry soldiers, he wasn't quite sure. Suddenly, the tension was palpable.

"Hold!"

The tone of command in Sorak's voice quelled the murmurings. Nasa had taken a step forward but halted. It was one of those moments where one false move could have provoked a disaster. It would be better to let Sorak deal with the situation.

But it was Pastak who intervened, along with her colleague.

She and the other officer in the group came and stood one each side of Sorak as Lenar struggled to his feet, confused, bemused, frightened by the undertones that had emerged.

Pastak knew that she had to explain. The soldiers, whilst clearly accepting Nasa and Lenar, were having difficulty in understanding the relationship between Sorak and Nasa and now apparently between Lenar and Desak.

115

"Lenar is Sorak's son. Sorak escaped from the city to be free to favour the slave that she had feelings for. Lenar came, Lenar knows who his mother is, who his father is, that was the way that Sorak wanted it. That's the way it is, this is the way that it will be in the future."

The language was cumbersome; the language of the city didn't encompass such concepts as love, as feelings for another person of the opposite sex. In the days before the rebellion such relations between a woman and a slave would have meant certain death. It no longer did. But many of the women, the less intelligent ones like the ordinary soldiers, had no comprehension of this. Pastak herself wasn't entirely sure that she understood the way things were between Sorak and Nasa, but she trusted Sorak and took the situation as she found it.

Pastak waited for the soldiers to digest what she had said.

"If Lenar has feelings for Desak, there is no reason why he should not show them."

Pastak was emphatic, but she understood the confusion of the two soldiers who had intervened. Equally, she knew that she had to defuse the situation.

"Nasa belongs to Sorak, but Sorak also belongs to Nasa."

The concept of belonging, at least, was something that they could all understand, even if not a woman belonging to a man.

"And if Lenar wants Desak to belong to him, it can happen if Desak wants Lenar to belong to her."

The murmurs recurred, but they weren't hostile, more they were a symptom of each of the women trying to work what Pastak had said through their minds and to relate it to the evidence of Sorak and Nasa, and Desak and Lenar in front of them.

Pastak, unlike Sorak, with a grasp of the realities of the city, knew that what she had said about male/female relations didn't work in general because equality was not accepted by the male Senate and most of the men. But equally she knew that the soldiers still saw men as inferior and, although Nasa's prowess was well known, she had no idea whether her troops actually believed it. Nonetheless, Pastak thought that it was important that her soldiers begin to grasp the concept of equality.

The two soldiers who had challenged Lenar steered Desak away from him. In the confusion of his own feelings, he watched her being shepherded into the group of lounging troopers, unclear what to do. But there really was nothing that he could do.

"We should get some rest," his father said, conscious of just how fragile the situation was.

Sorak and Pastak, however, walked to the edge of the group and into the trees. Pastak was curious, anxious, envious in a succession of thoughts that an amazed Sorak watched track across her face. Neither knew quite what to say.

"Sorak…"

Whatever Pastak was going to say didn't get articulated. A crossbow bolt whistled by her, grazing her arm.

"Mother's heart!"

Pastak's exclamation was loud enough for one of the soldier's relieving herself in the trees nearby them to hear, recognise and react. The return fire from her crossbow was more accurate then the missile directed at her leader. The scream of the dying soldier was loud enough to bring all of the women to alert and for Nasa and Lenar to rush to Sorak's side.

Lenar's two quick-fire shots into the massing group of male soldiers did something to restore him in the esteem of the women soldiers.

"Seven of them," Pastak said, "that's unusual! Change of tactic?"

It was. The new triumvirate, about whom Pastak and the rest of them hadn't yet heard, had ordered larger patrols of male soldiers to search out the resistance groups. It made more military sense than small groups. But it was a calculated attempt to both eliminate the women's groups, but also to disperse the lower-grade male soldiers out of the city. If the soldiers never returned the new leaders would not have worried. They were intent on advancing the more intelligent of the city's men.

The battle was quickly over. All but one of the male soldiers was killed. The survivor was found hiding in the undergrowth. Again Nasa was appalled by the slaughter. But he also got a sense that Pastak herself would have preferred to have taken the men alive; but this was not a preference shared by the women soldiers.

"A boy," Pastak said, "now they are using boys to fight us!" She waved her troops crossbows down. There had been enough killing.

The young trooper was clearly terrified, but seeing Lenar he edged towards him, uncertain of what to make of the two men apparently on good terms with the women soldiers.

Having dealt with the bodies, the women settled back into their groups and resumed their leisure. Wary of Pastak's displeasure, they ignored the boy-soldier.

Lenar sat on the ground beside the lad and offered him some water. Then he asked him his name. A torrent of frightened words poured out in lieu of a name. Lenar could make little sense of it but, when the boy had calmed down, Lenar left him and went to talk to his mother and Pastak.

"Keeps talking about numbers. 147. Numbers that give orders?"

"Slave numbers?" Pastak mused.

In the end it was Nasa who pieced together the latest news from the city by in his turn talking to the young trooper. The old leader, Soran, it seemed, was dead. The city was being run by three black and brown men. Men who didn't bother with names.

After much talk with the boy, Nasa concluded that the new

leaders must be ex-administration slaves, a far more intelligent and focused leadership than that of the ex-quarry slaves.

"This is not good news!" he said to Sorak.

* * *

Further along the edge of the plain, Kragar was resting with her party in her base camp. They had observed the larger squad of male soldiers as they openly crossed the plain and headed for the Edge. Satisfied that they weren't intending to attack them, Kragar sent one of her soldiers to keep track of them and verify where they were heading.

"They ran into another resistance group, Kragarmam."

"And?"

"And nothing. There was a brief fight. From the bodies hidden in the bushes, six of the male soldiers were killed."

Since the soldiers' orders were never to make contact with another resistance group in order to preserve security, Kragar's scout didn't attempt to get close enough to see who the group that had been attacked and fought back was.

"There must have been survivors. I'm sure I could hear male voices."

"Not for long!" Kragar said fiercely, knowing the fate of any men left alive.

Kragar was not one of those amongst the women who were beginning to worry about the carnage amongst the former slaves and the impact that the declining numbers of men was going to have on the future of the city.

If Kragar had known about the new governing triumvirate she might not, however, have been surprised to find that they were very much concerned about the future numbers of men, but more especially the quality of the men remaining in the city. The menial groups had always outweighed the personal and administrative slaves and, although they promoted the breeding programme as actively as Soran had done, they, like him, tried to minimise the number of low-grade former slaves who were allowed to breed.

But even the breeding process was changing.

When a pregnant woman, a former administration clerk in the Senate House, was accosted in the street by the man who would be the father of her child, something new emerged. The man said that he wanted to know when the baby was to be born and to see it.

The woman was astounded.

Mindful of the past, the couple met at a dream-pit, the only place where men and women could mix if they wanted to, and talked all evening. The man was a former slave in the Senate library; so both parents, like Sorak and Nasa, were intellectually equal. It was the first of many meetings and many conversations.

15

"We need to know more," Nasa was clear that they shouldn't set off for the city without better information. But where were they to get it from? How long would they have to wait?

Since no one could make too much sense out of the information that the boy trooper had given them the excitement over yet more changes in the city quickly died down and slowly, as guards were posted, everybody else went off to their sleeping areas. Apart from the cooking fire, it was pitch black until the first moon arose.

Sorak and Nasa had settled down with Lenar beside them, but their son was restless and anxious. The soldiers had kept Desak with them. At first, they could hear her crying, but a hissed protest from one of the troopers finally frightened her into silence.

The night seemed unending to Lenar. As always, his parents were awake early.

Nasa had clearly been giving the potentially new situation some thought once he had woken up. What little that they had garnered from the frightened boy soldier simply told him that they needed to be even more cautious. No one could be considered reliable, or trustworthy. If the city was in turmoil

121

again they needed to know both which parts would be safe for them, as well as Desak, and which they had to avoid. How they were to obtain this information Nasa still remained unclear about. For Sorak, the only way seemed to be to simply go to the city and find out exactly how things stood when they got there; not a very reassuring option.

Pastak drew Sorak aside again as she had done the previous evening. Sorak sensed that the former tenant was unhappy about something, or at least wanted to share her thoughts with her as an ally and as a friend.

"Sorak, things have got to change. A new administration is a new problem but the way things have been going the death rate amongst the men is so high that there will soon be a problem with breeding. Unless this new administration changes things, and the larger patrols don't suggest that they are going to let up on hunting for us, we will be left with very few of the sort of slaves, men, who will produce, well... well people like us, people like mangeneers, like administrators."

Sorak didn't know what to say. Pastak, a professional soldier, wasn't given to long speeches, let alone ones as profound as the one she had just delivered.

Yet something inside Sorak's mind immediately recognised that she was right. The well-ordered city had disappeared; in its place were warring factions, amongst the men certainly and possibly the women as well. The men had formed administrations, but they hadn't re-established a working relationship with the women, they had simply tried to replace them, to substitute identical male rule for female rule. But, as the result of careful breeding in the past, there was no reservoir of the necessary skills, talents and experience amongst the bulk of the men that now were needed. Such of the necessary capabilities that there were, were limited to a very small group of ex-slaves, all of whom were ageing, and for whom there was no immediate prospect of replacement.

"We have to work together with the men," Sorak said.

What might have seemed like a statement of the obvious, with the history of the city, was a momentous conclusion to draw.

Pastak looked at Sorak in wonder. The same thought was burrowing its way to the surface in her own brain, but Sorak had realised the truth instantly.

Free thinking. That's what living in the wilderness on equal terms with a man does for you.

Pastak couldn't believe that she had just had that thought!

She can't just deliver Desak and head off to the mountains again.

Pastak could believe that she had had that thought! Sorak seemed so much wiser than any woman that she had ever met, apart from the senior officers of her youth, and even they hadn't really understood what had happened in the city in the end.

"We need to know more of what is going on in the city."

Sorak repeated Nasa's caution. Pastak agreed.

But a sudden surge of tension amongst the soldiers attracted her. The boy soldier, it seemed, had disappeared.

"Disappeared, how can he have disappeared? Who was guarding him?"

The rather guilty looks from the soldiers told Pastak that no one had been guarding the boy, he wasn't seen as a threat and why would he want to escape into the forest?

"We'll patrol to where we met up with Sorak and then come back through the forest."

"Why don't they just let him go?" asked Lenar of his father. "What does it matter if he escapes? He won't last very long on his own."

"They need to protect the location of their camp."

Nasa knew that it wasn't a very satisfactory answer and he had always tried to share as much information and knowledge with his son as he could. But the new uncertainty that had crept into their future plans was worrying him, and he didn't want Lenar worried. It was their own location, not just that of the resistance group, that he wanted to protect, and the boy soldier knew where they were.

When Pastak's troops went on patrol, Sorak and Nasa stayed behind. There was a moment of more tension when some of the soldiers wanted to take Desak with them. But Pastak insisted that she be left with Sorak so that she could be taken into the city to the safe house.

This rather forced Sorak and Nasa's hand, although it delighted Lenar. They needed more information about what was going on in the city, but short of waiting an indeterminate time until someone escaped and contacted them, there was no way to obtain it. As Sorak had always thought, essentially, they might just as well leave straight away.

"Maybe we should cross the plain from here when it gets dark," Nasa suggested rather tentatively.

Both he and Sorak were aware that if they worked their way further around the Edge they were in danger of running into Kragar again. Nasa for one didn't want to do that, he didn't trust the black former tenant.

But the benefit of working around the Edge would be a much shorter distance to cross the plain to the city.

"But the shorter distance has more risk," Sorak suggested. "It's much more likely to be used by the male patrols."

This was something that Nasa acknowledged as true. They would cross the plain from where they were.

Since they wouldn't leave until it began to get dark, they had time to spare. Used to their busy life in the valley, neither Sorak nor Nasa were very good at doing nothing. Time dragged once they had sorted through their belongings, discarding what they no longer needed and generally sought to lighten their loads. Lenar, in his turn, made a perfunctory effort to do the same, but with Desak watching him with big eyes that no longer showed fear, his packing wasn't very well organised. None of them found it possible to fill the vacant time with sleep.

Then, at last, it was the moment for them to get going.

As the distant star disappeared over the mountains and the light faded, the four of them gathered in the trees ready to move off. But their son hesitated.

"Lenar?"

Sorak, again sensitive to her son's acute hearing, looked questioningly at him. What had he heard?

But no explanation was necessary. They all then heard the movement somewhere back in the trees further into the forest, but close behind them. Sorak and Nasa loaded their crossbows and urged Desak and Lenar to move towards the edge of the plain.

But Sorak was uncertain. Since the movement was coming from the direction that Pastak had taken it was hardly likely to be another patrol of male soldiers and, in any event, it didn't sound like a big party.

"Mother's heart, it's the boy soldier," Sorak whispered as the lad cautiously emerged, his hands held above his head.

"The women would have killed me," he said. "I want to go back to the city."

The remark was addressed to Nasa; wary of Sorak, he was effectively seeking his protection.

Nasa wasn't sure how to react. Things had changed so dramatically since they had stumbled upon Kragar's group, the male soldiers, and the knowledge of the upheavals in the city, that he found any new situation, however seemingly small, a challenge. Desak's unexpected arrival and the decision to see her back to the city had determined broadly what they should do. But the fact that everything was supposedly so different in the city didn't make it any easier to determine a safe course of action, both to approach the city, and when they got there.

He didn't want to be burdened with this boy, but what could he do?

Sorak, I need your help here! We can't abandon this boy, but we don't have enough food to feed him.

Nasa was suddenly aware that he had reverted to times past when he had looked to the then young officer for guidance.

But we must head into the city. We have to deliver Desak to a safe place. We've taken on that obligation and we must fulfil it.

Then the moment was gone. The old Nasa quickly resurfaced after the moment of doubt.

"We must go quickly now that the distant star has gone."

Sorak noted that Nasa had made no response to the boy, he simply gathered up his backpack and walked out onto the plain. They all, including the boy, fell in behind him. Sorak was aware of the unease in Nasa, but was reluctant to question him.

They were well out onto the plain; it was pitch black with only the suggestion of the first light from the second moon. They all instinctively kept very close together.

Sorak was amused and pleased to see that Desak was holding firmly onto Lenar's hand. The niggle in the depths of her mind told her that the increasing closeness of the two would have to be addressed, otherwise there would be trouble when they got to the safe house. As with any mother, Sorak was aware that her son was no longer a child, he had more than once proved himself as a man, but she was still protective of him and was even beginning to feel left out as his relationship with Desak blossomed.

She was brought back to reality by Lenar shrugging off Desak's hand and seeing him push himself up on tip-toe, his characteristic stance when he was listening hard. The grunt was Nasa clamping his hand over the boy soldier's mouth. He too had heard something.

Desak was looking anxious again, but now had sufficient control over herself not to make a sound when she saw what Lenar was doing.

The moon was beginning to create enough light for them to see and understand Lenar's pantomime, but also to see shadows that he was indicating that were moving in parallel to them but in the opposite direction. It was another party of male soldiers, but they appeared to be herding a number of women in front of them. There wasn't time to wonder what was going on and why they were heading away from the city.

"Fire," mouthed Sorak.

The soldiers halted. They appeared to have detected Sorak's party but were uncertain about their numbers and intent. As Nasa signalled their party to the ground, the thud of a crossbow bolt and a scream said that contact had been made.

None of Sorak, Nasa, or Lenar had time to check who had been hit. Returning fire brought down two of the male soldiers but, to their astonishment, a disorganised melee ensued as the women captives turned on the remaining soldiers, pulling them to the ground and disarming them.

When Sorak, with Nasa and Lenar behind her, approached, a ghastly silence had descended as the women strangled the three remaining men.

"Hold!"

Sorak immediately intervened as the women, not ex-soldiers but familiar with arms, covered Nasa and Lenar with the retrieved weapons.

"They are with us."

There was sufficient a pause for the women to realise that it was Nasa and Lenar who had shot the first two soldiers. There was puzzlement, but crossbows were lowered.

"He's dead."

Now with enough moonlight, a tearful Desak came over

to the group to report that the original shot fired at them had killed the boy soldier.

Nasa was angry, and for once Lenar knew why. The carnage amongst the former slaves and the casual way that any woman with the opportunity seemed prepared to kill them was causing him great distress.

Sorak understood and the beginnings of a purpose for going back to the city were seeded in her brain.

"We are going to the city," Sorak said with a gesture at the women to both seek an explanation of who they were and to understand whether they were likely to travel with them or want to push on and contact a resistance group.

Part Two

16

The women who Sorak and Nasa had rescued had been recaptured by a male patrol, having escaped from the city after hiding in the vegetable gardens. Where the male soldiers were taking them was still a mystery, although the women themselves believed that they would have been killed in the forest if Sorak and Nasa hadn't turned up. Reprisals like that had happened before. Needless to say, the women had no desire to go back to the city.

Nasa attempted to explain to them how they could contact the resistance groups, but they clearly were still suspicious of him.

"Believe him. It's your only chance of avoiding more patrols."

Sorak, angry and contemptuous of these women who couldn't let go of their old status even in the adversity that they had endured, simply wanted to resume her journey to the city to deliver Desak. She really didn't care what happened to them. With a profusion of thoughts coursing through her mind, Sorak was conscious that she had lost patience with people like the women, and Kragar, who seemed only to want to put the clock back. Pastak was the only woman that she had met since leaving

131

the valley, and since understanding the changes that might have been taking place in the city, who seemed to accept that the future had to be different from the past.

There was no way that they could bury the dead out on the plain even if the rescued women had been willing to help. But the released women couldn't get away from Sorak and Nasa quickly enough. Recognising that the party that had rescued them were militarily superior, even if they couldn't understand the relationships it exposed, all they wanted to do was get to the Edge and seek out someone safe like Pastak, or one of the other groups, as urgently as possible.

"What will Pastak do with them?"

Lenar's question was very much to the point. Already having acquired the party of mangeneers the last thing that Pastak would want, Sorak would have supposed, was yet more hangers-on.

Unbeknown to Sorak and Nasa, the forest fringes of the plain were filling up with escapees, many of whom offered no contribution to the resistance groups whatsoever. And most of these women were simply waiting for the resistance groups to attack the city and restore them to their old lifestyles.

Pastak and Kragar, and the other resistance leaders, had started to suspect that the city authorities had deliberately weakened the city security to allow more and more women to escape. Realising that a large proportion of those who had left the city posed no military threat, they saw them as imposing an increasingly unwanted burden on the resistance groups. 147, the former women's Senate Administrator's chief clerk, and the most powerful of the members of the triumvirate, would hardly have quibbled with this analysis. Anything that debilitated the resistance groups made sense to him.

But the loss of both women and men, and, in the case of the men, more often than not permanently, was beginning to be seen now as a problem by the more astute leaders of the triumvirate, rather than a consequence of the takeover of the city by the elite men.

An attempt to take a census to assess the true numbers of the city population was never going to be successful. With the fractured state of relations between men and women, and the large areas of the city not accessible to the male administration, such an endeavour was always going to be doomed to failure.

But much as Sorak in particular would have understood the problem, her preoccupation, once they set off into the night again, was to reach the city and find a way in before the distant star arose again. How difficult it would be, would be a first test of both their determination and the extent of control that the male authorities had.

"So how will we get into the city, Mother?"

It was a question that was beginning to exercise Nasa as well as Lenar. Lenar was more willing to ask.

"The easiest way is through the sewage treatment works, but apart from anything else, the smell we would pick up would be hard to get rid of and tell everybody how we had come into the city."

Lenar didn't understand why this made both his parents laugh until Nasa explained it to him that their original exit that way was still vivid in their memories. Entry by such a route, needless to say, had no attraction for Lenar.

"I reckon Red, the gate in Outer Four, is the best option. It's close to the area of the military barracks and the inner wall gate. Kragar seemed to think it might be controlled by ex-soldiers. It's a risk, but all the gates are a risk."

Kragar hadn't been able to give Sorak and her party very much guidance on how to enter the city, recognising that the situation was always going to be fluid and that decisions would always have to be taken on the day.

In the light of the second moon, the city was looming large

on the horizon. A curious feeling of anticipation and of dread coursed through Sorak's mind. To get to the gate in question they would need to swing wide around the walls to avoid the sewage disposal area. Nasa began to do this.

Lenar was carrying Desak on his back again. She appeared to be asleep. Sorak's worry about her son's reaction to their leaving the young girl at the military barracks increased as they got closer to the city. But it wasn't her only worry. Unsure of whether their group would be seen as unusual, or a threat, she was concerned by any potential reactions to them, first by the defenders of the gate and then by the women that they would have to seek out.

She need not have worried.

Kragar's prediction proved correct. The gate in Outer Four was indeed controlled by ex-soldiers. Not only that, the guard on the gate was commanded by an aging capral from Sorak's own old red platoon. Even more to Sorak's surprise, it appeared that they were expected.

How could they have known?

Sorak didn't really have time to think this out before they were surrounded by the gate guard but she later realised that communication between the dissident women in the city and the resistance groups was far more extensive than she had imagined. How this communication was actually managed, she never did find out.

"Sorakmam!"

The capal's delight at seeing her certainly told Nasa that his partner had not only not been forgotten over the cycles of the distant star but had become revered in a way that he hadn't expected. He saw this as a good sign.

Several of the soldiers, like the capral, and Sorak, were of an age but at least three of the troopers were young women. This was another surprise, but it seemed that out of sight of the male administration women soldiers had been quietly trained over the years. And many of these younger soldiers were battle-trained in a way that Sorak had never been as a result of the sporadic warfare between the men and the women. And Sorak was as respected by these younger troopers as much as by the older soldiers.

Nasa was treated with the same respect as Sorak, but it was Lenar who really attracted the interest. The rumour machine had already circulated the knowledge of Lenar's existence, but the soldiers, like every other man and woman that they had come across, had never met someone who not only knew their mother, but also their father as well. This was a phenomenon that they were going to have to get used to.

The fact that this knowledge of children and parents was changing in other single instances hadn't yet percolated down into all of the outer areas of the city where the dissident women were based. But the seeds had been sown in the minds of the women who now met Sorak and her son.

Lenar was embarrassed by the attention since he had no understanding of the true situation in the city in the past or even the present. He had been surprised that Desak didn't know who either of her parents were, but he had had no reason to suppose that this was a generality of the population.

"This is Desak. She was rescued from a male patrol by Kragar. We're taking her to the red platoon barracks for safety."

Both Nasa and Lenar noted Desak's renewed agitation, but since the girl was often agitated they didn't register it as of special concern. Sorak, however, sensed that there was an increasing wariness, even suspicion, in Desak's reaction as they had approached the city.

Since the distant star was now fully over the horizon, the guard capral began to urge Sorak's party to go with them through the derelict food gardens to their barracks.

"The mangeneers' barracks were partly burnt down recently by the slaves," the capral said as they skirted around the damaged building. "If we keep close to the sewage works no one will bother us."

Both Sorak and Nasa looked at the rundown state of everything. The whole area had mixed memories of Lenen and their final escape from the city, but they couldn't help being saddened by what they were seeing. How widespread the dereliction was within the rest of the city, neither had any way of knowing.

Although Sorak always thought of the barracks in Sector Four as the red platoon's, it had housed other platoons as well. Now, as they approached, it seemed deserted. But as the capral led the way into the building, however, they were greeted by two elderly officers still in their old uniforms who came hurriedly out to meet them.

"Sorak, welcome."

Our old capan!

The other ex-officer, another old capan by her insignia, Sorak didn't recognise, but she was too focused to realise that Desak clearly did know who this second woman was.

"Come with us."

The instructions clearly didn't include Nasa and Lenar but when his son started to follow Nasa held him back. Under the surface he could feel the tension. These were like the women on the plain, they hadn't been able to accept that change had taken place. Not for the first time, the wisdom of returning to the city was raised in the back of his mind. Delivering Desak was an obligation that they had now met; she was delivered. Nasa was torn between a desire to get out as quickly as possible and a vague feeling that there was something that he and Sorak could do to bring an end to the warfare between the men and the women.

And how do I suppose that I'm going to do that?

He had no idea. He needed to talk things through with Sorak. He had sensed that something of her former role as an officer had been reawakened, but he wasn't sure how real the feeling was to her. Sorak herself was not conscious of this. Meeting the capans had put her on the defensive as it looked like they still held their positions of authority. That worried her, as she didn't have a very high opinion of her own ex-capan. Her knowledge of the other capan was coloured by a clear sense of the rise in Desak's anxiety levels at the sight of her.

"We are glad that you have returned," her old capan said as she led Sorak and Desak into what used to be one of the communal areas of the barracks. "It has been a long time."

Sorak was well aware that it had been a long time, but the reactions of the two women told her that she had changed far more than they had.

In the communal area she was greeted by around twenty women, who stamped their feet in welcome. The enthusiasm of the welcome was something that she hadn't been expecting. It puzzled her. It was going to be a long time before she understood the mythological adulation in which she was held. She had become a heroine, attributed with more qualities of rebellion and self-determination than she would have recognised. Nasa, in his turn, had been equally revered, but in a far less effusive way. But in the present company men were largely ignored.

They seem to be expecting something of me. But what?

As the women surged around her, touching her as if they didn't believe it was her, there was a reverence about the older women that bothered her. She saw herself as an old soldier, no longer in service, with a family life; that was all that she needed, all she wanted. Yet she sensed very quickly that they were expecting more and she couldn't understand where the expectation could have come from. It would never have occurred to her that it was seventeen cycles of idealisation. The vision of her and Nasa over the cycles had long since parted from reality.

Then it was put into words.

"You will lead us," the ex-capan said, "the women will again rule in the city."

No, no, no. Things have changed. The women will never rule again, not on their own, not at the expense of the men.

Suddenly, in a moment of clarity, Sorak recognised again what Pastak, but not Kragar, was seeing. The clock could not be put back, the men were free, and they could never be enslaved again. The future was about working together, about living together, about stopping killing each other before it was too late.

But one look around told her that that was not what these women wanted to believe! They wanted the myth of Sorak to become reality. For Sorak there was no way that that was going to happen. At least so she would have said if she had been asked. The pull of another valley, another peaceful, fulfilling existence, was still powerful somewhere in her mind.

"We should go to the dream-pit and celebrate."

It wasn't the capan, it was a younger woman dressed in a mixture of old civilian and military clothes. It was then that Sorak realised that there were actually several younger women in the group, not saying much, keeping themselves to themselves, until now. She felt encouraged; these would be more aware and interested in the future than the old women living in the past.

In our little world we have grown so different. Yet, maybe we had just leapt into the future.

She began to relax. She felt herself to be so different from the older women, older though she herself was. Yet with Lenar and Desak and these younger soldiers, and sadly the dead boy soldier out on the plain, there had to be a future, and it had to be a future of men and women equally.

We have to work for a different future.

"Yes, we should go to the dream-pit," Sorak repeated, pulling herself back to the young woman who had offered the invitation, and back from the uncertainties that she knew were lurking in her mind.

And she meant with Nasa and Lenar, not just with the women. She would soon know if that would be possible. It was. The young woman gestured them to join her and Sorak.

"We must wait for Desak," Lenar said when the party was made up and was ready to go.

But Desak had disappeared into the barracks with the capan whom Sorak didn't know.

They didn't wait.

It was soon obvious that the proposal to go to the dream-pit by the younger women at the barracks was an effort to get Sorak away from the ageing ex-senior officers. So preoccupied was she by her own feelings that it was only as the party set off did both she and Nasa detect the underlying tension. Neither were very clear what it might mean.

"What's going on here?" Nasa wanted to know.

He recognised that he was a respected bystander but that that could turn to hostility if he overstepped the women's expectations of him. And he was far from clear what these were.

Poor Lenar set off with his parents in some anxiety. Desak's rapid disappearance worried him. She had hardly left his side since they had left the forest, but the moment they arrived at the barracks she was gone.

"I think the young women are unhappy," Sorak responded. "The old soldiers don't seem to have recognised that things have changed, they just keep trying to live the life they always did…"

"But with nothing to do and nothing to look forward to."

Sorak wasn't surprised that Nasa had got straight to the heart of the matter. And he had picked up on exactly the same issue as Sorak.

"But the dream-pit?"

"To get away from the old women, to get us away from the old women. I'm not sure what they expect of us, of me, but I don't think we are going to be able to get away from here like we had planned."

"But we can't live in the barracks. We'll have to find somewhere else."

Sorak knew that Nasa was right but equally moving to somewhere else would distress Lenar.

Not for the first time, Sorak cursed the day that Desak had wished herself on them.

The pounding intensity of the music as they walked into the dream-pit instantly invoked memories. Memories that with the passage of time had mellowed. The aggressive posturing of Mareck, the belligerence of the other officers, all seemed natural. Even the memory of Lenen being beaten down by Mareck and her rescuing her seemed like a romantic episode.

Lenar was momentarily overwhelmed.

Not too much appeared to have changed. There were no slaves serving drinks, but the golden caroc still seemed to be flowing. All the seats were occupied, there seemed to be no posturing between the women, no fighting, and the displays of aggression seemed to be a little artificial.

But as Sorak walked in with a return of her old confidence the noise level dropped.

I must be the oldest woman present.

Somehow that wasn't a surprise. But it wasn't Sorak's presence at first that drew the attention. That only came when the young women from the barracks let it be known who Sorak was. It was Nasa and Lenar. This was a dream-pit reconstructed in an area of the city where men simply didn't go.

But here were two men walking into the room with the confidence of any woman, Nasa because that was how he was and Lenar because he had no idea that his presence was so unusual.

But in fact, as Sorak quickly noticed, Nasa and Lenar weren't quite the only men present.

Much to her further surprise, at the back of the room where the music hadn't totally penetrated, there was what she recognised as a family group.

She couldn't believe it.

Sensing her amazement, Nasa focused on the group too.

The woman was openly breastfeeding an infant whilst the man looked on with every sign of pride and pleasure.

"They live in the old mangeneers' barracks, what's left of them," the young woman who had invited them to the dream-pit said. "They can't live anywhere else."

Sorak got no impression of what her companion might have thought about the situation that she was describing, but she clearly wasn't hostile. There seemed to be no such feeling amongst the other women either.

"We don't talk about them at the barracks."

That was something else that didn't surprise Sorak. She nodded in acknowledgement that her discretion was also being sought. The older officers would not have understood.

The idea that the woman had come to know the father of her child wasn't strange to Sorak, obviously, but it did set her wondering how many more such couples there might be. With the breakdown of the norms of the old female-led society, it seemed to her to be entirely likely that there would be others. And if there weren't, should not this be something to encourage?

Mother's heart, just enjoy yourself, and let Nasa and Lenar enjoy themselves!

Sorak wondered whether this was going to be possible.

17

Everybody seemed to want to talk to Sorak. Leben, the young woman who had extricated them from the military barracks, and who Sorak quickly recognised had her own agenda, carefully managed the access to her. But what Leben's agenda was, Sorak had yet to work out.

"Not everybody will be happy to see you," Leben said, "Since the men took over the women have fragmented."

It would be some time before Sorak got to fully learn about Leben and her background. But Leben was something of a kindred spirit to Sorak. Highly intelligent, brown-skinned; in the old days she would have been an administrator, maybe even a senator. But Leben had thrived in the uncertain environment and had grown into an independent and self-confident young woman; something that didn't necessarily make her universally popular. Whilst the older women still held sway, they didn't encourage too much free thinking, too much spontaneous action. The contradiction in this reaction with their adulation of Sorak's independence of spirit didn't seem to suggest itself to the capans and the other old women still in authority.

With much of her earlier years shrouded in mystery, as a grown woman Leben found her way to the barracks of the old

Senate Guard and joined a group of dissident women. But the women were only dissident in that they refused to work in the tanneries and other processing factories that made clothing and other necessities. Until Soran took over, the male administrators largely ignored them, just starved them of food, but didn't see them as worth creating more problems for themselves by forcing them to do work that they didn't want to.

"Soran executed the three oldest women," Leben told Sorak when she eventually got around to talking about herself.

"Two of us captured a soldier, cut off his private parts and sent them to Soran. And then we escaped the city to the Edge. I spent some time with Kragar, you know who Kragar is?"

Sorak knew who Kragar was.

"But Kragar's only interested in going back to the past and killing as many men as she can."

The way that Leben made her criticism of Kragar probably told Sorak more about the young woman and her beliefs than an hour's conversation might have. It also confirmed to Sorak that she might be able to work with Leben in some way in the future.

"But we can't go back to the past," Sorak said almost without thinking.

But at the dream-pit long before this conversation Sorak's questioning look had urged Leben to explain why everybody might not be happy to see Sorak, or at least the Sorak they thought she was, or wanted her to be. One word stuck in her mind.

"Fragmented? What do you mean by fragmented?"

"There are three groups of women," Leben said, "the collaborators, the passive resisters, and the active resisters. The collaborators are mainly old and elderly women who protect themselves by working with the male administration. In Soran's days there weren't many of them, he didn't trust them and often killed them without reason. The triumvirate appear to encourage them, mainly for their skills, but otherwise treats them with contempt. So far, and we aren't talking very long, the triumvirate have avoided killing any women within the city. They still hunt the resistance groups at the Edge, but personally I think that that is more to keep their low-grade soldiers out of the way."

The more she listened the more Sorak was impressed by Leben.

"And," she said, "how do the other women treat the collaborators?"

"The passive resisters, like that lot at the barracks, avoid all contact with them. The active resisters, within the city do the same, or if the opportunity arises they will sometimes attack them. The active resisters outside the city, that depends."

Sorak didn't really need to ask. Pastak would tolerate them, try to convert them to the resistance, Kragar would more than likely attack them, perhaps even kill them.

"And you?" asked Sorak.

"I'm a passive resister biding my time to become an active resister. There are many women around the city who know that we can't go back to the past. They know that we will have to find a way to live with the men or the city will die. Believe it or not there are men in the city, former high grade slaves, who believe the same. Not many and they are all old men. Until the triumvirate came, the men running the city have been former quarry slaves and the like; now that has changed, there has to be an opportunity. All the women are looking for is a lead."

The last statement was one that gave Sorak a nervous feeling in her stomach. Not only did she wonder how true it was but also whether Leben meant anything specific by making the assertion to her.

"But?"

There had to be a 'but', otherwise some sort of rapprochement would have been under way.

"But, although 147, we think, could possibly be amenable, the others are thought to want a male dominated society with women with fixed roles, rather than being equally involved. It's about lack of trust, about safeguards. And it's about the uncertainty over where the triumvirate's supporters stand as a whole. There are diehards here just as there are amongst the old women."

Sorak was beginning to have a problem absorbing what Leben was saying; her lack of contact with the city over the last seventeen cycles of the distant star had made it hard for her to appreciate the various shades of view. And the shades of view were more complex than Sorak could have first imagined. But the conversation had to end.

There were many other women, all much younger than Sorak, who wanted to talk to her, to ask about life outside the city, how she had survived. And almost every woman in the room, maybe bar the nursing mother, wanted to know what it was like living with a man on equal terms. Sorak knew that she was going to have to satisfy them.

But as Leben looked wistfully at Lenar, Sorak knew that there was a whole range of other questions that the women would want to ask but probably never would. All the women still expected to breed and one of the things that had persisted through the cycles was the mechanical way that this was done.

Breeding will have to change.

Somewhere in her brain, Sorak recognised that the intimacy of shared breeding, as she and Nasa had experienced it, was one of the most potent means of forging a more equal relationship between the men and the women. But how could that be conveyed to the generality of the population against the ingrained stereotypes from the past?

The booming music fascinated Lenar. The noise, the gyrating bodies as the young women danced together were utterly beyond his experience. And as Sorak seemed to be deep in conversation with Leben, and Nasa was surrounded by a circle of other women, in their turn fascinated by seeing a man so obviously confident in the company of just women, Lenar was lost and uncertain.

Then one of the women, more a young girl of Desak's age, reached out and took Lenar's hand. At least this was within Lenar's experience. But when she gently pulled him towards the dancing area, Lenar stiffened. Dancing was not within his experience.

Fortunately, Lenar was never far out of his father's notice.

"Lenar," Nasa said softly, seeing what was happening and being aware that the young woman might resent being rejected.

But a sudden commotion intervened, the young woman scurried away to rejoin her original group and Lenar looked questioningly at Nasa.

The music stopped abruptly. The musicians all retreated into the seating area and the shelter of their fellow women. Fear came and went from their faces as a small body of armed women surged into the room.

Nasa pulled Lenar to him and joined Sorak.

"Now what?" said Leben, moving towards the arriving party.

Sorak made to follow her but was restrained by Nasa. Cautious as ever, with armed and unknown women in the room he wasn't keen to draw attention to himself or Sorak and Lenar, not yet at least.

"What is going on?"

Sorak's respect for Leben grew on the spot. As direct as she would have been she knew that the only way to defuse a potentially difficult situation was to get things into the open. Her boldness worked.

The capral in charge of the soldiers responded to her demand.

"We were patrolling near Sector Five; we were confronted by a patrol, six men, creeping through the buildings. They appeared to be heading for the old mangeneers' barracks."

The bloodied state of all four of the soldiers told its own story. That they had made it to the dream-pit in turn suggested that they must have driven the men off, at the very least. In fact, after a brief but intense encounter, the male soldiers withdrew.

Sorak eventually did join Leben.

"We need to know why they were looking for the mangeneers' barracks," Leben said quietly.

Sorak, assuming that the men now directing the soldiers were more intelligent than the old quarry slaves, supposed that it was an intelligence gathering patrol, that's what she would have been sending out. Again, unbeknownst to her, she was correct.

She didn't get the chance to voice her thought.

"Sorakmam!"

The capral leading the soldiers breathed the name with a mixture of surprise, reverence and disbelief.

Leben had chosen to address the capral because she was obviously older than the other soldiers and therefore of assumed seniority.

A jumble of images flashed through Sorak's mind, all centred on her old enemy Mareck, with no explanation. But images of Mareck leading the hunt for her and Nasa all those cycles ago quickly lapsed into images of patrolling and platoon rivalry. Why?

"Sorakmam," the capral said again.

Then she knew. This was Mareck's blue platoon capral.

"Risak!"

"We still need an explanation," Leben interjected impatiently.

But she had lost control of the situation. It was as if she and the other women from the barracks weren't there.

Risak moved forward and saluted Sorak. Knowing her better than anyone in the room except Nasa, Risak hadn't exactly hero-worshipped Sorak, but she had never understood

Mareck's hatred of her. How could she? Sibling rivalry had been inconceivable in the city, and Mareck's relationship to Sorak had only been known in hindsight. But Mareck was long dead and Sorak was here in front of her. For reasons that she would have found hard to articulate she felt relieved, and more hopeful than she had for many cycles.

But the excitement had passed. The dream-pit came to life again.

"Now we have someone to lead us!"

As the music had resumed, only Leben and Sorak, and Nasa, who had joined them, heard Risak's statement.

Another jumble of images forced their way into Sorak's mind, of their valley, of the joys of motherhood, and of the peace of their previous existence, again with no explanation.

But Leben's matching look of exultation in response to Risak, and Nasa's look of anxiety chased the images away. Sorak knew that her life had changed again.

18

If Leben had given it any thought she would have also identified that there were three groups of men emerging. The city was now being run by a group of black and brown ex-slaves led by 147, 136 and 182, who deliberately refused to take names in order to reinforce their image of not being a self-serving elite in the eyes of the other men. With them were others of the former administration and clerical workers who had, in former times, been centred around the Senate. They had been aloof in the old days and they were still aloof now, but since they had introduced a level of stability they were tolerated rather than being regarded with any sort of respect or affection.

There was also an amorphous group of ex-personal slaves, formerly employed by military officers, mangeneers and higher administrators, as Nasa/1562 had been, largely now without a role. Potentially small in number they were the most vulnerable of the ex-slaves and tended to keep a low profile. But they were the group still most willing to breed since that had been one of their principal functions in the past. It was from this group that Desak's father had been drawn.

Finally there were the former quarry workers, gardeners, and workers in the tanneries and other manufacturing activities.

These were the most numerous of the men, the least intelligent or educated and consequently the most feared by the other two groups. But easily cowed when the city leaders weren't drawn from their ranks, they were regarded as the bedrock of the male administration, providing both the soldiers and still some of the manual workers. Many of these men were content to resume their old roles, rather than be forced into the male authorities' service.

* * *

The triumvirate operated on a majority vote basis and 147 was outvoted on the proposals to bring the warfare between the men and women to an end. 136 and 182 had proposed that all women should be disarmed and killed if they resisted. 147's objections stemmed from the fact that in almost every clash between the genders, it was the women who usually won, unless the men were in overwhelming numbers or they had caught the women off guard. The men held power not by force of arms but by their stranglehold on the administration. 147 simply didn't believe that disarming the women could be achieved without substantial bloodshed and, worse, by the invasion of the city by the women now living outside in the forest behind the Edge.

He was totally behind the notion of ending hostilities, his concern was how to achieve this with a minimum of casualties to the men, whilst maintaining the triumvirate's authority.

But first what the triumvirate needed was clear evidence of where the armed women were living and hiding, and how many of them there were. With that information, plans could be made to neutralise them. The clash between Risak and the patrol investigating the old mangeneers' barracks was an example of what 147 most feared. In this case, despite the women soldiers all being wounded in some way, Risak prevented the men from being killed. Captured, they were disarmed, stripped and delivered back to the edge of the area controlled by the triumvirate. 147 felt exonerated, but the incident did nothing to reduce the determination of his colleagues to proceed with the disarmament project. Risak's gesture of conciliation went totally unnoticed.

"The patrol met the women deep into Sector Four before retreating to Sector Five, but they had no idea whether they were living in the mangeneers' barracks that they were looking for."

147's report was simple and to the point.

Another patrol had been in the area where the encounter with Risak had taken place. The three male soldiers were in a quandary. It was obvious that something was going on in the old military headquarters on the edge of Sector Six. Adjacent to the closed arena, scene of Sorak's epic encounter with Mareck that finally led to her escaping from the city, the area like Sectors Seven and Eight was very much no-man's land between the heavily guarded areas that were centred on the old Senate buildings and the old residential areas that were originally occupied by middle-ranking administrators but were now only sparsely populated. It was an area that also contained the birthing houses and the schooling facilities for the girls of the various categories. It was the area where Sorak herself had been born, schooled and eventually trained as a military officer.

Slow of thought, and well aware that they were no match for women soldiers, the three men hesitated.

Suddenly, the rumble of voices from the headquarters building that had attracted their attention was overarched by a scream. It was the scream of a young woman or girl, not that the men were acute enough to understand that. Their instinct was to retreat. Since the triumvirate had come to power, fighting between men and women was discouraged where possible, so retreating when the situation was uncertain was acceptable.

And the situation seemed to be uncertain until a young woman, screaming again, burst out of the headquarters building and ran unseeingly straight towards the three troopers.

Naked to the waist and with her hands tied behind her the fleeing girl stumbled and froze at an arm's length from the leading soldier. Only aware of figures blocking her flight the girl crumpled onto her knees.

The noise from the building was cut off instantly as two old women and an elderly black man appeared in the doorway momentarily. None of them were armed. Confronted by the patrol, weapons at the ready, the soldiers were almost uncertain of what they had seen, so rapidly did the three rush back into the building.

The soldiers closed around the young woman. With their cumbersome thought processes almost visible in the expressions on their faces, the three men were torn between the opportunity that a lone and unguarded woman presented to them, and their instructions to deliver any unarmed women that they came across to the Senate House.

Desak, for it was indeed the young woman rescued by Sorak and Nasa, stared at the three men; her brain shut down, she was incapable of any mental processes. She didn't any longer have the power to scream.

Delivered to the supposed safety of the military barracks in Sector Four, her terror at the sight of the capan who Sorak didn't recognise was not fully appreciated in the excitement of Sorak's return. The capan herself couldn't have been more surprised, but she was quick to seize the opportunity. She quickly had Desak spirited away from her friends and had her bound and her mouth stuffed with a dirty rag. Urged away from the barracks by Leben, Sorak, Nasa and Lenar had left for the dream-pit before Lenar's anxiety had begun to overwhelm him.

Dragged through the derelict buildings and food gardens, Desak had been brought to the old military headquarters in the distant Sector Six by the capan and her mangeneer 'friend'. Secure from interference, they had intended to abuse Desak, as they had done before, and before she had eluded them and escaped the city, only to be caught by the patrol of men soldiers killed by Kragar.

The old black ex-slave, servant of the mangeneer, born with a mental deficiency due to too much in-breeding but allowed to live, provided the two women with creature comforts as they contemplated resuming their maltreatment of Desak. But with the desperation bred of past experience, Desak freed her mouth, stunned the mangeneer with a head butt and let out the scream that the three male troopers heard. With the agility of her youth she evaded the capan and ran out of the building. Confronted with the patrol, Desak's tormentors beat a hasty retreat, what else could they have done?

Incapable of coherent thought, Desak could only stare at the soldiers and sob.

But duty prevailed. Aware that such a pathetic figure, as Desak presented, would provide very poor sport, one of the troopers untied her hands and gestured her to accompany them. Having little familiarity with the city, Desak had no idea where she was being taken, but as she walked with the men, who in the end showed no inclination to even touch her, her awareness of her surroundings began to increase.

Lenar, Lenar!

It was the only thought that came into her head.

Desak's brain had started to function again when it was obvious that the soldiers weren't going to abuse her, but as she was marched into the administrative building next to the destroyed Senate House, her fears resurfaced and panic began to set in again.

Nasa would maybe have recognised her surroundings. As she was led further into the building and down into its bowels she was eventually housed in one of the cells of the underground prison. It was one of the few parts of the Senate buildings that had survived the original rebellion intact. Thrust into darkness, there was only a faint light coming from the corridor through a fanlight. She felt utterly bereft.

Perhaps it was fortunate that her whole thought processes had shut down again. Otherwise she might have wondered what else could happen to her in her wretchedness. She couldn't even conjure up an image of Lenar, and that sent her off into another bout of body-wrenching sobs, until she collapsed into an exhausted sleep.

She was awakened by being shaken. So devoid of coherent thought was she that she never registered that she was being shaken gently. The cell was bright with light from several oil lanterns. There was no smile on the face of the black man who was standing over her, but there was no malevolence either. Instinctively she recognised this.

"Come with us," the man said.

It was then that her brain switched back on and told her that the black man was accompanied by two male soldiers who viewed her with uncontrolled distaste. The black man however, seemed to have recognised authority and the soldiers merely glowered at her.

She was led back through the white-walled corridors, up ramps and then into a luxurious chamber, the like of which she had never seen before.

The two soldiers from the prison didn't enter the chamber, but there were two others, better dressed and armed with short swords.

"I'm sorry but it is necessary."

The black man gestured and Desak's hands were again tied behind her back. She wasn't as roughly treated as she had been by the lustful capan, but she was still restrained and helpless.

"You were being held against your will?" the man said.

Somehow reassured despite her bondage, Desak nodded. He

seemed almost sympathetic. Of course what Desak didn't know was that the military headquarters had been under surveillance as a possible entry point into the women-held areas of Sectors Four, Five and Six. The capan and her companion were in the wrong place at the wrong time and subsequent action by some of the triumvirate's more competent troops had ensured that the capan would molest no more young girls.

It was a raid that would have repercussions.

"Before you were taken to the military headquarters, where were you?"

The questioning was gentle but Desak knew that she was expected to give an answer. With no concept of the strategic importance of intelligence, Desak naïvely simply told the truth.

"We had just arrived at the barracks."

"We?"

"Sorak, Nasa, Lenar and…"

As she struggled to remember other names Desak suddenly sensed the deep silence that had descended on the people in the room.

"Sorak?"

A more acute observer than Desak would have noted the careful way that Sorak's name was articulated. Here there was no reverence, no expectation; more there was uncertainty, concern, bemusement at what the information imparted was going to mean to them.

147, for it was he who had been told of Desak's rescue from the old headquarters and was interrogating her, knew who Sorak was, but only by reputation. He knew her story, or at least the idealised story of her escape from the city. He knew that she had taken a favourite slave with her, and that it was the illicit relations with that slave that had forced her to leave the city. That the slave, and 147 shrewdly assumed that the Nasa to whom she referred was the former 1562, was still with Sorak, and had returned to the city as well, intrigued him. He had also heard the tales told by the soldier who had returned from the pursuit of Sorak of what had happened during the hunt, and of the slave 1562/Nasa's vital part in defeating the pursuing party. This was even more embedded in the folklore. To the former slaves, 1562/Nasa was a much more important figure than Sorak.

147 needed to think. He preferred to do that alone, so he dismissed Desak but had her confined to a small room in his quarters rather than sent back to the prison. He was sure that there was more that she could tell him about this Nasa and Sorak.

* * *

As Leben organised help to treat the soldiers' wounds, Sorak and Nasa settled comfortably away from the noisiest part of the dream-pit side by side on a sofa. The arrival of Risak and her troop brought the two of them back into the realities of the present and of life in the city as it now was. But Sorak was disturbed. She understood what Leben meant by the women being fragmented, but equally it was clear that Leben had visions of the women working together to… Sorak wasn't sure what Leben wanted the combined women to do. She seemed to recognise that they couldn't turn back time to re-establish the female dominance, but what she truly wanted in its place was not clear to Sorak. What she herself wanted in its place wasn't clear to her either, but the ideas forming in her brain disturbed her they were so radical.

"Mother, father, can we go back now?"

Outside the second moon was waning. Lenar knew this and his anxiety over Desak was mounting unbearably. Why he was anxious he probably wouldn't have been able to explain but, as both his parents sensed his unease, they were both surprised and both secretly glad that their son was showing the finer feelings that they had sought to encourage in him. If they had known the true situation with Desak they would have been even more concerned for their son.

Leben joined them.

"Part of the mangeneers' barracks is still habitable," she said. "and part of the Mech Division barracks in Sector Five is too. I suggest that you move in there."

Leben didn't say that the other family was hiding in the damaged mangeneers' barracks and it was better not to draw too much attention to them.

"We will go back to where we left Desak and see that she is settled, and then in the morning move on."

Neither Sorak nor Nasa had any idea what they were now going to move on to. They needed to think and talk. They both were beginning to feel that there was something for them to do, but neither could clearly define what that might be yet.

The red platoon barracks were silent but Sorak's old capan was still awake and obviously looking out for them. She gestured Sorak aside.

Sorak's body language did nothing to allay Lenar's anxiety as the capan briefed his mother.

19

147 was disturbed by what Desak had told him. He knew that he would have to share the information with 136 and 182 but, in truth, wasn't sure what it was that he would be telling them. They would have known about Sorak and Nasa, everybody did.

So Sorak and 1562, Nasa she called him, are back. Why? Why had they come back?

But why they had come back was the question that he couldn't answer, yet inevitably it would be asked. Clearly, he had to talk to Desak again, even supposing that she knew.

The decision to attempt to disarm as many of the women as possible having been made, the triumvirate had planned to meet that very evening to finalise their instructions to their soldiers. If Desak had anything more of use to tell him, with the distant star already waning, he needed to question her urgently. Which was what he did.

"You were captured at the military headquarters. Is that where Sorak and 15… Nasa are hiding?"

147 had an old crippled ex-personal slave who had worked for Crenan the old Senate Administrator, managing his household. Crenal, he liked the idea of having a name, had taken charge of Desak and 147 hardly recognised her when she

was brought back to him. Crenal had taken away her old shreds of clothing and provided her with a hastily constructed tabard that reached to her knees and was belted with a length of rope. Lenar would have been captivated by the appearance of a clean and tidy Desak. And, unlike his parents, in his ignorance, he would not have seen anything unusual in her having been fitted with an old slave collar. Fitting women used in domestic service with such collars had become a normal practice. Desak fingered the collar nervously, all too conscious of its significance.

"Are they hiding at the military headquarters?"

Since Desak didn't know that the building that the old capan and her 'friend' had taken her to was the old military headquarters, her only answer was to shake her head.

"They were going to a dream-pit," she said.

147 didn't bother to ask which dream-pit, he had by now realised that Desak wouldn't know.

"So, what is Sorak planning to do now she is back in the city?"

Of course, this was what 147 really needed to know, but on the evidence so far of Desak's shocked state he didn't have much confidence that she would be able to tell him.

"I ran away from Kragar and they were just bringing me back to the city."

Once she had started talking, 147 was shrewd enough not to say anything. He had heard of Kragar; she was on the triumvirate's 'most wanted list', but he didn't suppose that Desak's escape from Kragar, whatever that signified, had been in the city.

"Lenar said that Sorak and Nasa were looking for a new home. The valley where they had lived had been overrun by wild animals that had killed all of their beasts."

This didn't make much sense to 147 and it confused him as it seemed to suggest that Sorak wasn't going to stay in the city.

Although he realised that Desak was much more intelligent

than she seemed, in her current fearful state 147 sensed that he wasn't going to get the information that he needed. She clearly had no idea what Sorak's intentions were. That Sorak herself had no idea as she and Nasa returned with their son to the barracks didn't occur to him.

Crenal had taken Desak away to the food preparation area of the house. With 136 and 182 and the other leaders of the group due imminently there were domestic things that she could do to help him. Crenal, unlike 147, was very conscious that as Desak recovered her self-confidence her desire to escape would re-awaken and, with his limited mobility, there would be nothing that he could do to stop her if she ran away from him. Keeping her busy was one way of keeping track of her.

But as 147 had readily recognised, Desak, in her normal self, was certainly highly intelligent, and she herself had quickly realised as Crenal hurried her about with food preparation chores that it would be easy enough to escape, but not knowing where she was she had no idea to where she might escape. And she remembered Nasa's dictum when they were tracking through the forest, unsure where the next patrol might be, 'watch and wait'.

Arriving at the main room of 147's residence, 136 and 182 were accompanied by several others of the lesser leaders of the triumvirate, mostly black or brown, but not all. Some of the men were wearing uniforms similar to the ones that Desak had seen the women officers wear. Carrying around trays of drinks, a task so unfamiliar to her that it took all her concentration, she had little chance to register very much about these men. But she did get a sense that they might have treated her more roughly if the triumvirate members hadn't been present.

Flitting in and out of the food preparation area, as they all sat down for their meal, Desak again needed to concentrate hard to avoid creating some mishap that might get her punished. Whatever they were talking about, all she heard were occasional words, but Sorak's name was one of the words that came up quite frequently.

147 made no effort to identify Desak to his colleagues and the other men present, or why he had taken such a personal interest in her. She couldn't have known that having got all the information that he thought that he could from her, she had passed out of his consciousness.

The meal was soon over. Desak was locked in a small room by Crenal, nothing more being expected of her until the return of the distant star.

Despite his reservations about the achievability of disarming the women, or as many as they could, 147 knew that they had to make a start on the activity. One of the disadvantages of the stability that the triumvirate had introduced to the city was that it gave the dissident women the opportunity to organise themselves better and to infiltrate more and more areas of the city. 182 had been the first to recognise that there would be some point in the future when these women, in concert with the bodies of ex-women soldiers now scattered around the Edge, felt confident enough to directly confront them. It was a confrontation that they had every chance of losing as, although they had increasing numbers of soldiers, they couldn't match the quality of the women troopers. 182 knew that such a confrontation had to be avoided.

Disarming women was, in 147's mind, a simplistic approach, not that he would have been able to articulate his thoughts in such terms. Deep down in his mind, like Sorak, like Leben, like Pastak, he knew that some sort of accommodation was going to have to be made between the men and women.

But disarming women was what the meeting was about.

"As best that we can tell, the greatest concentration of women is in Sectors Four and Six. Armed women that is. The women in Sectors Two and Three are largely civilians. They don't have many arms, and many of them are beginning to work with us."

The report was given by a rather obsequious brown-skinned man who had, pre-rebellion, worked as a clerk in the military headquarters. A self-taught and self-appointed military leader he was one of the oldest men present. The plan to achieve the disarmament was largely his.

"So," said 147, "if we work through Sectors Two and Three, and the civilians, it should be easy enough to collect what arms that they have, crossbows and swords presumably. But it will also signal to the other women, the ex-soldiers, our intentions. Do we want that?"

147 had tossed a stone into the pond! The ripples of conversation got heated, cooled, got heated again, but in the end, it was decided that as the official administration of the city they were entitled to call for all citizens to hand in their arms in the interests of public safety and public order. But for 147 this wasn't very convincing.

Crenan and the long-gone women's Senate Administration would have been proud of them. 147 was in despair. Even the most intelligent men present, the former administrative slaves, and the younger post-rebellion men, couldn't seem to reach beyond imitating what the women would have done in the past.

The call to surrender all weapons was passed out to Sectors Two and Three on the certain knowledge that it would disseminate to the rest of the city. A deadline was included.

And once we pass the deadline?

147 was all too conscious that they had comprehensively avoided the issue here.

*　*　*

The meeting between Kragar and Pastak was frosty. The time that they had both spent in the forested wilderness beyond the

Edge had reinforced their basic underlying characters. With almost nothing in common, they had both always sought to minimise contact, but an urgent problem had arisen.

Aloof, arrogant, contemptuous of those paler-skinned than herself, Kragar had learned virtually nothing from her experiences since the rebellion and the overthrow of the women's control of the city. She still saw herself as one of the elite, without recognising that there no longer was an elite. The fact that the troops that she now commanded were a ragtag of ex-soldiers, none of whom where Senate Guards, was a constant reminder to her of what she had lost, and what she was determined to recover. The meeting with Sorak and, more particularly, Nasa had been a huge shock to her. But, against her rigid mindset, she had learned no lessons from her contact with them. Lenar she had effectively erased from her consciousness.

Pastak, on the other hand, had immediately recognised, once she had thought through the implications of the rebellion, that her world and her role in it had changed forever. For her the changed status of the men of the city could only be a good thing even if she couldn't visualise exactly how the change would play out. Unlike Kragar she had left the city because of her opposition to what was happening there rather than to form a platform to try to reverse events. The ex-soldiers that she had gathered around her she had tried to educate towards her own view, and although she was, like Kragar, on the triumvirate's 'most wanted list' her priority had slowly become avoiding killing the male soldiers, rather than Kragar's, to kill as many as possible.

As Sorak had discovered, Pastak was all too aware that the city couldn't survive without a thriving male community.

The two resistance group leaders had met on the day Sorak, Nasa and Lenar had gone to the dream-pit and Desak had been captured. In a sense, the meeting had been forced on them when their troops had almost come to open fire on each other when

Kragar was pursuing, and Pastak was avoiding, one of the more enterprising male patrols. It was a serious situation that had to be resolved.

Kragar, as was her want, blamed Pastak's troopers for the debacle, without regard to the fact that it was her soldiers who had strayed a long way from their patrol area.

"The last thing we need is to fight each other."

Pastak, as was also *her* want, sought to defuse the situation. "We need a better way to communicate with each other. That will give us a better chance to avoid the patrols."

From the expression on her face it was obvious that avoiding the male patrols was the last thing Kragar had in mind.

"We need a better way to communicate so that we can be sure to locate the patrols and deal with them, not avoid them," she said.

But attacking the male patrols wasn't the only thing that Kragar was interested in, so, uncharacteristically, she let the matter pass for the moment; she had something else that she wanted to say that she considered to be much more important.

"I think we must be ready to move back into the city now that Sorak has returned."

It was a statement that took Pastak completely by surprise. There had been nothing in her conversations with Sorak that had suggested that she was intending to get involved with any of the action in the city. Like herself, Sorak seemed to have sensed that there had to be a major change in attitude both by the triumvirate but also by the dissident women, if any sort of lasting relationship was to develop.

Aware that Kragar only wanted to go back to the pre-rebellion world, Pastak resolved to have no part in any military action in the city that was initiated by or involved the black officer. If her troopers wanted to be involved then they had better join with Kragar.

Back at their own encampment, Pastak said as much to her

soldiers. She was gratified to find that none of them wanted to join Kragar. But they did raise the possibility of taking action against the city of their own.

But Pastak couldn't help wondering what Sorak might do. From her brief conversations with her she was convinced that a return to a sedate life in some remote hidden valley was no longer going to be a part of Sorak's future. But what was?

20

The trip to the dream-pit had given each of Sorak, Nasa and Lenar, in their separate ways, food for thought. Meeting up with Leben, for Sorak, was probably the most noteworthy part of the evening. Meeting up with Risak and the soldiers was probably the most disturbing because it signified that the warfare between the dissident women and the men now running the city was both real and dangerous.

I need to watch out for Leben. She thinks differently from the other women I've met so far, but what role is she likely to have?

Had she known, Sorak would have been even more troubled to know that what role she, Sorak, might be willing to play, was precisely what was exercising Leben's mind too. For Leben, Sorak was an opportunity out of nowhere that might turn the campaign against the triumvirate into a potential success, rather than being a string of futile gestures.

Nasa, apart from realising that Sorak seemed to be quite at home at the dream-pit, and seemingly at ease with the people there, saw an opportunity to relax and to observe just how differently people were behaving from previous times. But he was still not sure yet how much of what he was seeing represented womankind in general. He recognised Sorak's view that things had to change in the relations between men and women, but a dream-pit didn't seem likely to be the best place to make judgements on the progress of any such changes. His concern that Sorak was getting drawn into something that they didn't understand yet was a worry to him.

Lenar had only one thought. It was a thought that originally troubled him, but once he had drawn the comparisons with his parents, he became reconciled to it. All he wanted was to be with Desak.

Sorak's old capan had been an unexpected resident at the barracks. The soldiers and the few civilians living there were committed to resisting the triumvirate, but the capan, Sorak recalled, had not been noted as a powerful clear-cut thinking individual and certainly not a decisive decision-maker.

But the expression on the old woman's face as the three of them approached the entrance to the barracks building on their return from the dream-pit expelled any such thoughts from Sorak's mind.

As the capan clearly wanted to talk to Sorak, Nasa instinctively drew Lenar to one side, but Lenar had already switched into anxiety mode.

"The girl, Desak," the capan started hesitantly.

Sorak's enquiring look forced her to go on. Something clearly had happened.

"Rillak knew Desak as a child when she was working at the category training school."

Rillak was the other elderly capan whom they had met when they had first arrived. Something stirred at the back of Sorak's mind: Desak had reacted to the old woman in an unexpected way.

"Rillak liked young girls."

Sorak's mind raced onto the implications of the capan's

statement without registering the past tense. Desak was a young girl!

"As soon as you handed her over Rillak had Desak taken to her quarters by a mangeneer friend, and when you left for the dream-pit it seems that she took her to the old military headquarters in Sector Six, where she still kept a room.

"What happened next is not clear since we only have the word of a brain-damaged slave to rely on, but Desak proved to be more resistant to Rillak than she had been in the past. As I understand it she must have escaped and ran off screaming. As she left the building she ran into the arms of a male patrol."

Sorak's anxiety level rose again. Desak had gone from one desperate situation to another.

"The old slave says that the soldiers took Desak away. He was very clear about that. We have no way of knowing to where. But the soldiers came back and killed Rillak and the mangeneer. They didn't bother with the old slave."

It was only later when Sorak revisited what the capan had said again did she feel no regret for the death of the old woman.

"When the soldiers came back, they came in strength and occupied the military headquarters. As far as we know they are still there."

There was more, but Sorak didn't hear it. Her military-trained mind told her that the first soldiers would have taken Desak back to their barracks, to their officers, if they had any. Desak would have been terrified. Her experience with soldiers had not been good!

You can't think such thoughts. You must concentrate on what the capan knows.

"The old slave? Brain-damaged. Do you believe what he was telling you?"

"He wasn't telling me, Sorak. He wouldn't have told me. But he's not the only ex-military slave that we have here. 1847 and 1633 pieced together what he told them, but it took them so long to get the information out of him that the trail had long gone cold."

Sorak's instinct was to make that judgement for herself, but she had a much greater priority. She was aware of Lenar fretting in the background. His father's efforts to manage his son's anxiety weren't working.

He has to be told.

Having given her report, the capan hurriedly retreated, knowing that Sorak would have a whole raft of questions that she wouldn't be able to answer. Despite their difference in rank in the past, the capan had a hearty respect for Sorak, and always felt intimidated by her.

"I will show you to your quarters."

Sorak was relieved that it was Leben who had quietly joined her and made the offer. Still unclear where Leben fitted in to anything, she was just grateful for a friendly face as she began to bend her mind to how she was going to tell her son what had happened to Desak.

"Your son will be sad," Leben said.

Sorak hadn't realised that the young woman had observed the brief passages between Lenar and Desak before the old capan had spirited her away. But having no idea of the background Leben had no suspicions of Rillak's intentions. If she had been paying more attention maybe… but Sorak didn't do regrets like that. What had happened had happened.

"The capan isn't much use," Leben said. "We don't take much notice of her. But 1847 said that the soldiers who came back, according to Rillak's slave, ex-slave, were elite headquarters troops. How he knew that I have no idea, but Rillak's ex-slave, before his brain began to fail was said to be able to remember amazing detail. 1847 was sceptical but Rillak's man described the uniforms of the soldiers who returned. I've no idea what they were nor had 1847, but they were nothing like any of the uniforms of the other male soldiers that we have seen. So they could very well have been what the old man said that they were. What that means we have yet to find out."

Leben took the three of them to the old Mech Div. Barracks as they had decided earlier. They weren't embedded into Sector Four as the old mangeneers' barracks were, but they were much more accessible to the rest of the city. A couple of elderly ex-soldiers were to be found in the food preparation area. Much to both Leben's and Nasa's amusement they readily supplied Nasa with food for a late evening meal. Old habits had yet to die in odd places in the city!

"We must talk again," Leben said but didn't wait for a response from Sorak.

"So, mother?" Lenar said.

Carefully Sorak explained what the capan had said and what Leben and 1847 had added.

Lenar didn't have a very comfortable night, but both of his parents were impressed by the mature way that he heard what was to be said, and the sensible questions of clarification that he asked.

"We will find her," he said, aware that neither Sorak nor Nasa were likely to offer such a solution to his problem when they had no idea how they might deliver it.

21

Still no clearer on why someone as astute and free-thinking as Leben appeared to be was just hanging around the old military barracks, Sorak bent her mind to the information that she had been given that formed a background to the abduction of Desak by the male soldiers.

Unable to sleep, she lay beside Nasa and let things flow through her brain. But Desak didn't turn out to be her major worry.

"Apparently the triumvirate have ordered all citizens to hand in their weapons at control points in Sector Three and Sector Five."

It was the last thing that Leben had said before she left.

Sorak wasn't sure what stationing male soldiers at the old military headquarters had to do with Desak's disappearance, but she could certainly see what it might have to do with forcibly disarming the women.

If, as Sorak had always assumed, the probing patrols into Sector Four were for intelligence gathering, the triumvirate would by now know that the barracks there represented the largest concentration of women soldiers in the city. Other areas, she had been told, like Sectors Two and Three, mainly contained civilians, commercial workers, ex-administrators and mangeneers, some of whom were thought to be cooperating with the male administration. There were pockets of women in other parts of the city, but Sorak had no idea how many, or their disposition towards the male administration. Sectors Seven and Eight, small in size and complex, largely the old commercial districts of the city, were no-go areas. Largely destroyed by the rampaging slaves in the immediate aftermath of the original rebellion, they had seemingly lain derelict and deserted ever since. Neither Leben nor the other women had any idea whether anyone now lived there.

In Sector Four the women were well organised and well armed, but following her conversations with Leben she had reservations, which she had already shared with Nasa, about the quality of their leadership. Old ranks still seemed to be respected; for Sorak, this reflected the rigid mindsets of the past, yet she knew that the younger women were probably much more capable than they were given credit for.

Sorak also knew that the women patrolled the sewage plant area and the food gardens to ensure that they weren't taken by surprise by an attack on their rear. But based on their geographic situation in Sector Four, and the occupation of the military headquarters, containment, she supposed, was the triumvirate's objective.

But the capan and the other officers I've met don't seem to have given much thought to the male soldiers being more enterprising.

"It only needs one good officer to join the men!"

It did, and one had.

Surveying the area around her from the roof of the military headquarters in Sector Six and assessing the means of access to Sector Four, Marwek, late of the Senate Guard, contemporary of Kragar, and renegade, was confident that the armed women could be confronted. There might be a few casualties amongst them, which 147 didn't want, but 136 and 182 didn't care about, but even if they disarmed half of them this time it would strengthen the triumvirate's position considerably.

"So, what if Sorak *is* there?"

Marwek had only just heard the rumours about the return of Sorak to the city. Less arrogant and more realistic than Kragar, she found it hard to visualise how, heroine though she might be, Sorak could deter a determined attack on Sector Four.

And as Sorak herself, finally falling asleep and then being prodded awake again by Nasa, organised herself for the new day, Marwek was meeting with a group of sullen male caprals in preparation for the day's action. All of the caprals were in their middle years and had served briefly in the quarries or food gardens, but once again being subject to the authority of a former Senate Guard tenant was not popular. However, since many of their troopers were now younger men with no experience of the pre-rebellion world, and no ingrained automatic obedience, the lives of these ageing caprals trying to maintain military discipline seemed to them to be no less stressful than their days in servitude, Marwek notwithstanding.

But Marwek, nonetheless, was a good officer, and gave her orders simply and clearly. She had soon realised that there was no point in explaining the strategy to the caprals, she just needed to give them enough of a view of her tactics to allow them to organise their men.

Rigid mindsets from the past were something that Leben had also had to battle with. One of the reasons that she liked Sorak, despite her being much older than her, was that she didn't have a rigid mindset.

Awakened as the distant star broke the horizon, Sorak wondered what the new day would bring.

"Welcome."

As much as to distract Lenar, after they had all eaten, the three of them headed back to the Sector Four barracks. Nasa knew from her behaviour that something was worrying Sorak, but long experience had taught him to wait for her to tell him rather than to ask. Sorak marched straight into the capan's office.

Leben was there with the capan and two other ex-officers, former tenants whom Sorak didn't know. The conversation was clearly fraught.

"Leben says that we shouldn't reduce the patrols in the sewage area and food garden to reinforce the access from Sector Five." Sorak immediately recognised the petulant whine of the capan's voice, still unable to make a decision.

Despite Leben being a civilian, the two tenants appeared to understand the military sense of what she had been saying. There were already women troopers guarding the access from Sector Five, but with a mixture of narrow streets between high-walled, ochre-coloured buildings and the tight barrack-like blocks of the officer's training school it would have been hard to defend, even with ten times the soldiers. To Leben's non-military mind, better to let the attackers through into the open areas of Sector Four overlooked by the barrack buildings where they could be fired down on with less risk.

Marwek understood this too, but was more interested in closing off an exit from Sector Four than fighting over it.

"I think Leben is right," Sorak said.

There was a sense of foreboding permeating the officer group that Sorak found depressing. The triumvirate's declared intention of disarming the women had seemed to demoralise the capan, but the tenants seemed reluctant to take action without her authority, despite Leben's obvious prodding of them to do so. Sorak had no such reservations.

"We need to be prepared on all fronts," she said, in a tone that would have induced some deep memories in Nasa. But he would have quickly acknowledged that the situation needed Sorak, the forceful tenant, to be back in business.

Events were about to overtake them.

"Capanmam," an ex-under tenant whom Sorak recognised from her desert patrolling days rushed into the capan's room. Her report was brief and to the point.

The women soldiers hated patrolling the areas around the sewage plant. Not only was the smell so foul that they had all had to bind parts of their undergarments around their faces, but because there was no one working in the area any more the sewage had overflowed out into the open spaces and a river of filth had formed and flowed into the nearby buildings. The guard barracks that Sorak had occupied all those cycles ago were now inaccessible without walking ankle deep through the evil-smelling sludge and voracious animal life.

But something was wrong.

Risak, promoted to tenant by the capan, and back on duty after treatment for her wounds from her earlier encounter with the male patrol, called for quiet. Apart from Sorak, Risak was probably the best of the former soldiers still active. A contemporary of Sorak, she was nonetheless a fit and vigorous leader, much respected by her troops.

The nearby vegetable gardens were more exposed, but they were a much more wholesome place. Risak knew that her troopers would prefer to be there than wallowing in sewage, but some instinct made her hesitate. The dull flutter of a crossbow bolt as it flew past the patrol immediately justified Risak's caution. Exactly where the bolt came from, Risak didn't see.

"Disperse!"

Risak's sharp order was instantly obeyed. Experience had told the women that since the advent of the triumvirate, the male soldiers always moved in a compact group when on patrol. Inexperienced, nervous, especially the younger men, they sought the comfort of close order every time. How effective a male patrol was, was entirely down to the man in charge. The first signs were that this present patrol wasn't very well led. On Risak's order a well rehearsed routine ensued. The women, once they had located the patrol spread out around them and sought to encircle them. On this occasion it was a manoeuvre that proved instantly successful.

Recognising their peril, the ageing male capral, once a worker in the very food garden that he now ordered a retreat into, sought to find cover where none existed. Overgrown and a tangled mess of dead and dying vegetation, the patrol found it almost impossible to move at any speed back the way that they had come and towards the inner city wall gate.

As the women soldiers began to hurry forward, weapons primed and trained on the now-cowering group of eight men, a stand-off developed. The women were outnumbered and therefore facing a superior number of weapons, but they were trained, experienced and not fearful; the male soldiers were none of these things. An urgent silence prevailed as the two groups identified each other.

Surrounded by the women and menaced by their crossbows, Marwek's careful tuition had come to nothing. She had sent the lowest grade of the soldiers available to her to the sewage plant and food gardens because she reasoned that this was likely to be the least patrolled part of the sector and the easiest to secure the weapons of the soldiers that they did meet. It was a major misjudgement that taught Marwek a useful lesson.

"Throw down your weapons!"

Risak's order was given clearly but both men and women knew that it carried a threat.

But the order was instantly obeyed. Some of the women soldiers seemed to perhaps regret that it had been done so. The follow-on from the rigid mindset, as both Sorak and Leben worried about, was still the willingness to kill men on the least provocation. Risak's orders were to kill as a last resort, but she was another one of those who were beginning to see how counterproductive such slaughter would end up being.

The under-tenant was despatched to report the incursion to the capan and two of the soldiers, having gathered the crossbows and other weapons from the men, were despatched to the triumvirate's nearest collecting point to hand them in.

It was only when the patrol straggled back to a furious Marwek that the apparent first fruits of the disarmament project turned out to be their own weapons. No one, it seemed, was game enough to tell the triumvirate members of this piece of gamesmanship by the women.

Marwek had undoubtedly misjudged the situation at the sewage plant, but that was only a relatively small part of her overall plan.

147 had never been to the old military headquarters before, either in his original slave incarnation or now in his role of a triumvirate principal. He was to meet Marwek. 136 and 182, in particular, were wary of the former Senate Guard tenant, if not intimidated by her. Her virulent hatred of other women was something that they couldn't understand. But 147 had had some contact with her when she was very young when he was working for Crenan, the old Senate Administrator and Nasa's original protector. Marwek had saved 147 from a beating by Kragar for some trivial infraction that earned his gratitude but Kragar's enmity. In the present situation such things created important bonds.

Marwek had fourteen soldiers lined up for 147's inspection. The special uniforms, already a matter of curiosity at the Sector Four barracks, drew his attention, but only as an introduction to the men wearing them. None of them had the slouching demeanour of the ex-quarry slaves, yet some of them had a sallow, battered look about them that was unfamiliar to him.

All but five of the soldiers were formerly employed in the

Senate prison. Rough, tough, regularly abused by the Senate Guard, Marwek was one of the few people who even knew of their existence. Along with five condemned men whom she had found at the open arena, and used to train the others, they were a formidable unit.

The changing administrations over the seventeen cycles of the distant star since the initial rebellion had produced a range of misfits; Marwek had sought some of them out. Shrewd, capable, but a female misogynist, she had seen the opportunities presented by the triumvirate to work out her dislike of her fellow women in a good cause. And the misfits were ideal for her purpose.

The recovery of the weapons, such as there were, from Sector Three had gone to plan. Populated by a mixture of civilians but including some of the birthing houses, the sector had become another no-man's-land where the triumvirate's forces were reluctant to go, and the women soldiers were reluctant to risk clashes with them anyway. But it was where there was the most cooperation between men and women. But unlike the soldiers, who tended to see the world in black and white terms, many of the civilian women, even having lost their jobs initially, realised that eventually they would have to be called upon to return unless the city was to descend into chaos, starvation, then total collapse. 147, at least, understood this.

For their own reasons Sorak and Leben and a few others of the more enlightened women in Sector Four would have understood the women's thinking.

As 147 left the old military headquarters, Marwek despatched four of her warriors by a circuitous route to Sector Five. Nervously waiting for them was a group of civilians, mainly older women, from Sector Two.

The next part of Marwek's plan to try to disarm the women of Sector Four was in play.

The boundary between Sectors Four and Five was indistinct and it was only the narrow streets between those high ochre-coloured walls of the buildings that signified that it was Sector Five. Sector Five contained some of the training schools for not only the military but also the various civilian categories. It was where Sorak herself had grown up and been trained as a soldier, but had failed to be brainwashed into total obedience to the norms of the city. It was not Marwek's ideal choice for a battleground.

Sector Four was more open with wide squares marking the areas between the different barracks of the various military units. It was here that Sorak lived as an adult and military officer and where her own personal rebellion was seeded and developed. It was here where she and 1562, the Nasa of the future, first met.

The four soldiers roughly herded the old women out of Sector Five into the barrack square that marked the beginning of Sector Four. The twenty women were positioned in groups of four or five in the streets and entrance ways to the square. Nervous, frightened, the women weren't very clear what their role was, although being caught in the crossfire seemed to be their most likely fate.

A patrol of four women soldiers emerging from Sector Four suddenly found themselves confronted by five brown and white women at the end of the main street entering the square. A single crossbow shot striking the leading soldier in the shoulder halted the patrol. Pulling their injured colleague into a doorway, the other patrol members sought to locate who had fired at them. Hidden behind the taller civilians, the male soldier was invisible to them. A second crossbow bolt fired over their heads and rattling off the wall of a building was enough for the patrol to hurriedly retreat. They were clearly being forced to stay in Sector Four.

"We checked the other routes into Sector Five."

The capral in charge despatched the injured soldier back to the officers in Sector Four to report.

"They are all blocked off by groups of civilian women covered by soldiers. It was impossible to say how many soldiers."

"This is different," Sorak said to Nasa as they congregated in the barracks' communal area. "Whoever's in charge knows their business."

That was a worry, but they didn't have time to speculate.

"Sorakmam, we are being attacked from two sides."

Risak had returned from the food garden area leaving the under-tenant in charge. The capan ordered her back to her post, but her orders were increasingly being ignored.

Marwek's plan, once again, was simple. Block off escape, which had been achieved into Sector Five, but not to the sewage plant and food gardens and the city gates. This would have confused the women and given her significant freedom of movement. It would have left her free to move into Sector Four to try to draw out groups of women soldiers, overcome them and disarm them. The capan's orders to disperse around the barracks to cover all points would have played into Marweks' hands.

Hiding behind Sorak's authority, Risak had seen the risks of dispersal and had tried to keep the garrison of soldiers in two tight groups and to confront the attackers as a body. With upwards of thirty women soldiers facing only ten of Marwek's the triumvirate's plan was doomed. Surprise had been lost and a direct confrontation even by the best male troops was inadvisable.

Forced to consolidate her own troops to counter encirclement, Marwek soon found that she was going to have to surrender some of her soldiers if she was to withdraw safely. Having briefly committed herself to the intrusion into Sector Four, she had to scurry to safety. She was furious.

"Disarm them, don't kill them!"

Sorak's order rang out loud and clear and into the hearing of the former Senate Guard tenant before she withdrew. Marwek knew now for certain that Sorak was back and active in supporting the women of the city. It was very much food for thought for her. So far, the quality of leadership amongst the women had been fragmented and poor.

Sorak's order wasn't quite carried out. At least two of the male soldiers, isolated in their efforts to retreat to the old military headquarters, were later found with their necks broken. Near one of them, the body of one of the younger women soldiers was found with her throat cut. It wasn't clear what had happened, but neither Risak nor Sorak could persuade the young soldier's companions to enlighten them. But all three deaths were seen as a defeat in their dealings with the triumvirate.

Retreating towards Sector Five, the largest party of male soldiers brushed aside the civilian women but found themselves outflanked. Surrounded and with their crossbows at the ready they waited. All five men were previously condemned to death; having nothing to lose, they stood their ground. This was just the sort of situation that Sorak had wanted to avoid. The tension rose. The death of the young soldier called for revenge.

"Hold!"

Sorak's order was greeted with murmurs of dissent, but neither she nor Risak had time to identify the dissenters. The tension heightened.

"Lower your weapons."

It was an order to both men and women.

Equipped with the short stabbing swords that the women soldiers also carried, the five men threw down their crossbows but drew their alternate weapons. The women reciprocated, ignoring their officers in their lust to punish the men who had killed their comrade.

Again, neither Sorak nor Risak were able to intervene

before a fierce battle developed. Unable to separate the fighting groups, all that they could do was watch helplessly as the five men were finally cut down, taking seven women with them.

Sorak was distraught. In all, nineteen men and women had been killed that day.

"This has got to end!"

But within the excitement of the battle and its aftermath, not even Risak heard her.

22

Marwek's report to the triumvirate principals was brief and economic of the details of what had actually happened in Sector Four. But 147, at least, was shrewd enough and knowledgeable enough to recognise that, in fact, things had gone badly and that disarming the women was probably not achievable. He made no effort to share his thoughts with 136 and 182.

"And you have confirmation that Sorak is there?"

182 knew the least about the history and mythology surrounding the former officer, although he was well aware of Nasa and the mythology surrounding him. But he had sensed that Sorak's return to the city was a potential cause for concern. He too didn't share his thoughts with the others, although he suspected that 147 had similar concerns.

"She was directing the women soldiers," Marwek said, without adding that Sorak was also urging her troops to avoid killing the men. She wasn't sure what this signified.

Marwek was naturally cautious in her dealings with the three men but she was also increasingly confused over Sorak; what was she doing now that she had returned, and just what was her attitude towards the men? She displayed her caution by saying very little.

However, 136 put her on the spot by demanding to know how many of their soldiers had been killed. He wasn't mollified to learn that they had killed more women than men who had died.

This has got to end.

It was a thought that 136 and 147 both had in common with Sorak, if for different reasons.

* * *

Sorak, Nasa and Lenar gathered once again with the capan, the other officers and the bulk of the women soldiers in the communal area of the barracks. Patrols were still out to make sure that there were no male soldiers left in Sector Four. Sorak noted some new faces and learned that about fifteen other women soldiers had hurried to Sector Four from other parts of the city when they had heard of the confrontation. The reinforcements were more than welcome.

The civilian women used by the male soldiers as human shields were invited to join them, although they were hesitant, fearing reprisals for their cooperation with the triumvirate. Mostly they just wanted to get back to the Sectors where they normally lived and to avoid any further trouble.

"That was too well organised," Nasa remarked once they had all settled into groups, and relaxed. Sorak knew exactly what he meant.

"There was a woman in charge."

A brown-skinned civilian, by far the oldest woman present, a former worker in the office of Crenan, the Senate Administrator from before the rebellion, made the statement in absolute confidence, having overheard Nasa's comment. Sorak's challenging look forced her to say more.

"She was wearing full uniform, helmet on and visor down, rare these days. The slaves did exactly what she told them to do."

Something was niggling at Sorak, Nasa immediately noticed

"And?" Nasa said, forcing the woman to say yet more.

She shook her head. She strongly suspected that the woman was Marwek, she too had known her in the old Senate offices, but knowing the temper of the women that she was mixing with, she wasn't prepared to give a name until she was sure that it was the right person. Unaware of Marwek's existence, Sorak had nonetheless assumed that the woman in question had to be a renegade military officer; with the skill displayed she had to have been. This was a concern.

The old woman eventually drifted away, anxious to rest and then return to Sector Two the next day.

Another civilian who had been hovering in the background, apparently wanting to speak to Sorak, now approached. She rather peremptorily waved Nasa and Lenar away, putting Sorak immediately on her guard.

"They are planning to kill the woman and child."

It took Sorak a moment to understand that the woman was talking about the family hiding in the mangeneers' barracks. Another of the old brown-skinned women who had survived the post-rebellion purges, she seemed to take no account of the father. Why the woman was giving her the information Sorak couldn't imagine, but she seemed fearful and she didn't stay long enough for her to ask her.

When Sorak rejoined Nasa, Lenar was no longer there. In the friendly social atmosphere of the communal area of the barracks, the presence of the two men having been accepted, neither Sorak nor Nasa thought to worry about their son.

But, as they sat quietly together, Nasa continued to sense Sorak's distress. The confrontation that they had just witnessed would do nothing to ease the friction between the men and women. Yet Nasa recognised the struggle in his partner's mind between her desire to re-establish their old lifestyle somewhere, and her desire, more her need, to see what she could do to help the situation. Like him, she was appalled by the casual nature of the killings.

For Nasa, however, Desak's disappearance and its impact on his son was just as much an incentive to stay.

* * *

"So, did the soldiers say anything that you heard?"

Lenar, unable to contain his angst over his loss of Desak, and aware of just how powerful his feelings were becoming, had slipped from the communal room at the military barracks whilst his mother was talking to the aged brown woman, and headed for Sector Six. Lenar didn't know the area that he was heading for was Sector Six, he had merely picked up the information on where it was and where to find the person there to whom he wanted to talk.

Only recently having been introduced to the city and to tall buildings, Lenar, to Nasa's increasing surprise hadn't been in any way intimidated. He seemed to have inherited his mother's ability to visualise the layout of the city, with Nasa's added ability to focus only on what around him was important to him within the whole activities.

Notwithstanding, Nasa would have been astonished just how quickly Lenar was able to find his way to Sector Six and to locate the ancient black man who had served the deceased capan in the old military headquarters.

Able to focus sharply on anything that attracted his attention, and retain an amazing amount of detail of what he had observed, the poor man was also subject to violent fits that threw him into uncontrollable spasms of body movement that left him exhausted and often injured. The emancipation of the male slave population after the original rebellion, however, didn't affect him as the capan had kept him hidden for many cycles of the distant star. In the old days, people like him would have routinely been killed by the women. The capan's motives were selfish and driven by her need to keep her perversions a secret from the old military authorities.

Used to fending for himself in the years after the rebellion, the old black man barely noticed the passing of the capan, and not really understanding caution or suspicion he was only too pleased to talk to Lenar.

Young, inexperienced and used to a bucolic life, Lenar never hurried unless the situation he was in called for urgent action. So dealing with the vagaries of the old black man, and Lenar never knew whether he had a name, didn't bother him. That there was something wrong with him was obvious, but beyond Lenar's experience; since they seemed to be able to converse adequately, he simply asked his questions and kept asking them until he got an answer that he could understand.

The soldiers who first captured Desak, it seemed, didn't say anything; they were frightened and simply wanted to get away from the sector. The soldiers who came and killed the capan and her friend were different.

How different?

"Senate Guard."

The man repeated the description again and again but Lenar could get nothing more of use from him. Having previously met Kragar, he knew who the Senate Guard were. Elitism wasn't something that he would have understood, but he was well aware that the Senate Guard was special.

If they sent Senate Guards, something must have been important.

Lenar felt that this was obvious, but didn't suppose that it was Desak, whom they couldn't then have known about. But it did set him to wondering if the return of the soldiers was nonetheless prompted in some way by their having captured her. It still didn't make sense.

But they are likely to know where she is!

However, his musing still couldn't tell him who 'they' might be and therefore where he might find them.

23

As the second moon started its second journey around the planet, Sorak and Nasa finally accepted that Lenar had gone missing. In her heart, knowing how intense he could be, Sorak wasn't entirely surprised. And she had a good idea why he might have headed off into other areas of the city.

Nasa also thought he knew why he had gone, but really had no idea where he might have headed.

He's gone chasing after Desak.

In the normal course of events, Nasa would have been proud of his son's perseverance and enterprise, but under the conditions within the city, and recognising that Desak had after all been captured by triumvirate soldiers, his only feeling was one of intense anxiety. His son's simple view of life wasn't going to be much help to him. Nasa could have had no idea how wrong he was.

But there were other pressing problems.

Sorak, who was torn between believing the old brown-skinned woman's warning about the threat to the young family in the mangeneers' quarters and rejecting it, only latterly became aware of Nasa's agitation. Sorak had a clearer idea where her son might go if their suppositions over his motives for leaving were true.

"If he's gone looking for Desak, he'll head for Sector One and the old Senate and Administration buildings."

"But, Sorak, how will he find them? He knows nothing at all about the city."

"You taught him well, Nasa, he will find his way."

Sorak wasn't sure that she believed what she had just said, but, as the first light of the distant star was appearing, the possible risk to the young family was beginning to bear down on her more and more. She explained what the old woman had said to Nasa.

As ever, his response was both common sense and practical. He could see every reason why the older, backward-looking women might want to eliminate the family. And, unlike himself, Sorak and Lenar they were highly vulnerable.

"Maybe we should just go and look," he said.

The mangeneers' barracks really weren't that far from the Mech. Div. accommodation where they were staying.

"Lenar will be back by the time we return," Sorak said.

She wasn't sure that she believed that either!

Needless to say, both Sorak and Nasa went fully armed.

* * *

The couple and their baby hiding in the old mangeneers' barrack block weren't without names, it was just that Sorak and Nasa didn't know what they were.

It had been Leben's suggestion that the family had hidden themselves at the old barracks when she observed the hostility shown to them by both of the old capans. This hostility had abated, but largely because one capan was dead and the other was increasingly ignored. Leben saw to it that the couple were supplied with food, but there was a problem approaching as the mother's milk was slowly proving inadequate for the child.

Milk was available from the beasts kept in the area between

the walls in Outer One, but this was not generally accessible as far away as Sector Four, and certainly not in the present circumstances. Nonetheless, Leben had noticed that there was very little husbandry of the animals and that they were slowly working their way around the city between the walls looking for food. So milk may well soon be available near Sector Four and the mangeneers' barracks, but the need was more immediate.

Servak was herself getting concerned. The baby was thriving, but as time passed she worried more and more about the future.

Why didn't I just let the baby go?

Knowing nothing about Sorak and Nasa, the young mother Servak's instinct to want to be associated with her child was at first incomprehensible to her, but in the chaos surrounding the end of Soran's leadership it seemed to make sense to protect the child herself so she took herself away from the birthing centre before her time there was complete. 697, breeding for the first time in the same febrile atmosphere, was no more clear in his mind why he had gone back to the birthing centre than Servak was why she had instinctively escaped it; they had simply run into each other, in effect, in Sector Five, both frightened and uncertain. But recognising each other, 697 particularly was reluctant to leave Servak and the baby at risk from marauding women and ignorant men.

Servak, knowing that men were now being given names just like women, began to call 697 Horan. He accepted the name and, just like Nasa, began to gain in confidence and power in their relationship. It was a cycler, one of the violent rain storms, occurring just as the distant star was setting that changed the course of their existence.

Seeking shelter in the derelict entrance hall of what had been a senior officer's dream-pit, they were joined by a group of excitable young women equally avoiding the downpour. The anguished cries of the baby, a sound that the other women were unfamiliar with, exposed them. With Horan retreating further into the building for his own safety, the young soldiers crowded around Servak and the child. This was an entirely new experience for them, but they meant mother and baby no harm.

Uncertain, curious, confused, the women swept Servak along with them when they went on to their own dream-pit, where Sorak, Nasa and Lenar were to arrive a few circuits of the distant star later. Horan followed the group at a distance, but was picked up by a patrol, and he joined the rest of the party in Sorak's old capan's room. At first he had been frightened to admit his interest in Servak and the baby, but to save himself from injury by the soldiers he had had to explain the situation.

The capan, as usual, was uncertain how to act; the young soldiers urged her to let them stay, and Leben, who had invited herself to the meeting, made her proposal for them to live in the old mangeneers' barracks. The capan had no choice but to agree.

Although well settled, Servak and Horan were never relaxed. The morning after Sorak's rather vague warning from the old brown-skinned woman, Horan was looking out of the window into the central courtyard of the barrack block that they were occupying when he was aware of shadows thrown by the distant star. They were moving shadows.

"Servak, there's someone out there!"

They had chosen to live on the third floor at the top of the building to give themselves the best views of the areas around the barracks and, as a consequence, the best security.

"Men," said Servak.

Horan couldn't imagine how she knew that they were – it was the masculine gait of the shadows – but he was immediately worried. Women they had every expectation to fear, their cohabitation was contrary to everything that the old pre-rebellion society believed in. And they knew that the old capan at the other barracks was not sympathetic and was only carried along by the young soldiers. They had no way of knowing why the men were there, but Horan had come to believe that all men would be hostile to them as the triumvirate appeared to be just as insistent as the former women's Senate on segregated breeding.

Neither Servak nor Horan had any military knowledge or experience. He had a rather ancient sword, but had no confidence in his ability to use it.

"Quiet!" Servak said.

There were definite sounds of approaching footsteps. The baby was asleep; Servak laid him down, not wanting to communicate her anxiety to him, causing him to wake and cry out.

The footsteps were becoming more hesitant, more disorganised as they got closer, as if the individuals were searching for something rather than coming directly to their destination.

And then Sorak and Nasa were in the room.

"There are men in the courtyard," Horan said nervously.

Both he and Servak knew who their two visitors were, Leben had talked about them on one of her visits. Something of their fading confidence returned.

"We saw them," Nasa said, "they are searching the building; looking for you no doubt."

Why, whoever these men were, were coming to kill the family even the old brown-skinned woman didn't seem to know. Independent initiatives, not always approved of by the triumvirate, were not uncommon; and it wasn't only the women that Servak and Horan had scandalised.

Nasa had hung back when they had first arrived at the mangeneers' barracks to check if there was anybody else around. He had quickly detected the three men. He, like them, didn't know where the couple were, but realised that it could only be them that they were looking for; the mangeneer's barracks were otherwise largely derelict. Alerting Sorak they had made their way to the top of the building; it was the obvious place to hide. Why the searchers hadn't also thought that and headed straight up the building tended to confirm to Nasa that they were indeed male soldiers, ex-quarry slaves, or the like, with not much intelligence or enterprise. That didn't mean that they weren't dangerous.

Servak stood by Horan who fidgeted with his sword. It was obvious to Sorak and Nasa that he wouldn't be any use in a fight, and a fight seemed inevitable.

Nasa signalled to Servak to take the baby into the darkened corner of the room. Horan followed her, happy to be dismissed from the action. More footsteps; they were getting closer.

Sorak and Nasa stood one each side of the door and waited. Sorak had already noted that the male soldiers had a tendency to move en masse, rather than individually, and that was how she expected them to eventually enter the room.

It's going to be hard not to kill any of them!

Nasa was just as keen as Sorak to prevent any more unnecessary deaths, but at such close quarters he wasn't confident that it would be possible; the men had to be confronted.

Sorak was wrong, these men were less craven than those that she had come across before. One of the tallest men that she had ever seen walked boldly into the room. Whether he was expecting to find anyone there they had no way of knowing, but seeing the bedding and the other signs of occupancy he paused, peered into the gloom, saw Servak, and collapsed into an untidy heap as Nasa struck him on the back of the head with his crossbow butt.

A strangled cry, more like a sharp sigh, escaped the man as he hit the floor.

Neither Servak nor Horan could be sure of what happened next. A jumble of arms and legs, a surge of grunts, groans and cries of pain filled the air and then a quiet settled in the room much as the three bodies had settled in a tangled heap on the floor. It was all over in the drawing of a few breaths.

Servak's scream echoed around the room and then out into the corridor, but it was quickly cut off when she realised that Sorak and Nasa were the ones still on their feet.

Sorak and Nasa exchanged a soldier's clasped arm salute and then pulled the three men onto their backs as Horan provided a feeble light from an oil lamp.

The following day, wrists bound, the three male soldiers were marched back to the barracks in Sector Four. Without even consulting the capan, Sorak and the tenants organised a prison in the old food preparation area of one of the barrack blocks. The women had little food to spare, but Sorak's determination to prevent more killings was accepted and given practical force. And there was plenty of room in the prison for many more captured soldiers.

Ignoring the capan completely, Servak and Horan were invited to move from the mangeneers' barracks back to Sector Four. The idea of families as a form of society gained recognition, if not universal acceptance, amongst most of the soldiers, led by the younger ones. Horan was found work to do, as a former office slave, organising the management of food supplies and the other scarce necessities of the women's lives.

Sorak and Nasa returned to their worries about Lenar, who had not reappeared when they returned from the mangeneers' barracks.

24

Kragar was steadily becoming impossible to live with. She was frustrated, or more accurately, probably, she was bored. Conscious that not a single male soldier sent out from the city under any administrative regime to kill or capture the dissident women had ever returned, the triumvirate had banned any further excursions. Kragar and her resistance colleagues had nothing to occupy their time. Unused to inaction, they had no idea how to cope with it.

"The women soldiers always win!"

147 knew that it was a highly unpalatable truth, but a truth nonetheless; there was no point in denying it. And 147, if not the other members of the triumvirate, was aware of the implications of the increasing death rate amongst the male soldiers. Reluctance to breed and a reduced number of women available to breed had slowed the birth rate, and the triumvirate's efforts to prevent what they considered to be low grade former slaves from breeding was causing resentment as well as depressing the numbers of new citizens being born. Managing population growth was becoming a major problem for the leaders.

Selective breeding, to regulate the number of men, had been

abandoned immediately after the slaves became free, but after seventeen cycles the post-rebellion generation were yet to fully make their contribution. Mature women in the intervening period had adhered to the former rigid numerical restrictions on how many children they could bear. None of the male administrations had been able to improve the situation.

"Something has to be done to end the warfare between the men and women."

147 had joined the growing band of people to recognise this fact. Without cooperation between the genders nothing would happen, but as things stood he had no idea how to achieve this, and the population would consequently continue to decline.

Kragar, on the other hand, didn't recognise this crisis at all. In a heated argument with Pastak at one of the gatherings of resistance leaders she had insisted that killing as many men as possible was the only way to persuade the triumvirate to surrender power back to the women. It was a completely blinkered view that took no account of the longer term.

"That is never going to happen," Pastak had argued.

"Then we must make it happen," Kragar had responded, "We must invade the city, take control of the troops there, and force the triumvirate to hand back the administration."

Pastak couldn't believe what she was hearing.

* * *

Despite his father's concerns, Lenar, with the absolute confidence of youth, and a little help from an aged and disabled black man, had no doubt that he would find his way to the administrative area. His conviction that that was where Desak would be was less firm.

When it came to it, Lenar had had little difficulty in finding the administrative offices in Sector One. Nasa only discovered later that his son had realised that the old capan's former slave, limited as his intelligence was, was his best clue to Desaks' disappearance with the soldiers. Having visited the old man in Sector Six, it also didn't take Lenar long to appreciate that Sector One, or rather the administrative area, was next door. What he was going to do when he got there he had yet to give any thought to, but he had no doubt that he would know when he got there.

Thanks to his mother's careful foraging for suitable clothing, Lenar didn't look like a soldier, even though very few of the male soldiers themselves had a full uniform. Men carrying swords, even crossbows, when not soldiers, was uncommon, but not unknown. But since, unlike his mother, Lenar found the crossbows used by the women soldiers and inherited by the men cumbersome, when he crept away from the Sector Four barracks he didn't take his with him.

Since empty or derelict buildings were all he knew of the city, walking carefully through the outskirts of Sector Six into the more open of areas of Sector One didn't attract his particular interest. The lessons from his father to only worry about the things immediate to his activity were well learned.

Sorak had worried about Lenar's understanding of the concept of city life when they had first arrived, but she need not have. She soon realised that he saw everything around him as what it was, rather than as what it had been or as she and Nasa remembered it, since he had no such foreknowledge. And being young, fit and healthy, the city was small in area compared to the valley and its surroundings that he had been brought up to range over. He had soon got used to the hemmed-in feeling generated by the tall buildings. In fact, Lenar had surprised his parents by how relaxed he had quickly become. Surprisingly, it was Nasa who found this the most difficult to accept, but his own experiences in the city, as a slave, pre-rebellion, had been more traumatic than he would have probably been prepared to admit.

But, as Lenar approached a large paved area soon after leaving Sector Six, it wasn't being hemmed in that caused him to retreat back into the security of the Sector Six buildings. To get where he thought he needed to go he realised that he would have to cross the large, open area. That would leave him very exposed.

"I shall have to find a way around the edge."

Talking to himself was something that Lenar did quite often. It gave him comfort.

The distant star was overhead; there were no shadows. From Lenar's point of view this was both good and bad. No shadows made it easier for him to see between the tall buildings; he had several times had the feeling that he was being watched. He was constantly on the lookout for both women and men. But shadows also gave him perspective and helped him judge distance.

"There's someone there," he told himself as he edged towards a group of single-storey buildings that formed one side of the open area. His feeling of being watched had become much more powerful as he had approached the open area; in fact, it was a tangible sensation rather than a feeling.

Running quietly on his toes, he retreated back into the buildings on the edge of Sector Six until he was able to work his way in parallel to the side of the open area. Eventually, he came to a narrow street that led him directly back to that area. He needed to take his bearings again. A movement identified a crouching figure peering carefully around the corner of the single-storey building at the end of the street. Whoever it was, was looking back to where he had just come from.

"Why are they watching me?"

Lenar was immediately alert to the dangers. Remembering Kragar, he knew that some women shot first and asked questions later, and increasingly so did the men. From the way that the figure was standing against the building he could see nothing that told him whether he was watching a man or a woman. But there was enough cover for him to edge forward. Why he was being watched got lost in his desire to know who his watcher was.

Throwing his arm around the figure's neck, the cry and the movement as she sought to stand up, told Lenar that it was a woman.

Used to wrestling with his father, Lenar tried to hold his balance as the woman used the arm around her neck to lever him around and down. They ended up rolling on the ground in a tangle of limbs as each attempted to get a firm hold on the other. The woman abandoned her crossbow in an effort to use both hands. The blow that she aimed at Lenar's jaw would have ended the fight there and then had it landed, but the blow that he was aiming, which did land, threw him off balance and her punch missed him.

Panting from the exertion, Lenar struggled to his feet, recovered her crossbow and unstrung it, and then took stock of the figure prone at his feet.

Used to the ex-soldiers of the resistance groups or at the barracks in Sector Four, all of whom were in uniform and clean and tidy, the figure before him was dressed half as a civilian and half as a soldier in clothes that were dirty and foul-smelling. Lenar couldn't contain his surprise.

The young woman, for she was very much of his and Desak's age, stirred, looked fearfully about her and, seeing Lenar peering down at her, pulled herself onto her haunches as if getting ready to pounce on him again. Tossing the disabled crossbow way out of reach onto the open area, Lenar braced himself, and waited.

A spike of angry noise shattered the wary silence between the two of them. It was coming from behind him. Lenar didn't dare look away from the young woman but she openly looked back up the street and started to make a bleating sound that sounded more like an animal than a human to him. His surprise ramped up.

He was immediately surrounded by a group of five other dirty and evil-smelling women, all of whom were menacing him with a range of weapons. Now on her feet, the young woman pushed herself in front of Lenar. Re-armed with a short-bladed knife she swung her arm to slash at him only to find herself back on the ground. A sharp kick in the ribs subdued her.

"So," the kicker said, "so who are you? And why are you here?"

The question was asked by an older woman who confronted Lenar with more caution than the younger woman. The voice was harsh but carried no menace.

"I was looking for the administration buildings, but I knew someone was following me."

A look of puzzlement crossed the questioner's face. The claim that Lenar apparently didn't know where the administration buildings were immediately made her suspicious. Everybody had good cause to know where these buildings were! She had more questions.

"Where have you come from? You're not a soldier, yet you're a fighter. How did you get here?"

"I came from the barracks in Sector Four."

Sorak having explained the layout of the city to her son, Lenar had a better idea of its geography than might have been expected. He found the system of sectors confusing but had soon grasped their inter-relations.

The older woman, the group leader, was suspicious again. What would a young male, non-soldier be doing at a military barracks? But it wasn't safe to remain too long out in the streets.

"Come with us!"

They moved off back into the low buildings skirting the open area. The young woman displayed her continuing resentment by jostling Lenar whenever she could until the leader ordered her back to retrieve her crossbow. Fearfully, the young woman did as she was told.

Finally climbing down into the basement of one of the buildings it was obvious that they had arrived at the group's base. The atmosphere was fetid and the smell beyond anything that Lenar had ever experienced.

The questioning continued.

Brought up to be truthful, Lenar answered all the questions fully. The leader, who had been the head guard at the closed arena, found Lenar's description of how he had got there, what was going on at the former barracks and the actions of the administration to attack the resistance groups credible, but it was when she asked why Lenar was there that all her suspicions revived.

The idea that Lenar was looking for a young woman captured by the male soldiers because he had feelings for her was more than she could understand. In the world that she now lived in men didn't chase after women, they took them as they needed them, and abandoned them as readily.

But it was only when Lenar was asked about who else was at the barracks at Sector Four that the woman got excited.

"I went there with my mother and father."

There were murmurs of disbelief amongst the other women of the group. It was the usual story. No one knew who their mother or father was! The leader asked the obvious question.

"Sorak and Nasa."

Being in charge of the guard when Sorak had her epic fight with Mareck, all those cycles ago, the leader knew exactly who Sorak was, and, as others had, assumed that Nasa was 1562.

Lenar was ignored whilst the leader explained about Sorak, about her role in inspiring the original rebellion, and much more. The excitement created was palpable.

In his carefully nurtured ignorance, Lenar couldn't understand their amazement at what he was telling them.

25

Sorak didn't get much time to worry about where Lenar might have gone. The old capan had suddenly bestirred herself and called a meeting of the officers and caprals, including, for the first time, representatives of those who had joined the group in the barracks in Sector Four after Marwek's attempts to disarm the women. Sorak wasn't specifically invited, but went along anyway.

The atmosphere was cold, even hostile, but it wasn't clear to Sorak why. Certainly following the arrival of the ex-soldiers from other parts of the city, most of whom weren't in coherent units, she sensed that a more aggressive stance seemed to be appearing, as if to justify their existence. This was instantly apparent as the capan opened the meeting.

"We must decide what to do about the recent attack," she said.

Sorak was incredulous!

What to do? If it had been left to you we would have been overrun.

Sorak found herself angry that the capan was suddenly trying to take control again. She suspected that this was as much to impress the newcomers as anything, but her respect for her old chief hadn't been high in the past and was virtually non-existent now. Things got worse.

"Leben, this is a military meeting."

For reasons that Sorak still hadn't had the opportunity to discuss with Leben, the young woman had made it her business to always sit in on the capan's meetings. Her contempt for the old woman was as great as Sorak's, although she probably hid it better. The capan's reaction to Leben was another surprise; she had largely accepted her presence in the past. There was a tense silence.

"She stays, Capanmam."

There was a subdued rumble of discontent at Sorak's intervention, but no one seemed prepared to actively challenge her. Sorak wasn't entirely sure why she had made the demand; but her instinct was to regard Leben as an ally. The capan looked angrily around at this lack of support for her desire to exclude Leben. She decided to move on.

"I have received a message from Kragar, on behalf of the resistance groups beyond the Edge. She says that we should prepare for a final battle with the male administration. They are planning an invasion of the city and asked us to make our dispositions to support the attack. They will let us know in advance when they plan to invade."

The capan's announcement was greeted with a mixture of cheers and cries of agreement. But Sorak was quick to notice that by no means all of the women joined in. There were clearly those present who were not supportive of such drastic action. No one wanted any more bloodshed, but there was frustration that nothing was happening to confront the triumvirate and the male administration. Some, like Sorak, were totally against the whole idea of military confrontation as a way of bringing things to a conclusion.

"We should not support this."

Sorak's response instantly polarised the room. There was

immediate hostility to her reaction. Somewhat to her surprise, the younger women soldiers seemed just as keen as their elders for a fight. Sorak's support in the room was more muted, but she knew that she had to put across her point of view.

"This is Kragar's plan, and I doubt that it is fully supported by all of the resistance leaders. Pastak, for one, I'm sure would not have agreed to it".

But it seemed that very few of the women wanted to hear.

Pastak, like Sorak, was clear that they, as women, had to come to terms with the men, either through the triumvirate and the administration, or by other means. More killing could not be the answer.

There was now more open hostility and jeers. Once again it was the younger women in particular who reacted against Sorak's intervention; they wanted action, they wanted resolution and a future; fighting and defeating the men was the only way that they could visualise.

"If we don't fight back, we will never recover control of the city."

Neither Sorak nor the capan saw who said this, but the statement was greeted with ragged cheers.

"We cannot go back to the past. The men cannot be enslaved again."

But Sorak's passion provoked an even more excited response. Many of the women stood up and began to jostle around Sorak and Leben and two of the tenants who tried to protect them.

It was obvious that most of the women present hadn't given any thought to the implications of their taking back control of the city. There seemed to be a tacit assumption that things would somehow just return to how they had been, even if the younger women weren't very sure what that meant or how it might be made to work. Since it had been happening de facto for most of their lives, the idea of coexistence with the men was simply accepted by the new generation. The issue was dominance, who was in charge. Dominance and subjugation was all that these women knew, and dominance by men was anathema to them.

"We need to tell Kragar that we support her," the capan said petulantly.

"No, we do not," Leben said, entering the debate for the first time.

The capan's face went white with fury. Dealing with truculent officers was one thing, being openly contradicted by a civilian was quite another.

"Remove her!"

Two of the caprals, who were most inclined to obey the capan, moved forward.

But a tenant from the old Mech. Div. stepped forward, hand on sword hilt.

A former colleague of Sorak, the tenant respected her freedom of thought and willingness to express an opposing opinion. Concerned also that their decisions be made in a proper and reasoned manner, she was worried that the weak capan was being carried along by the enthusiasm of the younger women rather than by the arguments. It was precisely the feeling that was beginning to emerge in Sorak's mind. They needed a proper process to make decisions in the absence of any formal women's organisation.

"Hold," the tenant said. "Sorak and Leben oppose this invasion. We need to know why."

The tenant faced down the jeers.

"We cannot go back to the past," Sorak repeated her mantra. "The slaves have all been freed. All the young men were never slaves anyway. Kragar wants a return to the world where women dominate and the men's only role is to serve them. This cannot, and must not, happen again. It will change nothing. The men will only rebel again. There will only be peace if we learn to live with the men, and with them taking equal roles according to their capabilities, with us. And we must urgently start breeding again, but in a way that makes the parents of the children born responsible for their development and training."

This time there was total silence, but the reactions of the women as they digested what Sorak had said didn't give her much confidence.

This is pointless, they simply aren't hearing me!

But Leben was and she was really concerned. The myths surrounding Sorak meant nothing to the younger women soldiers, largely brought up since the rebellion under the various versions of the male administration that had had no vision of the society that they wanted to create. To them, taking back control by force was the only option left. The sort of cooperative world that Sorak was envisaging was beyond their comprehension, and the older women would have been incapable of explaining it to them.

"I think we should leave," Leben said.

The tenants and caprals were losing control. Some of the recent recruits to the barracks were far less disciplined than those who had been there from the beginning, as a result of their time being hunted by the male soldiers. It wouldn't have taken much for them to have turned against Sorak and attacked her.

No one seemed inclined to stop Leben and Sorak from leaving the room. The capan futilely called for calm, but the younger women never listened to her anyway.

They found an anxious Nasa pacing the corridor outside the communal room where the meeting had taken place. He had heard the anger, but had no idea that it had been directed at Sorak.

"We have to leave," Sorak said. "Kragar is intent on invading the city and they are determined to join her. There will be nothing left to fight for by the time they are finished."

But Nasa wasn't just anxious for Sorak.

"Lenar has gone chasing after Desak," he said. "At least as far as I can find out he's disappeared into Sector One and the administration area."

This was hardly what Sorak wanted to hear.

"Go after him," Leben said. "Get him out of that area before the invasion."

Leben had accompanied Sorak and Nasa back to their quarters in the old Mech. Div. barracks. They had collected theirs and Lenar's things, and their weapons. They were ready to leave, but Sorak was determined to find out exactly what Leben was doing in Sector Four. They were placing increasing trust in her, but Sorak needed to know that that trust was well placed.

"What will you do, Leben?" Sorak asked. "You were just as against the invasion as me. Won't it be dangerous for you to go back to Sector Four?"

Leben laughed, well aware of Sorak's intent in asking the question.

Sorak hadn't noticed that she almost always wore a small backpack. Leben now shrugged her shoulders to reveal the pack.

"I'm not going back to Sector Four," she said. "There's no point. With that useless capan in charge nothing will change."

Sorak and Nasa waited for an explanation.

"I live in Sector One. I live in part of the derelict old Senate library; in sight of the administration offices, in sight of 147 and the other triumvirate leaders."

Nasa looked amazed. Sorak took a pace back from standing next to Leben and looked at her, hard and questioningly. This wasn't in any way the answer that she was expecting.

"There are women working with the male administration. I know most of them. They know everything that is going on. They will soon know of Kragar's planned invasion."

Sorak stiffened and laid her hand on the hilt of her sword. The conversation was taking an unexpected turn.

"Not from me," Leben said hurriedly. "I went to Sector Four partly to try to find out who was supplying information to the triumvirate. Someone undoubtedly is."

Not entirely sure whether to believe her, Sorak relaxed; but again her demeanour demanded an answer to the obvious question. If there was a traitor she would have to be exposed.

"I don't know. I couldn't find out. You saw how suspicious of me they were."

Sorak again wasn't sure that she believed Leben.

"You said partly about your visit to Sector Four. What was the other reason that you went there?"

Leben looked uncertain. Sorak wasn't sure how old she was, but had the impression that she had been born before the rebellion, but not necessarily many years before. What Leben now said stunned both her and Nasa when they understood the implications.

"147 worked for Crenan, the old Senate administrator."

Sorak knew who Crenan was. Mentor of her old friend Lenen from the cycles before they had escaped the city, she had favoured Nasa, and bred with him.

"147 knew who Crenan bred with. He also knew who the children Crenan produced were. Even in those days such things were known amongst the Senate and the black and brown administrators."

Leben paused, even more uncertain.

"And," said Nasa, "you are one of Crenan's children."

Attracted by the tone of Nasa's voice another thought had hardly started to surge through Sorak's mind when a crashing noise had both her and Nasa reaching for their crossbows. They were the only people living in the Mech. Div. barracks, if there was now someone there, and there obviously was, they could only be looking for them.

Grabbing their backpacks the three of them hurried out into the corridor as cries of pain and anger rumbled up to them.

There were women in the building, how many they couldn't tell, but from the chatter it sounded as if they were making their way up through the derelict building and someone had got hurt. Heading for the outside ramp, Nasa suddenly stopped, waved Sorak and Leben to silence and pointed.

Halfway up the ramp were three male soldiers clearly trying to hide from whoever was making the noise inside the building. Suddenly one of the soldiers rose up and fired through the ventilation gap in the wall. The shriek said that his bolt had found a mark. A melee ensued.

The soldier who fired had obviously seen that there were only four women soldiers in the room, one who was already injured and now one who was dead. The three soldiers clambered into the building swords drawn and attacked the two women still able to fight.

Nasa was first down the ramp, but it was Sorak who got in the first shot disabling a male soldier with a bolt in his leg as he bore down on one of the women who was lying at his feet. Nasa's shot similarly disabled a second soldier. The third was brutally cut down by the only woman soldier still on her feet.

Sorak signalled the two wounded male soldiers to throw down their weapons and go.

"No!" Nasa menaced the woman soldier as she took aim at one of the departing troopers.

Quickly gathering all of the weapons, from both male and female soldiers, Sorak tossed them across the ramp out onto the ground at the other side of the building.

"Go!" she said to the women soldiers as well.

Sorak had recognised one of the injured women as one of the more aggressive of the young women who seemed to object to her efforts to prevent the invasion.

Disarmed, the able-bodied women had no choice but to gather up their injured colleague and retreat, leaving the dead behind.

"Another time!"

"They were coming after us?" Leben questioned when they were alone again.

Clearly, they were.

Once again, Sorak recognised that things had changed, and not just in the security of their situation; Lenar had a sibling, not that that concept would have meant anything to him. And a whole new situation began to unfold.

26

Sorak was deeply shocked by the idea that the four women at the Mech. Div. barracks had come there to do her harm. So much so that it didn't occur to her to wonder what the male soldiers were doing there. They were just a patrol in the wrong place at the wrong time.

"We must get away from here quickly," Leben urged.

She wasn't panicking, but being more certain than Sorak of the women's mission, she wasn't keen to take chances. They could very easily quickly return in greater strength.

Sorak didn't set much store by her hero's status, if anything she regarded Nasa as the hero, but to have attracted the resentment of the group of women that they had left at Sector Four was beyond her understanding. She could simply see neither any point in, nor any likelihood of, the city being returned to female domination. You could not go back in time!

Leben led them out of the barracks and through a maze of back streets that she seemed to be very familiar with until they reached the edge of the open area that Lenar had recently come upon. Both Sorak and Nasa recognised that they were heading into Sector One; neither was very happy about this. This might be where Lenar could be, but neither of them were thinking about their son at that moment.

Leben was heading for the gate in the inner wall. How she knew that it would be held by the bunch of scruffy civilian women, neither Sorak nor Nasa thought to ask. Equally, neither of them had ever been to the section between the inner and outer walls to which Leben now introduced them. It didn't take the soldier in Sorak long to realise that the area would make a good hiding place. She also realised that Leben already knew that.

The area that they entered seemed to be open fields, well kept, with the vegetation cropped short. Nasa immediately recognised that they were in the area where the Senate had in the past kept the beasts from which they sourced their milk and meat. As Leben led them to the roughly constructed hut built under the city wall, they could see the herd of animals in the distance. The hut was in poor condition but the roof seemed sound. It had clearly once been where the former slaves who looked after the animals had lived. It also clearly had been used in the recent past.

The question of what the hut was now used for was obvious to Leben from Sorak's body language.

"It's a refuge," she said. "The women who work for the administration need a safe haven as there are still some of the older men who are violently hostile to them."

"But what will we do here?" asked Nasa.

He knew that Sorak wouldn't be able to just hang about in the hut doing nothing, it wasn't in her nature, and he still needed to locate Lenar and see that he was safe. But there were more basic considerations.

Leben pulled open a pile of firewood to reveal a stash of dried food.

"I will bring more when I come later," she said.

She made no attempt to answer Nasa's question. She, like

him, presumed that Sorak would find something useful to do. All she was doing was providing somewhere for them to retreat to and somewhere that they could use to rest and recuperate.

* * *

Sorak had been absolutely correct when she said the plan to invade the city from the Edge by the resistance groups was Kragar's plan and only Kragar's.

Relations between the black former head of the Senate Guard and Pastak had deteriorated to the point of open hostility. It was only Pastak's focus on the issue of building a resistance force committed to reaching an accommodation with the triumvirate, or whatever the current male administration of the city turned out to be when such an accommodation was achieved, that kept Kragar and her group at a distance.

"The old capan of the Armd. Div. and many of the younger soldiers have turned against Sorak because she advocates trying to work with the men in the administration."

Risak, another hyperactive soldier, and a supporter of Sorak and her view of the future, had escaped from Sector Four when it was clear that the status quo group were in the ascendant. With the capan unlikely to control the situation she saw no point in hanging around in the city. Avoiding Kragar, she had sought out Pastak as her most likely ally.

"There are three platoons of women in the Sector Four barracks," Risak said. "But there is another platoon or so who have moved into the mangeneers' barracks. These are mainly the dissenters; those who support Sorak's idea that we have to seek a permanent understanding with the men."

Risak was putting words into Sorak's mouth as she herself hadn't yet articulated very clearly what she was seeking to achieve. And finding herself at odds with the best trained force of women in the city was a setback to Sorak's thinking.

Pastak heard Risak out. The situation in the city was even more confused than she had realised. Pastak was aware that the ex-soldiers in the Sector Four barracks were the most powerful opposition group in the city, but she was also aware, although Risak didn't seem to be, that there were other armed groups around the city acting independently, whose support or opposition they needed to determine if they were to thwart Kragar's attempts at a military takeover. Some, who were civilians, they could count on; the ex-soldiers were more difficult to read.

"We need to contact Sorak," Pastak said as much to herself as to Risak.

Unspoken, they both realised that the preferred place for them to meet would be outside the city and beyond the Edge. But having had such a difficult journey to make it to the city, Pastak was unsure whether Sorak would want to leave it again.

* * *

Leben made her way back to the derelict Senate library. She had waited to leave the area between the walls until the second moon had risen for the first time and then ran quickly through the overgrown Senate gardens into the remnants of the library.

The stairs down to the library basement were lit by a feeble oil lamp. Leben proceeded cautiously. Nothing could be taken for granted. Dealing with the women who worked for the male administration was difficult enough, they were often fractious and overbearing to cover their fear and guilt, but they were also constantly suspicious of her and her mysterious comings and goings. And Leben was well aware that they had every right to be.

When she entered one of the old reading rooms, Leben was surprised to see not only the three women that she was expecting, but also the triumvirate principal 182 and an old woman whom she didn't know. She was careful not to show her surprise.

182 was probably the most reactionary of the three principals. He was opposed to 147's ideas of a rapprochement with the women. He was in favour of total male domination in the image of the past total female domination, without being aware that on both sides of the divide this position was being rejected. But he wasn't adverse to dealing with women when he saw it in his or the triumvirate's best interests.

182, in his turn, was equally suspicious of Leben's comings and goings and with her contacts with the women in the sectors of the city that the administration didn't control.

"Next time you make your way into Sector Four you will take Derrak with you."

Derrak was a former administration clerk; a quarter black, she was old, increasingly infirm and bitterly opposed to any idea of an accommodation between the men and women. She was the last person with whom Leben would have wanted to be associated.

"No," she said, "I work alone. Derrak is known to the women in Sector Four, as are all of the women known to support the triumvirate. She, like them, would be killed on sight. You can't want that."

As far as Leben knew this wasn't exactly true. The details of some of the women working for the triumvirate were known, certainly not all. The Sector Four women regarded them with contempt. There had never been any suggestion that they might kill them.

Derrak looked aghast. 182 hadn't said anything to her about his proposal. He knew that it couldn't be a serious suggestion due to Derraks' age, but he was much more interested in provoking Leben into some act of rebellion.

"Mother's heart!"

Leben had no idea who made the exclamation as the oil

lamp illuminating the room spluttered and then went out. All she was aware of was a surge of body movements, cries of pain and a gurgling sound that raised her anxiety level instantly.

Since the room was connected by an archway to the corridor there was no way of knowing in the gloom who had entered or left. There was just enough light from the lamps in the corridor to identify shapes. Then someone did leave the room. Leben wasn't sure who it was until she came back with one of the oil lamps. Whether anyone else had entered and left there was no way of knowing.

182's throat had been cut. Derrak lay half on top of him but with no signs of injury. They later supposed that she had died from heart failure.

One of the other women was bleeding from a slash wound down her arm; how she came by it wasn't clear, but there was no suggestion that she had also been an intended victim.

Leben and the other women left hurriedly, raising the alarm as they left the derelict library building.

27

Lenar had never met any women like the ones that he was now sharing a rather sparse meal with, not that he had actually met that many women. The only civilians that he had had anything to do with, and that only briefly, had been mangeneers and the like. But these civilians appeared to be from a sector of the city that even in the former days of female domination very few people had heard about. His father might have recalled warders in the Senate prison, but the experience had been so traumatic that it was doubtful that Nasa could have done so with any clarity. For Lenar virtually everything was a new experience and in his quiet, good-mannered way he saw no reason to fear these women.

In any event, he was virtually their prisoner and they his protectors.

That the leader of the group, Lenar eventually learned that she was called Quillat, remembered his mother, gave him some confidence, but the fugitive life that the women were leading made them nervous and quick to take offence. The enmity of the young woman with whom he had first tangled continued until the leader had had enough and, finding two staves, ordered her and Lenar up into the courtyard of the building that they were occupying. Sorak had taught Lenar stave fighting much to his father's surprise. It was another lesson that was about to stand him in good stead.

The other women made space. It was a rare opportunity for some entertainment.

Quillat seemed to have no doubt that Lenar would acquit himself well.

Handed the stave, Lenar faced the young woman, determined not to strike the first blow. But the young woman was in no way so inhibited and aimed a crashing blow at his head. He ducked and the force of her swing threw her off balance. Well fed and healthy, Lenar had a physical advantage despite the woman being taller. She was slow to recover herself.

Quillat couldn't help a rare smile. Memories of Sorak fighting Mareck filled her mind. And just as quickly as Sorak had demolished her opponent those seventeen cycles ago, so Lenar took the legs from under his opponent and deposited her onto her back on the tiled paving of the courtyard. With the breath knocked out of her, she threw away her stave and lay, arms stretched out in defeat. Much to the disappointment of the spectators it was all over in no time at all.

Back in the basement, as it grew dark, Quillat appointed sentries for the night and allocated Lenar a place to sleep. Notwithstanding the friendliness displayed to him he noted that it would be impossible to escape the basement without rousing those around him. But even conscious of the warmth of her body as the young woman had crept in to lie beside him, Lenar was too weary to even move away from her.

Next morning, Quillat chased the young woman away with a laugh. The defeated giving herself to the victor was an ancient practice that made no sense in the fractured world in which they now lived, but at least it signalled that the young woman's animosity towards him was over.

"This young woman. Why do you think that she will be in the administrative area?"

Lenar didn't need to be told which young woman to whom Quillat was referring. He had been completely honest, when questioned, as to why he was there, although what he would do when he located Desak he still had no idea.

"She was captured by soldiers, men, and taken away," Lenar said.

Quillat tried to hide her thoughts. For her, things didn't bode well. Lenar's innocence and naïve enthusiasm stirred something in her brain that troubled her, but along with him being Sorak's son, she decided that they would do what they could to help him.

She didn't give the girl much of a chance with the soldiers that they had come across. Recruited from the lowest orders of the ex-slaves they were a vicious and cruel lot. Lenar's ignorance was a protection for him and it took Quillat some time to realise just how little he seemed to know about the way that the male soldiers were likely to behave. And when she consulted the other women, even her hard-nosed former prison warders recognised that he was different. They didn't recognise gentleness or affection, things that had never been a part of their world, but they were affected by his obvious feelings for the young woman for whom he was searching. This was so unusual to them that even the less intelligent of them recognised it as something that was far from the lust that they had witnessed between men and women in the past. They were all as willing as Quillat to help him.

Of course, neither Quillat nor Lenar knew of 147's orders that captured women should not be harmed, nor that he had taken Desak into his household.

"There are women living in the burned-out buildings, the old Senate House and library, and there are women working for the administration. Some are held like slaves in the quarters of the leaders."

Quillat, although having had no military training whatsoever, was an efficient leader. Gifted with intelligence and common sense, she organised her small band into patrols and used them to keep track of all movements into and out of Sector One and the triumvirate administration building. As a consequence she knew not only the three principals of the triumvirate, but also the key figures who worked under them. She knew the names of all the women who actively supported and worked with the male administration, and those who did so under duress. She was also aware that there were other women whose role she didn't understand. She was equally aware of groups of dissident women in and around Sector One, but generally avoided them.

Quillat was just preparing to send out the morning's patrols when a group of three women whom Lenar hadn't seen before, one of whom was black, arrived hurriedly and in some excitement. The black woman it seemed was a captive. Her hands were tied behind her and she had a wedge of material stuffed into her mouth.

"There's big trouble," patrol leader said. "182 is dead. They've closed off all access to the administration area. We captured her hiding from the soldiers."

Quillat pulled the gag from the black woman's mouth and, with raised eyebrows, demanded that she explain herself. If nothing else, black women were increasingly rare in the male-controlled areas of the city.

One of the women meeting with Leben, she had been there when 182 was killed. She professed to have no idea who had killed the man, but working for, and living with, the head of the triumvirate guard, she was familiar with the petty jealousies and scheming that went on around the three leaders. She was sure that neither 147 nor 136 would have had a hand in 182's death. 182 had been causing dissent amongst the three by resisting anything that might detract from total dominance by the men, but he had been key to engaging the loyalty of many of the triumvirate officials. In many ways, he was a prime target for the women, and his death had sent shock waves through the administration.

"No one is allowed into or out of the administrative buildings and the leaders' quarters. Only trusted 'slave' women are allowed to be close to the leaders. 147 has ordered a hunt for the killer, but they won't find her."

No one seemed to be in any doubt that the killer was a woman.

Lenar wondered why Quillat didn't ask the black woman why they wouldn't find her, but another patrol had arrived equally excited by what had happened.

"The guard commander has been found dead. There has been fighting between the male soldiers. Many of the women working in the administration have escaped into Sector Six."

There was more. The triumvirate leadership was in chaos. Quillat had enough experience to know that they might be entering yet another period of the instability that preceded the downfall of previous administrations. It was a situation that she didn't relish. Like a growing number of women and men, she knew that an accommodation between the genders had to be achieved somehow, and soon, or the whole city would implode.

Like many, Quillat had underestimated 147.

28

The news of 182's death spread around the city in the usual rapid way. How it was spread no one was very clear. Sorak and Nasa were probably the last to hear as they were isolated in the area between the city walls and dependent on the return of Leben for news and sustenance.

But when she did return, Leben was in an uncharacteristic state of agitation. She had spent a couple of days in hiding in the derelict buildings behind the old Senate House and library waiting for the frenetic activity that followed the discovery of 182's body to die down. The activity was initially directed by the head of the triumvirate guard, but when on the second day he didn't appear in his office, the activities ramped up into an even greater frenzy. Then his body was also found.

The death of the guard commander was relatively straightforward. The ligature around his neck was obviously from a garment of the sort worn by the black woman who served him and who had disappeared. Her whereabouts, however, were quickly established, but as she tried to escape from Sector One the soldiers following were assailed by a burst of crossbow bolts and the black woman was seen to be being led off by a small group of armed women. The pursuit was halted.

147 and 136 were confused, and in their own separate ways anxious. Their rule so far had been benign. They had brought peace and stability to the city and they had never envisaged violence being used against themselves personally. Except that the peace and stability was fragile and there were many who wanted it to break down.

"The black woman couldn't have killed 182," 147 said. But he didn't seem entirely convinced by his own statement.

Had he known that in fact the woman had been at the meeting with 182, Leben and others, earlier, any conviction that he might have had would have disappeared.

Having too few people to leave the black woman under guard at their base, Quillat stuffed the material back into her mouth and marched her along with them on patrol. Long in the tooth, and suspicious, Quillat needed evidence to back up the woman's story before trusting her. Any false move and she was prepared to kill her.

* * *

On the third day after Leben had gone, both Sorak and Nasa were rested and their strength largely returned; the inevitable boredom set in. Sorak hadn't been in such good shape since they had left their valley, and Nasa likewise was equally relaxed. But neither could cope with inaction.

"We must move into Sector One," Nasa said.

Sorak knew that his anxiety over their son was unabated and that he still wanted to locate Lenar and satisfy himself that he was safe.

"Leben did ask us to wait until she got back.

"I know, Sorak, but why? Why doesn't she want us to know what she is doing in Sector One?"

Neither had an answer and some of Sorak's original concerns about Leben seeped back into her brain.

But eventually Leben came and brought them the news of 182's death.

Mother's heart, if this news gets to Kragar it will give her an ideal excuse to launch her invasion of the city.

Now back to her normal self, and the stirrings of her past causing her anxiety, Sorak found herself pondering on the next stages of any military action against the triumvirate. She was in no way anxious for there to be military action, more that her ponderings were about how it might be avoided.

* * *

Risak really didn't want to go back into the city, but both she and Pastak knew that there was no one else whom they could truly trust. The loyalties of the women in the resistance groups were often very personal and also very fickle. A powerful leader like Kragar was bound to attract great support, even if many of the women around her were less than convinced that an all-out assault on the city was all that was necessary to return things to where they used to be before the various male administrations. And increasingly there were those who were doubtful if this would be possible.

"We need to make contact with the decision-makers."

'Decision-makers' was an expression that Pastak had once heard Sorak use in her short stay with the resistance fighters. At the time, they were discussing the problems of knowing who amongst the people like Soran, in the past, actually held the power, and who were merely figureheads. Pastak was aware that the problem may well still exist, but she was sure that Sorak would know who they should deal with within the triumvirate. As she idled her time away waiting for Leben to return, Sorak would have acknowledged that she actually had no idea.

Risak's reappearance in Sector Four caused some surprise. What Sorak might have called the 'war-party' had prevailed mainly because the younger women soldiers were increasingly impatient for a resolution of the prevailing situation. The old capan had been confined to her quarters as she was steadily losing touch with reality. Because Sorak was known to be opposed to military action as a solution, Risak had the good sense not to ask after her directly. But she didn't have to wait long for news.

"The rest of the women are in Sector Six," she was told. This seemed to be code for those women who supported Sorak's approach.

The newly promoted tenant from the younger soldiers whom Risak had spoken to wasn't very communicative. Nonetheless she thought it worth the risk to enquire how many of these women there were.

"Ten. But there is also that civilian Leben, and several other non-soldiers."

"Leben?"

Risak knew who Leben was; but she didn't know where she fitted into the situation as it now was, and like Sorak she had residual suspicions.

"Leben seems to be able to move around the city at will. She's well informed about the triumvirate, and she knows where Sorak and that ex-slave of hers have gone to earth."

"Does she come back here very often?"

"She wouldn't dare," the young tenant said.

Risak's problem was still how to make contact.

But again, Risak's luck held.

A patrol led by a capral who had once been a bosom friend of Risak was about to probe into Sector Six. But in order to avoid conflict with the party of women who had recently decamped to there, the capral had suggested that they try to access the Sector from the area between the city walls and then back through the gate into the city adjacent to Sector One.

Risak invited herself to accompany the patrol. Her instinct

was that Sorak and Nasa were more likely to be in the Sector Six/Sector One areas than anywhere else as they were closest to the administrative area. And a vague memory of something overheard from one of the mangeneers who had escaped across the Edge came to mind.

"The burned-out Senate House and library are ideal places to hide. There are so many ways in and out. The old senators were up to all manner of tricks; and keeping them secret was a priority."

Risak still wasn't sure what the mangeneer had meant, but the ability of a lot of people to hide so close to the centre of administration had to be worth knowing about.

And it's just the sort of place that Sorak is going to want to know about.

Risak's confidence was entirely justified.

Once out of Sector Four, the patrol headed back towards the sewage plant and then out through the city gate. The capral divided the patrol of seven women, not counting Risak, into two. A group of three she sent on ahead with orders to locate a safe place for them to rendezvous and camp for the night. Risak and the remaining four she held back.

Something's going on here!

Risak's suspicions were aroused. The three sent on ahead were all older troopers from Sorak's and Kragar's soldiering days. The four she had held back were all young soldiers.

The orders were that once a campsite had been located, one of the three would make contact to direct the others to it. As the distant star began to wane, no contact had been made. Risak got the sense that the remaining soldiers weren't surprised. The capral ordered them forward to search.

"Mother's heart."

The patrol found three bodies. The capral this time was surprised. One of the women had been strangled, another had been stabbed in the chest, but the third had bled to death from a neck wound clearly inflicted by the stabbed soldier.

Risak was appalled at the savagery of what had happened.

"Capral," she demanded, "what is going on here?"

It was a dangerous moment for Risak since she had no idea what the answer to her demand might be. The answer that she got was unexpected.

"Risakmam," the capral said, gesturing at two of the women, "they were traitors. They were passing information to the collaborators. Leben suspected them. This patrol was set up to try to trap them. Something went wrong."

The role of the third soldier wasn't explained and Risak had picked up on the reference to Leben, so didn't ask.

"Leben. That young tenant said that she didn't come back to Sector Four anymore."

The capral grinned. "That's not to say that we, some of us, aren't in regular contact with her."

The capral explained. Risak listened in increasing disbelief. It seemed that there were more supporters of accommodation with the men within Sector Four than anybody realised. Some, like the capral and the four others of the patrol, felt it better to work from the inside to undermine the prevailing movement towards a military solution. The dissenters in Sector Six, the capral said, had made themselves ineffective by speaking out.

"There's a place we sometimes meet with Leben further along. A hut the slaves used in the past. When the distant star returns we'll have a skirmish, get a few wounds and then return with two bodies. I'm afraid that we failed in our duty to protect you, Risakmam!"

The soldiers all laughed.

The body of the strangled soldier disappeared some time whilst the first moon was casting its vermillion light. The capral didn't explain why it wasn't being returned to the barracks. And as the distant star rose again and they ate their meagre provisions, Risak set off under cover of the outer city wall to find the hut that the capral pointed out in the distance. Since the capral had implied that the old hut was a sort of meeting place that Sorak might use, Risak was keen to check it out.

Risak was much encouraged by the capral and her troopers, although it did nothing to reduce the confusion surrounding exactly how much support Kragar's invasion would have when it took place.

The herd of grazing beasts had moved progressively down the area between the walls and Risak had had to negotiate a way through them as she carefully approached the hut. Instinctively alert, she paused. The hut was occupied. She had no idea how she knew that, she just did. But with the herd now behind her she had no cover. She grasped her sword hilt.

"Risak, how goes it?"

It was the very woman with whom she so desperately wanted to make contact.

29

Sorak had been watching the herd when she noticed that some of the animals' movements had suddenly become hurried and disorganised as they were disturbed by Risak making her way through them. At first she didn't know that it was Risak, only that a woman soldier was apparently heading for the only place between the city walls where there might be people; the old herders' hut. Sorak's frustration at having nothing to do had invoked long lost memories of endless nights on foot patrol in the desert. She had had to cope with boredom then and she tried to school herself to cope now. But she was a different Sorak then, living in a totally different world. Then nothing was expected of her beyond the mindless military routines, now something was expected of her, but she was far from clear what that was. She had the sense that the women were expecting leadership from her but, in the complex situation that was developing, leadership to achieve what, she had no idea.

As she watched the woman soldier separate herself from the herd, a familiar figure consolidated itself in her vision, and she knew who it was.

Sorak had been feeling angry and confused ever since they had been forced to retreat to the old hut. Such a retreat was against all her better instincts. Leben's visit had been short and she had headed back into Sector One after only a couple of circuits of the distant star. Leben was certainly looking to Sorak for leadership, but she too recognised that there was no clear vision for her to relate to yet. Nasa had gone with Leben. Still tortured by his anxiety over Lenar, he could stand the inaction at the hut no longer.

Nasa was increasingly uncertain of his role in Sorak's future activities or in fact whether he wanted a role in them at all. For him, the past was something to move on from, not something to seek to recreate, not that he thought that that was Sorak's intention. But he also knew that there were emerging expectations of his partner that he couldn't ignore.

"If you expect to be contacted you will have to wait," he said to Sorak, "but no one is going to contact me, or be interested in what I'm doing."

Nasa was being realistic rather than bitter.

This was after Leben, through her usual unexplained channels, had brought word that the women in Sector Six wanted to speak to Sorak. Wanting no part of yet more violence, they had set themselves at odds with their Sector Four colleagues, but some of the younger women in Sector Four were getting belligerent. For these untried warriors, in their view, the idea of putting off any confrontation with the triumvirate cemented its hold on the city. Instinctive rather than active supporters of Kragar's approach to dealing with the men, they tended to vent their frustration on those who counselled inaction, as the Sector Six women appeared to be doing.

Sorak felt that she had no option but to wait for the women to contact her. She didn't want to appear to be too close to these women, some of whom she knew were very outspoken in their views. She was in sympathy with their reluctance to support more warfare, but Sorak's attitude was anything but passive. As she and Nasa recovered themselves physically they had also spent time discussing how the problems of the city might be settled. A dialogue with the triumvirate would have been Sorak's immediate objective, but she was as yet in no position to undertake anything to achieve it.

But before we try and contact 147 and 136, we need to decide what it is we want as an outcome for the city.

This thought seemed to be so obvious to Sorak that she couldn't understand why no one appeared to be trying to decide what the outcome might be.

Accommodation with the men might now be the acceptable outcome for an increasing number of women and, she supposed, men, but Sorak knew that they had to define in very simple and specific terms what 'accommodation' meant. And the women in Sector Six as well as those in Sector Four would have to contribute to the solution when it was determined, as it was important to heal the rifts in the women's ranks as well.

Not wanting to fight the men didn't mean that the Sector Six women would accept them as equals. Kragar and many of the Sector Four women undoubtedly would not.

For Sorak this was the key issue. How intractable an issue it proved to be she knew would define their prospects of success. Plotting a course through this matrix of positions, fight or not to fight, dominant or equal, was going to be far more challenging than anything that she had ever done before. And Nasa, for one, was far from clear why Sorak thought that she had to undertake such a task. But in the long hours of inactivity the feeling that this was what events had forced her back to the city to do was gaining strength in her mind. Whether she could have offered a satisfactory answer to 'why?' to Nasa she would probably have doubted.

"Sorak, well met!"

Risak felt a wave of relief as she and Sorak clasped arms in the soldiers' greeting.

Inside the hut Risak immediately saw that Sorak was alone.

"Lenar went off into the city to try and locate the young woman Desak. Nasa has gone after him as we haven't heard from him."

Sorak felt that she had to get Risak's unasked questions out of the way. Risak, like Pastak, seemed to accept the concept of the Sorak/Nasa family.

As the distant star began to drop behind the city walls Sorak shared what little food that she had left with Risak.

Risak explained how she had got there and then tried to explain to Sorak the fractures that existed between the various groups of women in Sector Four. This information confirmed what Sorak thought that she knew.

"The capan is confined to her quarters, the young women soldiers have voted themselves two new tenants. They are uneasy about hanging around whilst the triumvirate entrenches itself even more. They want action. But some are in favour of attacking the administration whenever and wherever they can; others want to wait until Kragar launches a full-scale invasion, yet others still want a combined attack with the women from the Edge, but Kragar is not popular amongst a lot of the younger women because she doesn't listen to them. They would like someone else to be in charge of the fighting."

"And what of the other women from the Edge, the other resistance groups?" Sorak asked. "Of Pastak, of the civilians?"

"Pastak will only join the attack when she is convinced the women in Sector Four, and elsewhere, have a plan for what should follow success in the attack. Again, this is a big issue, many of the women want to go back to the pre-rebellion days, as you know, but many others even in Sector Four know that peace can only come if the men have an equal share in the management and success of the city, and they can see a safe future."

"And the women in Sector Six?"

"Sorak, the women in Sector Six, and there are fewer and fewer of them as the sensible ones realise that doing nothing achieves nothing, the women of Sector Six are best ignored. Any attack on the triumvirate in Sector One will flow through Sector Six and they will have to take their chances."

"So, there's not much point in my waiting here."

"Sorak, Pastak, myself and others who see the situation as we do think that there are two key things to be achieved. We need to know exactly where all the women of the city stand, not just the soldiers. Many civilians are working with the administration, directly, maybe unwillingly, and that is helping the triumvirate run the city. Killing women is not in our plan, although Kragar believes that if we have to we have to. What we also need to know is what the other armed groups who, unlike us, are already active against the triumvirate are planning to do, and whether they would be prepared to work with the military to defeat the male administration."

Suddenly another whole new level of complexity opened up for Sorak; she had tended to only see things as just involving the military.

"The time for action has arrived," Risak said rather portentously. "The old capan, in one of her more clear thinking moments said, 'Sorak will make it happen'. And it's one of the few things that everybody seems to agree on."

"I wish I had their confidence!"

But Sorak wasn't much given to self-analysis and later, as she drifted off to sleep, exhausted by trying to understand how things might develop, and sharing the pile of animal skins with Risak, deep in her brain priorities were beginning to shape themselves. At no time did it occur to Sorak that she wouldn't play her part. And if taking the lead was what was wanted of her, that's what she would have to do.

Nonetheless, she woke up with just one thought: how was she going to make contact with 147 and how was she going to make him and the rest of them want to talk to them about the future?

* * *

For once, Nasa felt himself at odds with Sorak. His mind was increasingly dominated by the wellbeing of his son and his concerns over his capability to fend for himself in the hostile city. He knew that Sorak was equally concerned, but he had no understanding of her attitude. For Sorak, to show her anxiety was to belittle her son; he was a man, and as a man he had to deal with his problems. For her to in any way intervene was to indicate a lack of confidence in him. For his father, man to man, it was simply about helping if help were needed.

But Nasa had no idea whether it was.

"There's only one way to find out," he told himself, and since Leben was due to return to Sector One, he went with her.

Since Sorak seemed to want to make contact with the women in Sector Six, as well as Sector Four, Nasa decided that he had to set off in search of Lenar on his own; he was disinclined to wait any longer. He was well aware of the risks of heading into triumvirate territory, but since that was where he assumed Lenar had gone, he saw no choice. And with Leben's guidance and his own practical common sense, he was confident that he would find his son and the young woman who had so comprehensively captured his affections.

But things started to go wrong almost as soon as they made their way to the gate in the inner city wall. Normally guarded by a group of armed civilians of uncertain origin, as they approached they could hear the sound of fighting, hand to hand fighting.

"We must find another way," Leben said.

But Nasa had already crept forward to see what was happening. Of the eight gate guards, three were lying on the ground injured or dead, the other five were heavily engaged with seven or eight male soldiers. It was only the superior skill of the civilians with their swords that prevented them from being overwhelmed.

"Nasa..."

Leben, not being a fighter, was alarmed by Nasa unshipping and loading his crossbow.

Dedicated to not killing any of the male soldiers, Nasa was hard pressed to find a target so that he could disable him. Then as two men beat down one of the civilians who was desperately trying to defend herself, they exposed themselves. Quick-fire, Nasa lodged a crossbow bolt into the thighs of both men and they limped away to the shelter of the gatehouse. Inexperience told in the end as the male soldiers hesitated in their efforts to see where the new attack had come from. Disarming three of the men quickly, the women pressed their advantage, but the men's attempt to secure the gate had failed and the male troopers withdrew to nurse the wounds and their injured pride.

Leben showed herself to the gate guards as they menaced Nasa once the men had gone.

"Hold," said Leben, "it was he who just saved you."

As the civilian women began to recover their breath, Leben hurriedly explained what Nasa had just done. Since Nasa wasn't inexperienced as a fighter, he had kept himself well out of sight, so the women hadn't really seen him in action.

Once they knew who Nasa was, they surged around him only too happy to show their appreciation.

"The triumvirate have seized all the inner wall gates except this one," the leader of the gate guards said. "We brought in reinforcements, but we had to disperse as they tried to herd the beasts at us as a diversion. But the beasts just ran away around the walls."

As they were talking, two parties of well-armed but ill-dressed civilians, ten or twelve in all, joined them. It seemed that they had captured and disarmed most of the other male soldiers and sent them back into Sector One. The loss of weapons was beginning to become just as important an issue for the triumvirate as the loss of soldiers. Nasa was pleased to see that, unlike some of the soldiers, the civilian women were just as keen to avoid killing the men as he and Sorak were.

With Leben's continued guidance, she and Nasa finally arrived at her hideout in the derelict Senate buildings.

Nasa had been surprised as they worked their way carefully through the narrow streets towards Sector One just how many women there were in the triumvirate-controlled area.

"Passive resisters, mostly," Leben said, using the definition that she had given to Sorak. "Some try to undermine the administration if they can, but largely they just want to stay alive and be left alone."

Nasa found such an attitude hard to understand, but he acknowledged that most of the civilian women had very little choice.

"How will they react when the invasion comes?"

Leben shrugged. That was a worry for her too, since it raised the possibility of setting civilians against soldiers, something that no one wanted.

30

The messages that Kragar was getting back from the city were confused. Even then she was only being told what people around her thought that she would want to hear. She was aware that not all of the women camped in Sector Four supported the purpose of the invasion that she was planning, but being Kragar, she assumed that once battle was joined they would fight with her. She was probably right in most cases. But the only genuine common thread was everybody's desire for the stand-off with the men to end.

Equally, what Kragar also didn't know was that word of the planned attack on the city had already reached the triumvirate and they had started making their own plans in response. Neither 147 nor 136 wanted an armed confrontation but they were unlikely to be in a position to avoid it if it was forced on them. The superiority of the women soldiers was their permanent concern.

The news of 182's assassination had reached Kragar, but she had no interest in the politics of the triumvirate. Her focus was getting as many of the women soldiers from the resistance groups into the city as quickly as possible and as soon as possible. After that, all they had to do was fight their way into

Sector One and take control of the administration. This was Kragar's only plan. Her assumption, albeit rather rose-tinted, was that things would then resume as they had been before the original rebellion.

"Do we know how many soldiers that Kragar has?"

147 had called Marwek to see him. She was essentially the only effective military officer that the triumvirate had. But he and 136 were hesitating over giving her overall command of their troops since she was widely disliked and resented by the men who were already in charge of the triumvirate's military activities. Yet even these men, if pressed, would have acknowledged that she was the best that they had.

Marwek's animosity towards Kragar was well known and seen as a positive incentive for her. The fighting prowess of the male soldiers rarely matched that of the women. Marwek's strength was her recognition of this and her ability to mitigate its impact with planning and battle tactics.

"We must never get drawn into a head-on battle," she kept saying.

The narrow streets and complex geography of large parts of the city were made for guerrilla warfare.

Kragar had gathered the resistance group leaders to her encampment in the forest just inside the Edge. The whole area had taken on an entirely different character since the days when Sorak and 1562/Nasa had made their escape from the city those seventeen cycles ago. From virgin forest it had been turned into a small village with dozens of dwellings fashioned out of the branches of trees and secured against the sudden night-time downpours as well as possible attack. Attacks there had been, but the male solders, not unnaturally, tended to prefer ambush rather than direct assault.

In the centre of the camp was an open-sided building that was used as a communal gathering point. Answering Kragar's call it was full of the tenants and caprals who led the various groups of resistance fighters. In the way of these things, groups of likeminded women gathered together as they awaited Kragar's arrival. Knowing how to make an entrance, she knew how to keep them waiting.

Pastak had been rejoined by Risak who had brought one of the young new tenants from Sector Four back with her. Meenak was an outspoken young woman who had been recruited as a soldier as a child and had been put through training in the old way. She was very much her own woman and held the older officers, particularly the ageing capan, in contempt. Risak she had respect for because she had seen her in action, and because she only killed when it was absolutely necessary.

Meenak was aware of Risak's support for Sorak, but with the arrogance and ignorance of youth she had no understanding of the respect in which Sorak was held. She simply lumped her into the same category as Kragar and the discredited capan and took no account of her. It would be some time before this attitude changed.

Meenak, nonetheless, was careful to avoid expressing any opinion of Kragar.

A crescendo of stamping feet announced that Kragar had appeared. Not all of the stamping, however, could have been said to be friendly. There was instant silence when she raised her hand.

Kragar wasn't one for fancy speeches, or for providing more information than she thought necessary to achieving her purposes. In the present situation she was very conscious of the 'need to know' principle. Information, she knew, was getting to the triumvirate very quickly.

"When the distant star returns one more time we will move into the city."

Not everyone cheered. Kragar noticed that Pastak and several of the other more experienced officers were amongst the silent ones. They needed more information on what Kragar planned before they would be willing to commit themselves. Kragar had expected something of the sort but was nonetheless irritated.

"Some parties will need to be set to move as soon as the distant star disappears. They will need to be in position to enter the city by the Yellow and possibly the Green gates."

Pastak and Risak exchanged looks. The Yellow and Green gates were on the other side of the city from where they were positioned, but closest to Sector One and the administration areas. It made military sense.

"We will undertake that."

Risak and Meenak were both surprised that Pastak should volunteer so quickly, bearing in mind her previous caution. They would have expected her to wait until Kragar had outlined her intentions in more detail. But Pastak had already formed a view on the best way to attack the city and where she would have deployed her best troops. Securing and controlling access to Sector One as quickly as possible was a part of her thinking.

Kragar had been caught out. She had expected Pastak to argue about the plan, to demand to know what the objectives were; to try to impose her own ideas, it was the way that she knew Pastak thought. She was instantly suspicious.

However, Pastak had realised that entering the city directly into Sector One and taking control of the access into the administration area would require some really hard fighting, although she suspected that the men might not have the stomach for it, but she also knew that it was the best chance to prevent the triumvirate people being slaughtered by a vengeful Kragar. Once the women were in the city, Pastak knew all too well that the fractures in the women's thinking would be exposed. Part of her plan was to deny Kragar's thirst for revenge, as well as denying her the chance to re-establish the old women's system of control. Pastak, like Sorak, was a pragmatist, and she was better at reacting to events than forming them.

"I was expecting you to take command of the troops in Sector Four and organise the advance into Sector Six and then Sector One," Kragar said hurriedly, although this was something that she had reserved for herself in her mind.

Pastak didn't say anything; there was nothing that she needed to say. Risak, who by now had sensed what her colleague had on her mind, was surprised again when Meenak stamped her feet and shook her head.

"The troops in Sector Four aren't going to take orders from Kragar!" she muttered.

She was clearly heard but no one showed any reaction. How the resistance groups worked out their relationship with the women soldiers who had remained in the city was a concern to the more thoughtful of the women. Kragar's assumptions about her role in this relationship were treated with scepticism.

Risak grinned to herself, but she put a hand on Meenak's arm; there was no point in taking issue, Kragar was just thinking on her feet in the face of Pastak's initiative. Things would almost certainly work out differently.

It was Pastak whose raised hand quietened the rumbles of conversation that had begun to break out amongst the women. With a gesture she invited Kragar to continue with her briefing. It was important that they all knew what was on the woman's mind.

In the pitched darkness that followed the vermillion glow of the first moon, Pastak, Risak and their body of heavily armed troopers set out across the plain surrounding the city. It would be a long and arduous trip. Days later they arrived at the Yellow gate. They were careful to time this arrival as the distant star began to rise. It was important in Kragar's plans that the triumvirate knew that the invasion had begun. Kragar and the bulk of the resistance troops were by then within sight of the city wall and the sentries posted by the officers in Sector Four.

The invasion was indeed underway.

But, in the quietness of the night after Kragar had announced her plans and the various group's part in them, Meenak quietly slipped away from the camp and returned to the city to rejoin her colleagues there.

31

Lenar and Quillat both watched the black woman with interest. She seemed to accept the restraint placed on her, and even having spat out the material in her mouth made no effort to resist being gagged again. Quillat concluded that she felt safe, and when so many black and brown women had been killed, she was grateful for that. For Lenar, whose only experience of black women was Kragar, her unthreatening demeanour was something new.

Following the death of 182 and the uncertainties that that would be inducing, Quillat had decided that she would head into the administration area with a small patrol to try and gauge the situation. Still careful to avoid the young soldier whom he had first encountered, notwithstanding her apparent new-found devotion to him, Lenar pushed on ahead of the main body confident that being a man he was less likely to be fired on by any male soldiers that they might meet. They didn't meet any. At least they didn't meet any active soldiers, but they did come across a heavily bleeding trooper propped up against a wall as they emerged from one of the narrow streets that brought them to the piazza in front of the ruins of the old Senate House.

There was a moment of tension.

"No," Lenar quickly said, "we will not kill him, he is no threat to us."

But as Quillat moved to tend to his wounds, the man was getting more and more agitated. However, it was she rather than Lenar who sensed that it was something beyond the imminent fear for his life that was disturbing him.

"It's the black woman," Quillat said when she realised that the man's gaze kept coming back to her.

Eventually the man, understanding that he wouldn't be killed out of hand, seemed to calm down.

"She killed 182!"

It was a hissing whisper. Both Quillat and Lenar heard what the man said but none of the rest of the patrol did. The black woman, nonetheless, having seen the looks that she was now being given, looked discomforted for the first time.

Quillat quickly took her aside and told her what the man had said and was clearly asking if it was true. Slowly, the woman nodded her head, fearful of how the admission might be received. She need not have worried.

Quillat's response was to free her, now satisfied that she was not any sort of supporter of the male administration and therefore posed no threat.

"Adlan," the woman said, introducing herself.

"Do the triumvirate have any women slaves, Adlan?"

Lenar's question clearly surprised the woman. It was hardly what she might have expected from the only man in the group. She wondered how he could possibly have known that there were several serving in the triumvirate members' households. She nodded. She knew nothing of 136's arrangements, but certainly 182 had had three slaves; it was their knowledge that allowed the woman to get close to him and for her to kill him.

"147 may have a woman working in his food preparation area. What else she does, I don't know. There is some mystery about her. 147 has no interest in degrading women. He's too shrewd not to know that the triumvirate can't survive without them.

The information wasn't much use to Quillat or Lenar. However much she sympathised with him, Quillat wasn't in the business of rescuing young women from administration households, she was about disrupting and disabling their activities. And nothing that Adlan had said identified any of the women slaves as likely to be Desak.

"Something's wrong."

As the patrol crept around the edge of the piazza and into the ruined shell of the Senate House they were aware of much more activity in the undamaged parts of the administration buildings than they had ever seen before. There was an urgency, a tension in the atmosphere typified by the hurried way that the administration staff were observed to be going about their duties.

"Something's wrong," Quillat said again.

Adlan had disappeared, but Lenar could see that this wasn't what Quillat was concerned about. And, in any case, as Quillat made her dispositions Adlan returned. She had clearly made contact with someone friendly to her within the administration building. How she had done so so quickly no one thought to question.

She was obviously excited. The news that she brought was unverified but there seemed to be no reason not to believe it.

"A party of women have captured the Yellow gate, and more women have been seen in the desert approaching the Red gate on the other side of the city. This is more than the usual skirmishing."

Quillat wasn't sure that she understood what Adlan meant by 'skirmishing', but she realised that it probably didn't matter anyway; with this news they would need to regroup again and to prepare themselves for battle. She hurriedly sent a runner back to the rest of the group ordering them to remain outside of Sector One for the time being.

"Could this be the start of the invasion?" Lenar asked.

He hadn't been paying that much attention to what his parents had been discussing in the past days, but he was aware that Leben and the other women were expecting something to happen. And it was something that some of them, including his mother, were not happy about. Again, he was unclear exactly what an invasion involved, but his mother's concern about it was enough for him. The present excitement seemed to match her concerns.

Lenar knew all about Kragar, and his parents' distrust and dislike of her, but not knowing where the Red or the Yellow gates were, that the arrival of these women from the wilderness was the talked-of invasion was all that he could think of.

Quillat, who did know where the Red and Yellow gates were, drew Adlan away from the rest of the patrol and talked to her quietly. She was reluctant to commit herself without more information on what was going on, but not being far from the Yellow gate she also knew that she should be ready to help the women there. She didn't suppose that capturing the gate was their prime objective; attacking the administration buildings seemed much more likely. But having the gate in their hands and available for access and exit, however, made military sense to her.

"There are at least two platoons of male soldiers in what's left of the old Senate Guard barracks, maybe forty men," Adlan said, her grasp of the situation impressing Quillat. "Many of them young and not very well trained. How willing they will be to fight, we will have to wait and see."

But Adlan was a rarity. She was a black woman who had survived the purges after the initial rebellion because she was still a girl in school. During the next seventeen cycles of the distant star she had kept her head down, worked with the civilians who had come to terms with the various male administrations, without actually doing so herself. She had steadily built up a range of contacts, including Leben, some of whom she knew were biding their time, but many of whom had become committed to the male administrations, particularly the triumvirate, as they were more moderate and less vicious than their predecessors. Adlan was very clear where her loyalties lay, but she didn't judge those women who collaborated, it was the only way that they could survive.

"The women at the Yellow gate may just be there to block escape and provide a safe entry into the city. Until we know how many women there are we won't have any idea what their purpose is," Adlan confirmed Quillat's reading of the capture of the gate.

Although this all made sense to Quillat, it fed Lenar's impatience. He didn't want to get involved in any fighting. He understood how personally dangerous that would be for him, but he realised that if the women attacked the administration buildings it would give him an ideal opportunity to try and get into the residential quarters to hunt for Desak.

When the distant star began to fade, Lenar gathered his backpack and weapons and signalled to Quillat that he was leaving. To Quillat, Lenar's independent behaviour was a complication that she didn't need. But she had no reason to try and stop him in his quest for Desak, since he had no part in the male administration and, in any case, was Sorak's son. The novelty of knowing this last fact wasn't lost on Quillat; she was keen not to do anything that might offend Sorak. All of which said, Quillat still agreed with Adlan's rather sour view that Lenar was a man, and their priority in the short-term was defeating men, not supporting them.

It took Lenar much longer than he had intended to skirt his way around the administration buildings. As Quillat and Adlan had already noted, there were many more people about than he had been expecting. His experience was restricted to Sectors Four and Five, which were largely deserted other than the barracks. At one point he had to dodge into one of the occupied buildings to avoid a noisy bunch of male soldiers. But the people inside the building were moving around in a purposeful manner that he knew could bode no good for him. He was glad to get out again without being spotted.

Working his way deeper into the accommodation area adjacent to the old Senate complex, he was quick to notice that the quality of the buildings had changed.

This lot of buildings look in better condition, maybe that's where they live.

Lenar had no idea who 'they' might be, or how many of them there might be, beyond that Adlan had said that 147, one of the leaders, lived in a separate building the other side of the burned-out old Senate library. Lenar only had a vague idea what a library was and none of what it might look like, but the group of buildings that he was carefully approaching seemed like a good place to start his search. He had arrived at exactly the right place.

The building was two storeys and, although he couldn't at first see it, it was built round a courtyard. Again, in his ignorance of the design of city buildings, he couldn't know that the lower storey was comprised of working areas and storage. He eventually found a narrow passage through the building into the courtyard. He crept through, his sword at the ready. He had no idea what to expect.

"People!"

He froze. It was voices, a man and, as he listened, a woman, a young woman he judged as the voice was shriller than his mother's. They were in a heated argument.

Crenal, 147's household manager, was angry; Desak thought that he was always angry. Sometimes he grasped her by the slave collar that she had been made to wear and dragged her about the kitchen. She was strong enough to have resisted him, but she was sufficiently in control of herself now to know that that would simply lead to punishment, or worse. She had set herself to wait for Lenar to rescue her, so she waited. She had every expectation that he would. But Crenal could be exasperating and increasingly she found herself, if not physically resisting him, talking back to him.

In a pause in the shouting match, the young woman's voice sounded out in more measured terms on its own. Lenar's heart missed a beat.

"Desak," he whispered to himself.

He edged right to the end of the passage to see into the courtyard. He found himself under the first floor veranda which stretched right around the inside of the courtyard. Hugging the wall he shuffled himself quietly to a ventilation opening. He could feel the heat coming out as he got close. It was the kitchen and the voices were coming from the kitchen. His experience of kitchens was restricted to their home in the valley, but clearly this kitchen was much bigger.

He needed to understand the layout. He had to take the risk. Only by looking through the ventilation opening could he be sure that it truly was Desak and what the problems might be in rescuing her.

A sweeping glance as he bobbed up into the opening revealed that it truly was Desak and a limping old man, back to him, who were arguing.

"Desak," he whispered to himself again, this time in elation.

His scan had also revealed a door the other side of the ventilation opening, the way into the kitchen from the courtyard. He knew what he had to do.

But he froze again. There were more voices, this time two men, two men who were obviously walking along the veranda above his head.

There was no uncertainty this time; he recognised one of the voices immediately.

"Father," he mouthed.

32

Nasa's and Leben's trip to Sector One and the administration buildings had been eventful, but their personal relationship had been easy, relaxed and something of a surprise to Leben. Remarkably, it was the first time that she had ever been alone with a man, let alone an older man. Growing to maturity during some of the worst times of Soran's and the other male administrations, men were something to be wary of, to fear. But she had no such feelings about Nasa. Young as she was he treated her as an equal, with a confidence that she assumed had grown from living all those cycles with Sorak, unfettered by the rules of the city. She felt very comfortable in the relationship.

Leben, of course, unusually, had come to learn that she was Crenan's daughter, but she had no idea who the old Senate administrator had bred with beyond the obvious fact that he must have been white.

Nasa, having heard Leben's story and listened to her conversation with Sorak, however, was well aware that she was his daughter. But after all the cycles of living with Sorak and Lenar as a family he didn't think much of it. He had bred three times with Crenan, and previously three times with another administrator before Crenan had downgraded him as a personal slave and sent him to serve Sorak as 1562.

1562/Nasa had been far too intelligent for his own good working in the Senate offices. Being white, this would eventually, had not Crenan transferred him to Sorak, have led to his being sent to the quarries. Only black and, to a lesser extent, brown-skinned slaves had value in the closed environment of the pre-rebellion women's world; clever white slaves were a threat that hadn't been tolerated.

But nothing much of this remained in Nasa's consciousness, even if it had shaped his life. And it was Lenar, and only Lenar, of his offspring who was the subject of Nasa's concern.

"You should hide yourself in one of the derelict buildings away from the immediate administration area," Leben had said soon after they had arrived. "No one knows how many women are living in Sector One, apparently, nor how many of them are fully loyal to the triumvirate. You must trust no one."

Nasa knew this to be true, but the reality of his situation meant that he would have to trust someone amongst the men if he was find his way into their living quarters and to where he supposed Desak, and therefore Lenar, would be found.

* * *

With Risak and Leben gone, Sorak had no immediate means of contact with the women soldiers in Sector Four and, in view of the unexpected animosity displayed towards her, she hoped by only certain individuals, she was reluctant to seek the women out until she was ready. But she knew that she had to do something to counter the baleful influence of Kragar.

Time was running out. Inaction was never an option for Sorak. With Nasa gone too, the stirrings of her old military past and assurance in command began to surface. Her antipathy to Kragar was an added motivation. Almost without thinking about it she had taken on a role in what was going to happen between the men and women, even if she wasn't entirely clear what that role was to be.

As the distant star arose on the morning that Lenar had located Desak and was surprised to hear his father's voice, Sorak had decided what she had to do. She knew that Kragar's invasion was imminent; she had to prevent the clash between the incoming women and the troops of the triumvirate.

Then she was suddenly conscious that the herd outside the hut had become agitated. Sorak went onto alert as she wondered why. Carefully, she exited the hut through an opening that she had created close to the outer city wall, the hut originally only having had one entrance. What seemed like a group of women was trying to work their way through the herd. With the beasts milling around, their progress was slow and hesitant. Sorak didn't immediately recognise any of the women.

"Sorakmam!"

Sorak drew her sword, confused and, unusually for her, uncertain. She had been recognised.

Suddenly a number of the beasts, in their agitation, had started to stampede down the open pasture away from the hut, leaving the women exposed.

"Sorakmam?"

What is going on here?

It was the voice of a capral who Sorak vaguely recognised. As the herd dispersed, the group of six soldiers moved into formation.

"Kragarmam has ordered the soldiers in Sector Six who don't support attacking the triumvirate to be disarmed. Most of our group escaped to the Edge, they were planning to join Pastakmam. We were out patrolling when the order came. Rather than hand in our weapons, we escaped."

Sorak took time to digest what she was being told.

"So Kragar has actually arrived?"

"She's camped outside the Red gate, Sorakmam, waiting until Pastakmam has secured the Yellow gate."

The capral was clearly unsure of Sorak's potential reaction. The careful formality of her speech, irritating as it was to Sorak, showed her uncertainty, but she realised that the capral might not know that, like themselves, she was against attacking the triumvirate. She hadn't spent that much time in Sector Four and none in Sector Six, and had said very little when it was clear that there were those who didn't welcome her.

Sorak had had no idea that the resistance groups were planning to attack the city in two places, but for her Pastak's hand was clearly evident in the plan the capral outlined. Cutting off retreat from Sector One and the administration area made sense and wouldn't necessarily involve Pastak in too much fighting, but it gave her first access to the men running the administration, rather than Kragar. But, allowing Kragar to dictate the main battle was, in Sorak's mind, a mistake, however, she recognised that there was probably not much Pastak could have done about that.

But how are we going to stop Kragar from attacking the triumvirate troops?

She voiced the thought.

"We have to try and make contact with the triumvirate troops. When will Kragar start her attack?"

It was obvious that the capral, who knew nothing about diplomacy, wasn't sure whether this was a good idea, but Sorak knew that it was the only way to prevent unnecessary bloodshed. Instinctively, the capral deferred to Sorak.

"She was to wait one circuit of the distant star for Pastakmam to get into place."

From this timing, Sorak knew that the attack must already have started.

"We will come with you Sorakmam." The capral was

obviously desperate for someone to take command of her situation.

"No, no, what you should do is continue to work your way around the city walls. In the circumstances there won't be many male soldiers about, I imagine. You will have to take care at the Green gate, but you should be able to reach Pastak at the Yellow gate before the distant star goes down."

She didn't doubt that Pastak could use friendly reinforcements, however few. For herself, she needed to get back to Sector Four as quickly as possible to try to convince the soldiers there that instead of fighting the triumvirate they should meet with them and work out an accommodation that would allow normal life to resume without one gender dominating the other. It would have been a formidable task even without Kragar advocating death and destruction as an alternative. But, for Sorak, talking not fighting was the only way forward.

* * *

Leben headed off on her own into the maze of buildings that stood behind the old Senate complex, some derelict, some partly damaged, some intact. Nasa was happy to be left on his own, even if he didn't yet know how he was going to proceed.

I need a base, somewhere to retreat to if necessary.

He and Leben had discussed the situation in Sector One and the old Senate buildings. She was keen to give him as much information as possible since learning from experience wasn't really an option for him. Many of the men and the women in the administration area would be hostile to him for a range of reasons that Leben didn't see any point in explaining. Many of the women working for the triumvirate did so out of fear, but many from more complex motives that were generally driven by the desire to achieve a better life than they had under the old regime. For white and pale-skinned women under the black and brown-skinned women's rule, life could be harsh, dangerous and unfulfilling. Now they had opportunities. Nasa would have understood this.

But for these women and many of the less capable men, intelligent men like Nasa were a threat.

Since he and Leben had gathered some food on their way to Sector One, having followed what at first seemed to Nasa to be an absurdly tortuous route, he had enough provisions for several days and knew how to procure more. The food wasn't particularly healthy or substantial but from his former slave days he knew how to survive on a meagre diet.

Rising early as the distant star breached the city walls and cast long shadows, Nasa prepared himself for his venture into the administration's back yard. He was convinced that Lenar was somewhere within this maze of buildings. Leben's contacts had advised her that 147 and 136 were known to have female slaves. The concept had distressed Leben, but for Nasa it was almost like a signal of intent that the triumvirate wanted to establish a male version of the old women's society. This didn't augur too well for the future.

Of course, Nasa had no way of knowing that certainly in the case of 147 he was wrong. Accommodation with the women was an objective that had slowly seeped into 147's mind, and was very near to achieving articulation. More thoughtful and more intelligent than 136, 147 did have a vision for the future, but he was also willing to modify it as events unfolded.

"I need to find where 147 and 136 live." Nasa, in the absence of Sorak had reverted to quietly talking to himself.

But whenever he let his mind dwell on how things might change in the future his subconscious flashed a warning picture of his son in front of him. He was pulled back to his first priority.

Why he supposed that Desak was being kept as a slave in one of the triumvirate principal's accommodation he couldn't explain to himself, a premonition perhaps, but he needed to start somewhere and knowing where to find the leaders was going to be important.

Nasa had hardly carefully moved himself out of the basement where he had spent the night when he heard voices, angry voices, women's voices. Keeping within the shadow of the walls of one of the taller buildings he crept forward towards the sounds. As he edged around a corner two women had obviously been fighting with their fists. One of them, who had got the worst of the encounter, was wearing what Nasa immediately recognised as a slave collar.

He didn't have time to wonder what was going on.

With the 'slave' woman thrown down onto her back the other fighter crouched over her pinioning her arms. As she raised her arm to crash down a blow into the prone woman's face, Nasa leapt forward, grasped the raised arm and pulled his own arm around her neck. Crushing her windpipe he held her until she went limp. Checking that she wasn't dead and signalling the other woman to be quiet he dragged the assailant away and used her upper garments to imprison her arms. Pushing her out of sight in the entrance to a building, Nasa returned to the 'slave'. Standing taller than him, but with head bowed down, she seemed uncertain as to whether to run away or stay.

Nasa approached her carefully, trying not to frighten her.

Reasoning that she had been running away in the first place, Nasa gave her one of his rare smiles and led her into the burned-out lower floor of another building.

Clearly not an ex-soldier from her bearing, Nasa had little experience in dealing with low-grade female civilians, which was what he assumed she was. Clearly, however, he needed to understand what had happened to her if he was going to help her.

"Nasa," he said gesturing at himself.

"Deetak," she responded.

"Who were you running away from, Deetak?"

But the thoughts that the question provoked in her brain cut off her attempts to answer. As she looked down at Nasa pure terror filled her eyes.

"Deetak, I won't hurt you. I won't take you back. I can take your collar off and you can escape from Sector One."

Still she seemed unsure of him, but slowly, as her brain accepted that he was unthreatening, she relaxed. Her response all came in a rush.

"I work for 136. He's one of the triumvirate leaders. Learah, she runs his household, she beats me because I don't work hard. I ran away because she caught me talking to another slave who works for 147."

Nasa was instantly focused; it was possible that Desak worked for 147.

"147 has two women slaves. I was talking to the brown-skinned one. Crenal used to beat them regularly until 147 stopped him. Crenal runs his household. 147 isn't like other men."

But Deetak was becoming agitated again. Nasa could hear why. 136's slave mistress had recovered or had been found. She was demanding a search for Deetak, but whoever the man was who had found her was refusing.

It was apparent from the man's reaction to the demand made of him that something important had happened, that much Nasa could understand, and it appeared to have put the triumvirate into a panic. That surprised and encouraged Nasa.

Without asking he inserted his knife into the clasp that held Deetak's slave collar closed and prised it open. Bending it further open he tossed it into a pile of debris on the floor of the building.

She felt her neck in a gesture that Sorak would have recognised, giggled and walked up to Nasa and gave him a hug before he could resist.

"There are questions that I need to ask you," he said, "before I show you how to leave Sector One."

The conversation was brief. Deetak had met Desak at 147's house, but didn't know her name. But the description was good enough for Nasa.

Deetak had seen no strangers around 147's house, which was adjacent to 136's, but she admitted she wouldn't really know, amongst the men, who was a stranger and who was an administration official. At least she knew that there weren't too many visitors.

True to his word, Nasa took Deetak to the edge of the piazza that bordered on Sector Six, indicated the way that she should go, and then retraced his steps to where he had spent the night. The distant star was overhead as he carefully made his way to 147's accommodation.

He didn't get very far.

33

Lenar's limited experience of life often had the benefit of not allowing him to waste energy on speculating about things that he was never going to understand or to conceive an explanation for. Desak was his priority and Desak was all that he was going to think about.

So his father was there in 147's house. How he got there, why he was there, it never occurred to Lenar to wonder. His father was just there, he would have his reason, and all that he had to decide was whether to make himself known or wait to see what happened, since Nasa was clearly with someone else, and Lenar knew that they were in hostile territory.

And with Desak being so close to hand!

All he had to do, he told himself, was to burst into the kitchen, disable the old man, he had no idea that it was Crenal, or what Crenal was doing there, and grab Desak and head away back into the mass of derelict buildings that surrounded them. He didn't know his way around the area, nor who else might be there; certainly Quillat and the other fighters would be, but he was aware that there were likely to be other women who would challenge his being in Desak's company.

"But I need to get her out first!" he told himself.

Clearly his father and whoever he was with weren't going to come down from the veranda. Why would they? There was only food preparation, storage and the quarters for Desak and any other women enslaved there. With no signs of anyone protecting 147 or his house, he just needed to get on with it.

Lenar ducked below the sill of the ventilation opening and stood by the door into the kitchen. He didn't know if there was another way into the kitchen from inside the building; he assumed that there must be, it was a risk that he would have to take.

Gently he tested the door; it opened outwards but wasn't bolted or locked.

There had been no noise, no shouting for some time. He wondered whether Desak was still there. It occurred to him that she might have left the kitchen, or the old man had.

He knew that he was procrastinating, if not the word for it. He drew his sword. It was shorter than the military version that Sorak used, more like the cut down one that Nasa always carried.

"Desak."

He had flung the door open, leapt through the entrance and rushed towards the figure of the young woman that he had come to rescue.

The old man wasn't there. Lenar, notwithstanding his joy at seeing Desak, didn't neglect the precautions that he knew were necessary. There was indeed another entrance to the kitchen, the old man had obviously left that way.

Satisfied over his immediate security, Lenar turned his attention to Desak. He hadn't really registered that she hadn't made a sound, nor had she made any movement towards him. He soon saw why.

A chain had been attached to her collar and to the wall at the back of the kitchen. She had something wrapped around the lower part of her face and seemed unable to use her arms.

"Desak," Lenar muttered again, in both relief and excitement.

Snatching up a knife from the kitchen bench, as his father had done for Deetak, Lenar inserted the knife in the clasp of the collar and levered it apart. The collar and chain clattered to the floor. In the silence that followed, Lenar heard the gasp that the brown-skinned young woman who had entered the kitchen had uttered.

It was 147's other female slave. Having shared confidences with Desak, she understood the situation immediately. She knew that she had to help.

"Strike me down, make me bleed," she said urgently to Lenar, "then go."

Not bothering to release Desak, Lenar struck the woman full in the face and kicked her feet from under her. Bleeding heavily from the nose, she lay still as Lenar grasped Desak by the shoulder and pushed her out of the door, along the walkway and back through the narrow alleyway. He didn't have time to wonder why he had so rigorously followed the woman's instructions. Desak had looked horrified, briefly.

Sheathing his sword, as they ran towards the nearby burned-out buildings Lenar picked Desak up by clutching her around the waist, and holding her under his arm. He jogged rapidly to safety. Lost in the gloom of the narrow streets between the buildings, most of which were two or three storeys tall, he eventually found the entrance to one of the less damaged houses and pushed his way in. Desak tottered as he deposited her on her feet.

Recovering, Desak leant on Lenar, her eyes sparkling even in the semi-darkness of the room he had brought her to. Then free of the wrapping around her face and her wrists unbound she threw her arms around Lenar's neck and kissed him as he had never been kissed before.

"We should go further up," Lenar said, leading the way up the ramp to the next floor.

The smell was appalling and Desak hurried up the ramp again as Lenar discerned a rotting body in one of the rooms.

Searching through the rooms on the top floor they eventually found what had obviously been a bedroom. The divan was without bedding, but Desak immediately sat on the edge and held her hand out to Lenar.

If he had given any thought to it Lenar would have seen no benefit in his limited experience in the situation that he now found himself in. It was the first time that he had been completely alone with Desak and he sensed from her rising excitement that she meant to take full advantage of that. By comparison, after her experiences with the old capan and the groups of soldiers who had captured her, however removed those were from being with Lenar, Desak had experience enough for the two of them. She knew that men always wanted to couple with her, violently in her experience, but she also knew that they got pleasure from it; her memories were confused between pain and something more pleasurable.

She didn't think that Lenar would be violent, he had always seemed so gentle. As she explored his nether regions with her fingers she found that he was nonetheless showing the same signs that the soldiers had displayed.

Lying embraced on the divan, Lenar took considerable tutoring to start with until he began to understand what was required of him. Then, as he thrust hard into Desak, any inhibitions that his ignorance might have induced in him dissipated, and he gave himself over to enjoying the sensations that he was feeling. Desak's pleasure at their love-making was all too apparent to Lenar.

Brought up in the loving relationship between Sorak and Nasa, Lenar had no idea that they were doing something unusual within the ethos of the city. Desak, brought up in an entirely different world, was very aware that they were doing something unusual, but found it so delectable that she simply laid back and lost herself in the joy of being with Lenar.

34

Nasa was angry with himself at being distracted by helping Deetak, but he could hardly have left her to whatever fate the other woman had in mind for her. In any case, it was a valuable insight into the disorganised state that the relations between the women had come to in the face of the triumvirate's control of the administration. But he was no closer to finding Lenar and the dwellings of the triumvirate principals than he had been when he started.

As he penetrated further into the old Senate buildings, he couldn't stop himself from being increasingly torn between helping Lenar rescue Desak and helping Sorak intervene to prevent a confrontation between the retrograde women like Kragar and the triumvirate troops. The closer he got to the seat of power the more he realised that a military defeat, whichever way the battle went, would solve nothing.

He had no idea what Sorak was going to do. A practical man, he had little time for, or experience in, strategic thinking. Whatever it was that Sorak decided upon he was aware that one or two of the younger women soldiers seemed to resent her arrival and the deference that the older women showed her. This was something that Nasa, like Leben and Risak, and all the others who knew Sorak, couldn't understand.

Having rescued Deetak he hadn't been taking much notice of the distant star, so he wasn't sure how much light there was left.

But once again it was nearby noises that focused his attention.

Working his way back into Sector One he had taken a different route from the one that he had previously used. He hadn't intended to, but without Sorak's surefooted knowledge of the city, he had simply worked his way along a different street without any idea of where it might lead. He now realised that the area was inhabited, whereas his previous route had been devoid of people. There were clearly both men and women in the vicinity.

Instinctively dodging into the doorway of a building, but finding the door locked, he waited as the source of the noise, a mixed group of men and women, surged passed him.

She must have seen me!

Nasa was conscious of making eye contact with a black soldier, an officer, who was walking at a measured pace behind the group. The rarity of a black woman in authority had, unwisely, attracted his attention.

Marwek had seen him.

But if the frozen figure in the doorway of the building was the individual that they were looking for, for reasons that she wouldn't have cared to share, she was happy for him not to be caught. The search parties were a distraction for Marwek. In her rather fragile position within the triumvirate leadership, Marwek was forced to concentrate very clearly on issues that seemed to be important to 147 and 136.

* * *

The death of 182 had created problems for the triumvirate, apart from reducing it to two. 147 had no personal regrets over the death of his colleague, none of the three had been friends; friendship was not a concept particularly well understood by the men of the city. But it did expose him and 136 to increased pressures from the more senior figures that they had installed in the administration. No one had put themselves forward as a replacement for 182, but decision-making had become harder as not only was 136 increasingly reluctant to support 147's conciliatory approach to dealing with the women, but the other officials were claiming a say in these decisions. Previously they had largely accepted the three leaders' decisions without question.

As Leben had discovered, the triumvirate knew that the black woman who had killed 182 had been captured by a group of dissident women and would escape their justice, but her friends would not. Leben herself was not known to any of the senior triumvirate officials, so was under no immediate threat. However, she cut off all contact with the people that she had dealt with in the administration and returned to Sector Four frustrated that she would no longer be able to provide intelligence to the soldiers at a time when Kragar was likely to need it most.

Unknowingly, Nasa had found himself on the edge of the rising turmoil within the administration.

The mixed group of soldiers, led by Marwek, whom he had hidden from, had been returning from a futile search for another more recent assassin.

136 had been found with his neck broken by one of his female 'slaves' as she came to waken him on the morning that Kragar had arrived at the Red gate. Well aware that the cause of death indicated that another male had killed 136, the 'slave' was in a quandary. Happy enough that the man was dead, he had been very abusive of her, she was keen to give the assailant as much time to escape as possible, but her own life would be at risk if she delayed raising the alarm for too long. However, this was something that she thought worth the risk; the more uncertainty amongst the triumvirate officials the better.

She crept back out of 136's bedroom. Stepping again over the sleeping bodyguard, she hurried to the kitchen. She had no reason to be there other than to have been seen by the other 'slaves' to have been there, before announcing that she was going to rouse her master. She kicked the snoring bodyguard in the ribs before re-entering the bedroom, awakening him sufficiently to hear her scream when she found the dead 136.

Finding the 'slave' hysterical, the bodyguard knocked her down before checking that his leader was dead. He was. The bodyguard, in his turn, was in deep trouble since his being asleep had allowed the killer to gain access to 136.

Other household members arrived, roused by the screams and activity, and then finally the commander of the triumvirate guards. The 'slave' told her story, leaving the bodyguard to explain his failure. The 'slave' was allowed to return to the kitchen.

The guard commander, conscious that Marwek was in the administration building, to forestall her, hurriedly organised search parties but with no clear idea where to look.

147 was summoned, and Marwek arrived in response to the frantic activity.

"The killer will have long gone," 147 remarked when the situation was explained to him.

The errant bodyguard was led away, and Marwek, now aware that Pastak and her troops had just arrived at the Yellow gate, ordered the guard commander to recall the search parties. They had other priorities. As much to hide her anger and frustration, Marwek herself undertook to go out and recall the party searching down towards Sector Six. But she was also interested in how easily she could use Sector Six to confront Kragar as she advanced.

Her sighting of Nasa was stored in her brain rather than was forgotten. Marwek had also used the time she was out hunting down the search party to think out the implications of the death of 136. 147 was now in sole command, but his views on how the triumvirate should develop and on dealing with the dissident women, well known and debated, weren't, Marwek knew, universally accepted. Conscious of how fragile the administration was, and of past history, she equally knew that she had to do what she could to bolster 147 and to keep him on the course of accommodation with the women.

Conscious also that some of the senior officials, like the guard commander, were hostile to her personally, both as a woman and as a former Senate Guard tenant, she knew that she had to tread carefully.

"If he were the killer he would hardly have been hiding so close by, or at least he would have broken into the building."

In fact Marwek had no doubt that Nasa wasn't the killer. So what was he doing there? Suspicious and happy to have something to occupy her mind whilst she watched her back until 147, or whoever, had decided what to do first about Pastak and her invasion force, and then Kragar, she began to worry that she shouldn't have just left Nasa where he was.

"What if he was heading this way? Why would a lone man act in the way that he was?"

Marwek knew, now that the thoughts had surfaced, that she would have to go back to where she had last seen Nasa and to search for him.

Having very little confidence in the capabilities of the male soldiers, Marwek had collected a group of four other former women soldiers about her, two of whom were former Senate Guards. She called these two to her and they set off.

"We need to be careful. There was something confident about this man, and also there are groups of women out there who would be only too happy to cut us down."

Marwek had had reports of Quillat and her activities; she was clearly a competent leader and one, Marwek thought, to be avoided. She didn't expect to find Nasa where she had last seen him, but it was the obvious place to start the search.

"He can only be heading for the administration buildings themselves, or for the living quarters. I would think the living quarters, they are less well guarded."

She was thinking of the fate of 136 and his useless bodyguard.

From where they had picked up Nasa's last sighting, the route to the living quarters took them through some derelict buildings, some of which had signs of habitation, but these weren't of any interest to her.

They arrived at the living quarters without any signs of the man. But that quickly changed.

"Mam!" one of the soldiers gestured towards an area of small trees that verged upon the side of 147's residence. Marwek saw the shadow. She could see enough to know that it was the man that they were looking for; his confident manner was unmistakable.

Nasa had arrived some time earlier and had worked his way around the residence trying to understand the layout. Unlike his son, he didn't explore any of the three narrow passages that would have taken him into the courtyard.Nonetheless he established a clear picture of the house and knew that the kitchens would be on the lower floor. All he needed was clear evidence of Desak's presence, that should lead him to Lenar.

He wasn't about to get such evidence.

"Hold!" Marwek said sharply as the three soldiers surrounded him.

Nasa's heart sank. He knew that there were black and brown-skinned women still around but he hadn't expected to find them right in the middle of the male domain.

"Who are you, and what are you doing here?"

It was roughly demanded. Marwek was angry with herself. Sidetracked into hunting the mysterious lone male she had realised that she had given herself a problem. What was she going to do with this man now that she had arrested him? Why had she even wasted her time to chase him down? What instinct was it that told her that this man was different?

But his answers immediately justified her actions as soon as they were given.

"I am Nasa. I am here in search of my son and to give a message to the principals of the triumvirate."

The two soldiers gawped at Nasa; what he had said made no sense to them. They had never heard of Nasa, nor that a man might want to search for his son, let alone know who he was.

But Marwek knew who Nasa was. She knew about Sorak and their past. Why he was searching for his son she didn't know but that was of no interest to her.

What was of interest was the message for the triumvirate, and from whom. Marwek immediately assumed the message was from Sorak on behalf of the dissident women.

147 was still angry over the death of 136. But as his anger abated he began to feel fearful. Of the other two members of the triumvirate 136 was the closest to his way of thinking although he was in favour of taking the issue of an accommodation with the women much more gradually.

Now with his two colleagues dead, being the sole leader was a responsibility that frightened him.

He needed to think. He retreated to his bedroom. He told his staff that he didn't want to be disturbed but Marwek overrode the order. As she marched in even 147 was fearful of Marwek.

The conversation between the two of them was lengthy, and Nasa was beginning to worry that maybe 147 wouldn't want to give him a hearing. By now he knew that 147 was the only principal left and he had no way of understanding how he might react. The last thing that they needed was indecision.

Marwek had never been in 147's private rooms before and she was impressed by the sparse furnishings and the absence of any of the signs of wealth and power that she had been used to seeing from the old women senators when she was a young tenant. Marwek even began to feel the beginnings of respect.

147 had aged, she thought, he looked tired and at the present time, understandably, rather sad. But she knew that he had a brain as sharp as any she had come across in a woman and when needed an ability to make up his mind quickly and decisively. She explained what Nasa had told her but offered no comment or opinion. Needless to say, 147 immediately sought her opinion.

"You trust this man?"

147, who remembered Nasa as 1562 when working for Crenan, had no reason not to trust him, but he was aware that his judgement was seventeen cycles of the distant star out of date.

"I trust Sorak. I have never met her, but I have met some who have. If she wants peace between men and women, I would support that. The city has to have a future and we won't get that by continually killing each other."

147 didn't need convincing. He knew that the women beyond the Edge were planning, had in fact started, an invasion to try to reinstate women's domination, but he also knew that not all women agreed with that. What he didn't know was how to resolve the two points of view, and without bloodshed. Yet here was the possibility of a solution.

"I will see this Nasa."

Marwek acknowledged the order and went in search of the man.

Having made the decision, 147 felt relieved. Perhaps this would be a way to make contact with the women who wanted to live in peace with the men. Perhaps it would now be possible to get all of the women in the city to see men as at least no threat, if not as equal.

But he wasn't so sure how achievable it would be. There would be opposition from both genders.

271

He had told Marwek that he would meet with Nasa out on the veranda. As he waited for Nasa, Crenan, the old Senate, and a whole jumble of thoughts surged through his mind. So much was going to have to be changed.

He recognised Nasa. He was older, weren't they all, but he had the same confident stride and intelligent eye that Crenan had worried about all those cycles ago.

"You are welcome."

"I'm glad that we will be able to talk."

And Lenar was amazed to hear his father's voice.

35

Sorak's eventual journey back to Sector Four was uneventful, but first she spent one more night at the hut in the grazing area between the walls. She needed to rest and she needed to think. She had yet to make contact with the triumvirate, nor did she know that it was now a one man leadership. If she had known she would have been worried. The last thing they needed was a fractured administration with uncertainty over who held the ultimate power.

"Nasa, where are you, I need you."

It was a thought that had invaded her mind many times whilst she was on her own. But thoughts of Nasa only prompted worries about Lenar.

Sorak had total confidence in Nasa; he would find Lenar, he would find Desak, if she was to be found, but at what risk?

Sorak's soldier's instincts had been revitalised over the recent circuits of the distant star. Having run gently around the grazing area to exercise her body as well as her mind she approached the hut cautiously on return. She had no reason to suppose that someone might be there, but she skirted around the outside and made for the entrance that she had created at the back.

She paused and listened.

There was movement, she was sure of it; someone was in the hut, someone or something.

Peering into the gloom of the derelict building, the shape of a woman, moving around organising some bedding materialised in her vision.

"Leben!"

Her dusky skin in the gloom made Leben hard to recognise, but Sorak homed in on her characteristic body movements to identify the woman.

By the time Leben had turned and looked, Sorak had moved out of the highlight of the open space in the hut wall, but in her turn she recognised Sorak's voice.

"Sorak!"

Somewhat to her own surprise, as well as Leben's, Sorak gave her friend the sort of hug she might have given to Lenar.

"What has happened?"

"Many things, Sorak, many things, since we were last together. 136 is dead. There is only 147. That is not good news. The other members of the administration aren't all in favour of change. There are still some of the older men who want to be dominant in place of the women."

"Do you know where Nasa is?"

"No. We separated. He was convinced that the young woman that Lenar was looking for was being held in the living quarters of one of the principals. How he knew that, I don't understand, but with only 147 left, who knows what might have happened to her?"

"Nasa has amazing instincts."

"More importantly, Sorak, as I was leaving I met up with a group of women, ex-prison wardens, led by Quillat, who seems to have had contact with Lenar and saw him on his way. But they were heading for the Yellow gate, as Pastak has captured it from the men guarding it, and is waiting for the invasion to start."

This was news that Sorak wanted to hear, but also didn't want to hear.

"Kragar must have entered the city by now. We have to stop her."

"How can we stop her?"

"Leben, I have to meet up with the women in Sector Four before Kragar orders them into the battle with the men. Most of those who think like we do have by now either joined the resistance groups at the Edge, or are heading to meet up with Pastak in Sector One."

"But with her own troops and those in Sector Four, Kragar will have two companies of soldiers. Pastak has almost a similar number. I have no idea how many male soldiers there are but…"

"But it will be a disaster!"

"I will come with you, Sorak, but I fear that neither of us will be very welcome to the women in Sector Four."

Sorak knew this to be true.

"We have no choice!"

Taking a route between the walls, out by the sewage plant and then via the mangeneers' barracks, Sorak and Leben arrived at the communal area in the main barracks used by the dissident women in Sector Four at the time of the late meal. The area was full of women soldiers, young and older, and Sorak was disconcerted to see that the old capan was back with the company.

Leben had seen her too.

"What's she doing here?"

As the two of them entered the room and were recognised, an ominous silence settled on the women.

One of the younger soldiers who had been the most hostile to Sorak moved to confront her.

"What do you want? You are not welcome here."

But the young tenant, Meenak, whom Sorak had met before,

moved forward with two of her colleagues and stood beside the young soldier.

"Sorak," she said, "and Leben have a right to be here. They are welcome. They will not be threatened."

Rumbles of support for Meenak suggested to Sorak that the group was far less united than they appeared to be. That encouraged her.

"Tenant Kragar," Meenak said, "is due to arrive once the distant star arises again. She has waited until we have gathered our forces. Her fighters will base themselves in the mangeneers' barracks."

Since Sorak had expected Kragar to already be within the city, this encouraged her too.

The hostility subsided and Sorak and Leben were invited to join the old capan and three tenants at their table. The capan stared at Sorak as if she didn't know who she was, and Sorak realised that the old woman was no longer capable of leadership or even of coherent thought.

"Why *have* you come?" Meenak asked.

Less in awe of Sorak and her reputation, she was genuinely concerned that the arrival of the two women was going to cause serious dissent. Unlike many of the women who yearned for firm leadership and some sort of purpose to their existence – Meenak certainly wanted a purpose – the more time passed and the more conflict seemed inevitable, the more she realised that defeating and killing males wasn't the answer.

She hadn't quite got to the point of accepting that an accommodation had to be made, but she wasn't far off the thought. Sorak would have been pleased if she had understood the thought processes going on in the young woman's head.

Precisely how many amongst the gathered women would have agreed with her, Meenak was unsure.

"The triumvirate don't want conflict."

Sorak knew that this was an overstatement, but she also knew from Leben that it was supposedly 147's view.

"They want a peaceful coexistence with the women. They want joint involvement in the running of the city, and they want a resumption of mutually acceptable breeding."

This was undoubtedly a much more serious overstatement, but Sorak recognised that the women needed something straightforward as a reason to come to terms with the triumvirate.

"And," Leben added bluntly, "if we go on killing each other there won't be enough people to either run the city or to ensure its continued existence."

"We cannot go back to where we were all those cycles ago before the rebellion. All the administrations since have been based on replacing female dominance with male dominance, and each failed."

Sorak had no more to say. She needed the women present to hear the message as a simple choice and to decide what they wanted to do.

Meenak banged on the table with her fist. The room went quiet. In a few brief words she repeated what Sorak had said presenting it as the message from the male administration. She was heard in silence. But the silence was immediately overtaken by a fierce debate as the women understood that they had a decision to make that would undoubtedly define their futures and that of the city.

Sorak and Leben had no idea how the debate, or rather the convoluted range of conversations, was going. There was nothing that they could do to influence the outcome. Meenak had made it very clear, backed up by the other officers, that she and Leben must not now interfere in the process.

"Mother's heart," Leben muttered.

There was another silence as another group of women soldiers noisily entered the communal area.

"Kragar!"

The former Senate Guard officer moved to the capan's table. At the last minute she realised that Sorak and Leben were there. A look of pure evil flashed across her black face in recognition, before being replaced by a look of surprise.

"Kragar, you are welcome," Meenak said.

But Sorak perhaps wasn't the only one present who felt that the formal greeting was anything but sincere.

Kragar's untimely arrival had cut off the debate about whether the women should support the invasion and join the fight against the triumvirate or take some other action to open a dialogue with the administration. Whispered consultations between Kragar and some of her supporters within Sector Four quickly gave her an update on the state of things.

Clearly, she was not happy.

"We will move into Sector Six and Sector Two when the distant star returns. Anyone who has no stomach for the fight can stay here."

Classic Kragar. Just pursue your own agenda, never mind what anybody else thinks!

It was a thought that occurred to both Sorak and Leben.

And then Kragar was gone.

Nothing had been decided. Kragar's arrival, although expected, had paralysed the debate. The meeting with Sorak and Leben was clearly over. The officers and soldiers hurried from the communal area leaving the two bemused and uncertain women with the vacuous capan.

"We should try to stay with the officers," Sorak said, "and if necessary go forward with the troops."

"But we won't be able to stop the fighting. Kragar seems determined."

"We have to try."

Unaware of Marwek's overwhelming influence on the

triumvirate's military strategy, Sorak and Leben could have had no idea that the last thing that was on the triumvirate commander's mind was joining battle.

36

After his meeting with Nasa, 147 called Marwek and five or six of the senior members of the administration that he could trust to his private quarters. Whilst only desiring a peaceful accommodation with the women, 147 knew that he had to be prepared for the worst. There were those in both camps for whom a decisive military confrontation was the only way forward. Marwek was his only hope in this situation.

By this time, Lenar had rescued Desak and 147's other servants had found the brown-skinned 'slave' woman. Fearful of reporting Desak's escape, the male members of the household dealt with the woman's wounds and despatched her on some chore to the administration building. Fearful in his turn because of his own failings, Crenal said nothing. 147, in the end, never knew that Desak had disappeared.

147 made no mention of his meeting with Nasa, although Marwek was aware of it and suspected that things had changed as a result of this meeting. But she did notice that he had a renewed confidence and was more like the powerful administration slave that she knew from the past. She had mixed feelings; if this was to lead to positive action she would be happy, but if 147 simply wanted to maintain the status quo, she would not.

The administration officials were apprehensive. Their leader's situation report did nothing to quell their concern.

"We are being attacked by two bodies of women," 147 said; he saw no point in hiding the gravity of the situation. "The Yellow gate has been taken by one group and is forming a focus for any discontented women from within the city. A large group has arrived from the Edge via the Red gate to reinforce the women in Sector Four. Their total numbers are greater than the soldiers that we have available."

Whatever Nasa had said to 147, Marwek was quick to realise that he must have provided significant intelligence. From her knowledge of Kragar's rather rigid mental processes she was surprised at the two pronged attack, but although she knew that Pastak was a member of the resistance groups, she had no idea of her influence on the invasion plans. Marwek had never met Pastak, so she had no means of judging her capabilities.

147 knew what he had to do.

"Marwek will take charge of the troops and organise our resistance to the attack," he said.

A surprisingly fierce look from him quelled the rumble of dissent. He was fully aware that none of his subordinates had Marwek's military skills.

"Marwek has no love of the women in Sector Four, and understands the leader of the attack, Kragar, as a fellow former officer in the Senate Guard."

It was the only explanation that he offered.

Mention of Kragar, the most feared of the women in the resistance, ended the dissent. The officials knew that Marwek was the best that they had.

Marwek had no intention of making any direct attacks on the women ranged against her. She understood guerrilla tactics, she had used them briefly before and in the last few circuits of the distant star had identified several areas in the sectors separating them from Kragar's forces where they could best be used. Her key focus was going to be Sectors Two, Five and Six. With the quality of the troops at her disposal she saw guerrilla warfare as her only option, although her preference was not to join battle at all.

She knew that there were risks in her battle plan. Firing down on the advancing troops from the derelict buildings that they would have to work their way through was the safest way of combating them, but that opened the possibility of bodies of male soldiers being cut off and isolated. This was something that she was later able to exploit.

Marwek called together her small band of trusted former women soldiers. She gave each an area to be responsible for and to provide intelligence on.

"Since Kragar can't know all of the troops involved, if she sees you she won't know which side you are on. It's important to know the routes that she is using to advance into Sector One and in what strength."

Taking advantage of the confusion of not knowing which side a woman might be on at any given moment had benefits, but Marwek also knew that it was a tactic that could be used against them as well.

* * *

Pastak had been joined by Quillat and her irregular soldiers. Since Pastak had, as a young officer, been mainly involved in patrolling outside the city, Quillat's local knowledge was of a great help to her.

"We have the strength to overrun a large part of the administration area, but it is there that the men will fight the hardest and there that there will be the most casualties. But we don't want to kill any of the men if it can be avoided."

Quillat acknowledged Pastak's statement. Her less tutored mind found it hard to accept that killing the unruly ex-slaves and young men was to be avoided, but she was just as keen as Pastak to see an end to the fighting and a return to something like normal life. And Quillat accepted that normal life didn't mean life before the original rebellion.

Pastak's patrols had reported numbers of civilian women surrendering to them, and as time passed small numbers of men were doing the same. One capral reported that all the men that they had been approached by were elderly ex-slaves, not very intelligent, confused and only too happy to revert to being managed by women. Pastak was obliged to use a part of the Yellow gatehouse compound as a prison camp. The old men were given duties, but were not allowed to serve the women in the camp. There was to be no going back to former times, even if these old men wanted it.

* * *

Kragar's anger at finding Sorak and Leben in Sector Four and her suspicions that they were trying to undermine what she was planning to do didn't interfere with her firm direction of the troops under her command. She was a good soldier.

The biggest problem for the advancing troops was the need to pass through a mixture of narrow streets bordered by two and three storey buildings, and the open areas associated with both the military barracks and administrative areas. These were features of Sectors Two and Six, both of which led to Sector One.

Kragar's reconnaissance told her that although an approach to Sector One via Sector Six might be the easiest, the need to cross the piazza that divided the two sectors was a major risk. The area around the piazza was a natural site for an ambush. Totally familiar with Sector One from her days as a young tenant in the Senate Guard, she had a clear idea how she would proceed once she had got there; it was getting there against opposition that was the challenge.

"Kragarmam," the young tenant, Meenak, who had supported Sorak, saluted smartly, "a captured civilian in Sector Two says that the triumvirate troops are being led by a Tenant Marwek."

Kragar's face, never the most handsome, contorted into a look of rage that amazed the young officer. Meenak had vaguely heard of Marwek but had no idea that she was Kragar's contemporary in the Senate Guard, nor that they were reputed to be sworn enemies.

Since the advancing forces had the initiative, they took their time in spreading out into Sector Six and later into Sector Two. Kragar had allocated taking over Sector Two to the troops from Sector Four, and had deployed the resistance fighters that she had brought with her into Sector Six. Still not sure that she fully trusted the women who had stayed in the city, charging them with occupying the mainly civilian areas of Sector Two would keep them busy and gave them little chance to obstruct the fighting when it started. The terrain in Sector Two was not conducive to rapid military deployment.

Meenak reported her orders to Sorak, convinced, with some justice, that Kragar was trying to sideline them from the fighting whilst using them to secure large areas of the city. Sorak, by now, had identified the young tenant as one of the people that she would not have to convince of the need to come to terms with the men of the city.

"So, Kragar is going to advance through Sector Six."

Sorak understood the logic of this plan but doubted that Marwek would be drawn into a head-on battle with the experienced women soldiers, even if Sector Six was the ideal place to do so.

She was, of course, correct. Marwek had no intention of directly confronting Kragar.

"We will be in a better position if we accompany Kragar,"

Sorak said to Leben. "There isn't going to be much fighting in Sector Two."

Leben agreed, but she was no more confident than Sorak that they could prevent Kragar's troops from killing any man who came within their range. However, it was late, the distant star was setting; they would have to await its return for the action to start.

The attacking forces settled for the night in the derelict buildings of the Sector Six barracks and the old military headquarters, and in more comfort in the accommodation areas and open spaces of Sector Two. Runners between the sectors kept the officers abreast of the dispositions. Kragar had no expectation of action during the nighttime.

But for Marwek the nighttime was a period of opportunity.

As the second moon rose for the first time, bathing the city in a brief bright light, the dull thud of crossbow bolts finding their mark went unnoticed as the outlying sentries in Sector Six were brought down. Small groups of black-clad male soldiers hurried through the lines and into several of the buildings. Marwek wasn't happy that six women had had to be killed, but stealth was absolutely essential; she hoped that nonetheless the death toll could be kept low. That was up to Kragar.

As the second moon made its second circuit the alarm was raised as the sentries were being replaced.

"They will have got into the buildings," Kragar said, hurriedly roused from sleep.

She understood what Marwek was about. Why else had these particular sentries been killed?

Kragar knew that she had to either change her proposed route through to Sector One or run the gauntlet that she presumed Marwek had established. Being Kragar, she wasn't prepared to change the route and acknowledge that she had been outwitted. She continued to forge her way through Sector Six.

The orders to the male soldiers were very clear. Shoot to disable, not to kill. This wasn't popular, but Marwek's reputation was enough to secure compliance.

The tension mounted.

Leben, not being a soldier, was very nervous when she and Sorak set off with one of Kragar's patrols. The decision to head straight on rather than try and evade the areas where they supposed that Marwek had placed her sharpshooters, she knew, had exposed them as much as the troops.

Sorak, not having to move in formation indicated to Leben to simply walk as close to the walls as possible. Screams alerted them to the action as three soldiers were struck in the legs by crossbow bolts. It was obvious to Sorak as well as Kragar what the tactic was.

Disable, not kill. That pleased Sorak.

"We move on," Kragar said.

Well aware that they would be leaving small parties of male soldiers in their rear, something that Marwek had finally realised couldn't be avoided, she reorganised the marching order to protect their rear and flank.

"We're being channelled," Sorak said, also recognising Marwek's tactics.

Leben looked at her, not understanding.

"The shooting has been arranged so that we are forced to move along the main thoroughfare of Sector Six, which leads to the closed arena."

"Why?"

Sorak had no answer for Leben. At least she didn't until the troops began to bunch up and it became obvious that there was some obstruction ahead. Debris from the damaged buildings had been piled into the roads that led into the open area in front of the closed arena. Only one route was unblocked. It took them straight into the arena.

This is the last place I would have thought that Marwek would have sought a confrontation.

Recognising the poor quality of the male soldiers, Sorak was totally bemused.

Kragar ordered her troops back into the shelter of the buildings. From behind the barricades the retreating figures were assailed about the legs with more disabling crossbow shots. Much to Kragar's anger, some of the soldiers broke ranks in their hurry to get out of range. Her fury increased when she realised that she was no longer dictating the course of the action.

Sorak and Leben edged forward, notwithstanding the risk.

What then happened, Sorak couldn't have anticipated; nothing in her military training or life's experiences could have warned her.

There was movement as one of the barricades blocking one of the streets opened and two very nervous male soldiers appeared waving a white flag. Kragar had no idea what the white flag was supposed to mean, but nonetheless ordered her troops to hold their fire.

"Kragar!"

Marwek then stepped out in front of her two soldiers. It didn't take Kragar long to understand that her former colleague was seeking a personal confrontation

She moved out into the open area and, noting that Marwek was only armed with her sword, she threw down her crossbow before she then advanced towards her.

37

After his meeting with 147, Nasa headed for the kitchen and servants' quarters on the ground floor. Still in a panic over Desak's disappearance, and having no idea who he was, only the brown-skinned woman amongst the servants seemed prepared to talk to him, and even she took some coaxing.

Nasa's direct question of whether Lenar, whom he described, or Desak, had been in 147's house eventually elicited an acknowledgement that his son, at least, had been, but had left hurriedly. Desak's presence was denied, but Nasa had a feeling that nonetheless they knew who she was.

The brown-skinned woman's explanation, on questioning, of how she came by her wounds made no sense to Nasa. Lenar was never aggressive, so he pressed her for more information.

"That is not how it happened. Is it?"

With still no idea who Nasa was, she stuck with her story.

"Lenar is my son," he finally said. "I need to know where he is and that he is safe."

Nasa met with the usual incomprehension over his relationship with Lenar. But once she had grasped what she was being told, the information was enough for the brown-skinned woman to be more forthcoming.

"They headed into the bad buildings," the woman said.

The bad buildings seemed to be what the derelict remains of the Senate House and the accommodation of the old women senators and officials were called. As Nasa had come to realise, this was a vast area.

Having gained as much information as he could, he set off to start his search.

* * *

As the angry figure of Kragar marched out into the middle of the open area in front of the closed arena, Marwek moved a few paces further towards her and then waited.

Sorak, in her turn, moved out of the shadow of the building where she and Leben had watched the unfolding situation. Leben didn't follow her at first. Kragar was unaware of the movement. Marwek wasn't, but made no show of recognising Sorak's implicit involvement in what was about to happen.

"Klaan-curs," Kragar spluttered, resurrecting a long dead curse of the soldiers, "surrender your arms and withdraw. You have until the distant star is overhead."

"And then what?"

Sorak wasn't surprised that Marwek ignored the order to disarm, but she was surprised by the calm way that she demanded to know what would happen after any such surrender. Knowing that Kragar had declared her intention to kill any armed male soldier that she encountered, for Marwek it was an obvious question. For Sorak the 'what then' was more about how they first organised a peace process, and then reorganised the society of the city.

But Kragar was struggling for a response.

So Marwek got no immediate answer. Kragar's slow thinking brain had, in accepting Marwek's question, slowly realised that the former slaves could not just return to their former mistresses, the young males had had no mistresses, and many of these mistresses were dead.

After a long silence, Kragar eventually said, "Each man will be allocated a mistress or a working role. Any man who resists will be punished."

Sorak simply couldn't believe what she was hearing. Kragar still obviously hadn't seemed to have registered just how things had changed, or she chose not to.

"There will be no surrendering of arms. The men will continue to run the city; any woman who wishes to join them, and who has the skills needed, will be welcome. Any man or any woman will be able to breed with whosoever they wish, and they will be jointly responsible for the care of the children that they bear."

This, however, was something that Sorak could believe that she was hearing, but she had had no idea that Marwek had even known what the enlightened women were thinking.

But for Marwek it was simply 147's mantra, as quoted from Nasa, not that Sorak had any notion that Nasa had sold their vision of the future to 147.

As Kragar drew her sword and advanced on Marwek, it was clear that nothing that had just been said had lodged in her brain.

"Hold!"

Sorak bounded forward into the narrowing gap between the two women.

"Kragar," she said, "we cannot go back to the days when the women ran the city. We cannot!"

Kragar hesitated. She'd heard the words, but only as defiance of her wishes.

But as the leaders confronted each other a clash seemed imminent,

Then there were noises around them. Several bodies of women soldiers had emerged from the streets and buildings surrounding the open area, and male soldiers were pulling aside the barricades and forming up. The men were outnumbered, generally shorter than the women and inexperienced in fighting, but nonetheless determined that female domination should not be forced on them again.

"Kragar, there must be no more killing. The city will die if we keep killing each other. There won't be enough people to breed."

Sorak continued her urging.

Again, Kragar had heard the words but her brain didn't seem to be programmed to accept them.

Leben had joined Sorak. Marwek had quietly drawn her own sword as Sorak confronted Kragar.

"Kragar," Leben said, "Sorak and Marwek are right. If we fight now and kill each other we will be killing the city as well as ourselves."

This time Kragar only heard the defiance. Beside herself with rage, the blow that she aimed at Leben almost decapitated her. Forced back by Marwek and Sorak, who had quickly drawn her own sword, a furious Kragar raged incoherently.

Stunned by the violence of their leader, the young tenant, Meenak, ran forward and checked Leben for life signs. There were none.

Kragar's violence was finally too much for Meenak.

"Into the closed arena," the tenant said, "you must be punished for this."

Hemmed in by a cordon of angry women soldiers, Kragar was forced into the closed arena. Women and men in roughly equal numbers were allowed in and sat on opposite sides of the combat space. For Meenak this was the only way to forestall any fighting between the soldiers whilst their officers concentrated on Kragar's punishment.

Sorak didn't have time wonder how Meenak knew about the pre-rebellion way of punishing errant women.

But things were moving too fast for Marwek.

"No," she said, as the young tenant, having disarmed Kragar, prepared to execute her. "No, she deserves better than a criminal's death. Give her back her sword."

It was a tense moment. Meenak hesitated. She couldn't understand why Marwek should want to mitigate Kragar's crime.

But Sorak nodded to the tenant. Marwek, she felt, like Kragar, still hankered after some of the things from their past; and the honour of the Senate Guard was a powerful common bond. Death in combat in the arena was the punishment for Kragar's crime from the days that she yearned for. But there was no other criminal to act as her opponent. Marwek offered herself, even at the possible expense of her own life, to allow her former colleague to at least die with some dignity.

As the arrangements for the combat were being made, Sorak's angst at Leben's death welled up and shielded her to a large extent from the savagery of the reversion to the past that she would normally have vigorously opposed. However, Meenak had the maturity to recognise that if Kragar had been allowed to get away with killing Leben, she would have seen it as an endorsement of her warped way of determining the future.

Two wooden shields had been procured from the arena stores and the combatants stripped naked, as was the custom.

Both were skilful swordswomen and had not the circumstances been so dire, many of the women soldiers would have relished such a quality combat. But there was too much hanging on the result.

Sorak and Meenak knew that should Kragar prevail they would have to put her to death themselves, an action that might incite a violent reaction from the women soldiers who supported Kragar's view of the future of the city.

But they had no time to worry about such considerations.

The two combatants circled each other, each anxious not to be backed against the wall of the arena. The occasional dull thud marked a blow parried by a shield. Equally matched in reach, Marwek was probably the more agile, but Kragar had immense strength in her upper body. At this stage they were only testing each other out.

Then, whether from tiredness or by intent, they stopped their circling when they were out in the centre of the arena. A clash of metal heralded a change in the pattern of the fight as they engaged with their swords directly. A loud splintering thud followed as Kragar smashed her shield against Marwek's. It was a bad move as her shield disintegrated, leaving her with only the narrow centre portion. It was an opportunity. Covering her body with her own shield, Marwek rushed at Kragar, forcing her to stumble backwards.

Caught off balance, a groan from Kragar marked a slash across the thigh from Marwek that drew copious quantities of blood and, more importantly, slowed Kragar down.

Recognising that Kragar, wounded, was now at her most dangerous, Marwek drew back and covered herself with her shield again, with only her head peering over the top and her sword arm visible at the side. Kragar's rasping breaths were audible all around the arena.

Then, sensing that her wound was rapidly weakening her, Marwek began to move around her opponent forcing her to expend energy to always be able to present a defensive face to her. Having to drag her damaged leg, Kragar's movements were now cumbersome and slow, but she still managed to cover the vulnerable parts of her body.

As it began to be apparent that the fight couldn't go on for much longer, both the male and female soldiers readied themselves for what might follow.

Back in the arena, the circling continued and resulted in

Kragar eventually being backed against the arena wall. Then, almost as if she was tired of the battle and just wanted a quick end to the encounter, Marwek thrust forward with her shield, Kragar throwing out her own shield arm to try to maintain her balance. Marwek's stabbing thrust into her chest ended the contest and Kragar's life.

As Meenak came forward to check that Kragar was dead, Marwek threw away her sword and shield in self-disgust and headed into the bowels of the arena. Emerging fully clothed, she disappeared into the mass of derelict buildings without saying a word.

"Leave her!"

Sorak had recovered herself sufficiently to stop some of the women soldiers heading off after Marwek. She was afraid that they might do her harm. There had been death enough.

At Sorak's order the women soldiers were mustered in the open area outside the arena. As they did so the male soldiers formed up and marched back to the administration buildings.

There was still tension in the air and Sorak called the young tenant in charge of the Sector Four troops to her. A second tenant, almost as pale-skinned as Sorak, arrived with Meenak, her expression angry and uncertain. As Kragar's deputy, she had a difficult role to play. The anger that Kragar's death had generated needed to be dealt with, Sorak understood that, but many of the resistance fighters had followed Kragar because they too wanted a return to the past. Many of them knew Sorak, knew her history, admired her independence, but couldn't relate to her attitude to the men of the city.

"We should all return to barracks. There will be no attack on the administration area. There will be no more fighting."

In the event, Sorak had gained sufficient respect amongst Kragar's followers for her edict to be obeyed.

38

Awakened by the light from the distant star falling on his naked back, Lenar took a moment to recall where he was or, at least, to recall that he was laying on a bed with Desak. Where he physically was he had no idea. All he knew was that they couldn't be very far from where he had found Desak and heard the voice of his father. But exactly where the burned-out and derelict building that they were hiding in was within the city he was far from clear.

But the son of his father, it didn't worry him now that he was with Desak. Being lost in the city was one thing, but why his father had been there was another.

"Lenar?"

Desak had been awakened by Lenar's movements. She knew that she wanted him inside her again, but sensed that he was not as calm as he had been when they had first settled in the derelict building. Something of his confidence had disappeared.

"Lenar?" she said again.

"I heard my father in that building."

Desak was puzzled.

"Why would your father be visiting 147?"

Having little understanding of what was going on, and no understanding of the frictions between men and women, Lenar could think of no reason for his father to come from Sector Four just to talk to 147. Didn't the man have a name? He wasn't even clear who 147 was, except that he was important and kept women chained up. Neither was he aware that it was Crenal, 147's head of household, who had chained Desak to the wall. 147 himself had long since forgotten about Desak.

She could see that Lenar was in a quandary. She had long since learned that his face was open and transparent, he had no guile, what he was thinking was what was in his face. He clearly wanted to go back to the house and find his father, yet he didn't know how to achieve this, nor did he want to leave Desak now that he had found her.

"Lenar!"

The tone had changed. Rather than the almost plaintive, questioning tone, Desak now sounded alarmed. She had heard something. Lenar had heard it too, and he knew what it was.

"Women," he said quietly, hurriedly shrugging himself into his clothes and drawing his sword.

Someone was searching the building.

Gesturing Desak to silence, Lenar moved to stand by the entrance to the room and waited. This was back to the all-action Lenar that Desak knew and understood.

Two women, armed but not soldiers, peered through into the room, one older and one young. Seeing Desak sitting frozen on the bed, they advanced cautiously.

"You are welcome!"

The two women whirled around, swords raised, to find themselves facing a grinning Lenar. To Desak's total amazement the older woman and Lenar embraced.

"Quillat," Lenar exclaimed, manifestly pleased to see her.

It was part question, part explanation to Desak. Lenar had told her about his time with Quillat's group and their support in his search for her. As the younger woman with Quillat stood guard, Desak was herself treated to an embrace. Knowing her background, Desak found Quillat's behaviour extraordinary; from Lenar's description she had expected her to be hard and unfriendly. But the collapse of the old women's regime had given Quillat a new lease of life, and a life that was kinder and less brutal than that of her past in the Senate prison service.

"We have joined with Pastak," Quillat said by way of an explanation of her own.

Having met her, Lenar of course knew who Pastak was.

"She is holding the Yellow gate. The other women from the Edge have entered by the Red gate led by a former Senate Guard tenant, Kragar."

Lenar definitely knew who Kragar was!

"Something is going on in Sector Six, or was expected to be going on. All the male soldiers that the triumvirate could muster were sent there, but there was no fighting and it appears that the male soldiers returned to the administration area."

Quillat was clearly puzzled. She knew who Marwek was, but not her personal interest in confronting Kragar and her troops. Lenar and Desak, of course, knew even less about these events.

"Pastak has sent Risak to Sorak, to your mother, to find out what has happened. It's good that there was no fighting, but that doesn't solve anything."

Lenar and Desak could only listen. They had suddenly become bystanders, something that didn't bother Desak, but something that made Lenar even more anxious to make contact with Nasa. Something was clearly expected of his mother; that worried him even more since he only had a very hazy idea of his mother's former military capabilities.

"Pastak has started to occupy the buildings around the old Senate House and library. The male soldiers don't seem to want to try and stop her. We were sent out to patrol and to locate the living quarters of the triumvirate leaders, or leader, as there now seems to be only one left. 147."

"We came from 147's house," Lenar said as Desak suddenly became very agitated.

"You can take us there?" Quillat was quick to see the possibilities of Lenar's help.

Lenar would have been happy to help, but his concern was more about what would happen to Desak if they returned to 147's house.

"But Desak can't go back," Lenar said. "She was captured and made to work in 147's kitchen. They would kill her if they caught her, as a runaway."

Quillat didn't at first see the problem. They were going to 147's house to capture him. But Desak's obvious fear finally registered with her and she proposed that Desak go to the Yellow gatehouse and wait for Lenar there; she could spare one of her troopers as an escort. Neither Lenar nor Desak were happy about this, but with the prospect of also finding his father at 147's house, Lenar agreed.

At the time of Lenar's and Desak's conversation with Quillat, they would not have found Nasa at 147's house. Having urged 147 to try to make peace with the women, and feeling hostility amongst 147's followers, who were feeling vulnerable, after his conversation with the brown-skinned woman he had quickly helped himself to some food in the kitchen and left the area of the house.

Lenar, where would you go once you had released Desak?

Where Nasa himself would have gone was back to Sorak and the safety of the hut under the city wall. Although in his old slave days he had had no equivalent to the burgeoning young manhood that his son was experiencing, he had had undying feelings for a woman, and assumed that Lenar would want to spend as much time as he could with Desak before the realities of life caught up with them.

I'd find a safe place to hide and…

Memories stirred in the depths of Nasa's brain of a cold night beside a lake when he and Sorak became one physically as well as mentally, and the very youth that he was so anxious about was conceived.

Hide and couple with Desak was exactly what Lenar had done!

And find a building with a usable and safe upper floor was also what Lenar did, as Nasa would have done.

Amongst the burned-out and derelict buildings, seeking one with more than one storey narrowed the odds considerably. Recalling his brief time with Leben, Nasa had a reasonable idea where to head if he could first get his bearings. Far less sure of himself in the narrow streets and lanes of Sector One that stood behind the old Senate complex, Nasa moved cautiously. In fact, he was far from sure that he was still in Sector One.

"Mother's heart," Nasa whispered to himself with a laugh, as he plunged into the maze of buildings, "there are people even here."

Nasa, like most of the inhabitants of the city, really had no idea how many people actually lived there, and how many had then survived the upheavals of the last seventeen cycles of the distant star. As he crept along the narrow streets, keeping as close to the wall as he could, what he heard were women's voices coming from inside the building that he was passing. He halted. There was an entrance way that he would have to pass across.

But before he got the chance a group of nine or ten lean and hungry-looking civilians, some hardly wearing any clothes, and all armed with clubs or knives, had swarmed out of the entrance and surrounded him. The situation was more threatening than anything that he had faced so far.

"Hold!"

The measured tramp of a disciplined body of troops filled the silence that accompanied the action against Nasa.

A brief period of confusion ensued.

The civilians turned to face the armed women who had confronted them. Nasa took the opportunity to break out of the encirclement. What turned out to be a mangeneer, the leader of the civilian party, stepped forward to the head of the armed group and raised her hand. Weapons were lowered, but all of the women remained wary.

"Father!"

As Nasa separated himself from the civilians, Lenar caught sight of him.

"So, what is happening here?" demanded Quillat.

"We just wanted to know what a lone man was doing wandering around the bad buildings," the mangeneer said.

All was quickly explained. To the surprise of both Nasa and Quillat it seemed that there were many civilians, and again no one seemed to know how many, hiding in the old buildings or just living out their lives in the houses that they had always lived in in the days before the rebellion. They had food sources, they continued to run things like some of the food gardens and animal husbandry, and there were men who had joined them and bred with them.

A sub-world had developed under the eyes of the various male administrations that simply self-perpetuated without impacting the mainstream of what was going on in the city. It was very much what Sorak and her supporters saw as the future.

But the situation was fragile and rejected by the purists of both genders; consequently, strangers were not welcome. Nasa was obviously a stranger.

And all of this was going on within a few street blocks from the administration buildings and triumvirate living quarters. Nasa was incredulous; Quillat was suspicious, but for her anything was now possible. She was aware of such pockets of people getting on with their lives within the nooks and crannies of the city.

"We will have to trust them," Quillat said to Nasa and Lenar.

Quillat spoke briefly to the mangeneer leading the group and told her that they were on patrol and wouldn't trouble them anymore. Also, that they wouldn't be coming back that way. She outlined what she thought the civilians should know about the situation developing between the triumvirate and the invading women soldiers. It was cautionary.

"Stay out of sight. A confrontation is developing. When it's over, hopefully things will be different and you won't have to hide."

When they arrived at 147's house, Nasa remained in the background. He felt a little guilty. The other senior members of the triumvirate organisation had gone, leaving 147 and a small group of bodyguards who were easily overcome. Nasa couldn't believe that things had collapsed so quickly; it was less of an anticlimax, increasingly more of a farce.

147 was readily captured.

"Nasa, I hope that we can bring an end to this," 147 said.

39

Marwek's retreat from Sector Six and the closed arena was angry and unthinking. She was ashamed of herself at the rage that she had displayed in fighting Kragar. However much she had disliked her former Senate Guard colleague, she should not have lost control of herself, as she saw it, in front of so many people.

She also felt ashamed of herself because she perceived that Sorak and the other women who were seeking to come to terms with the male administration would not see her as serious about sharing their views. She was a killer and she recognised that killers had no place in the world that she thought that Sorak was seeking to create. Had she known, Sorak in fact didn't condemn her, she simply saw her as a product of her background.

And Marwek, as was Pastak, as was the young tenant Meenak, and the others of the women, were according Sorak a role in the future that she perhaps would not have wanted. But one thing was clear to Marwek: someone had to take charge of the situation, someone not driven by self-interest or a hankering for a past that could never be recovered. Who else but Sorak?

"I must find Sorak and make my peace with the women in Sector Four."

This Marwek realised had to be the starting point for any relationship with the other women.

But having now retreated right back into the area surrounding the triumvirate administration building and not being far from 147's living quarters, it occurred to Marwek that capturing and presenting 147 to Sorak and the other women would be an ideal way of restoring their faith in her. How she was to achieve this, in the urgency of the moment, she gave no thought to.

But, as she emerged from the narrow street opposite the entrance to 147's residence, she saw that she was too late.

* * *

Risak knew where to find Sorak. The hut built against the outer city wall, and with the wandering herd of animals no longer being properly managed as cover, was an ideal hideout.

But, nonetheless, Risak was a good soldier and approached the hut cautiously. Having travelled around the Edge with Pastak's armed group for several circuits of the distant star she was out of touch with immediate events and was therefore uncertain as to whether she would find Nasa with Sorak, or even their son. A runner from Kragar's group had arrived at the Yellow gate just before they were about to move into Sector One, but the runner had been delayed by having to evade a massive increase in male patrols as they prepared to defend the administration area. Risak had no idea of the outcome of the expected encounter, especially as she had had to frequently seek refuge in derelict buildings from bodies of male soldiers who appeared to be returning to their home area in good order.

None of this made much sense to Risak.

"Sorak will know," she told herself.

Sorak was aware of the outcome of the confrontation between Kragar and Marwek, but was ignorant of what was happening in Sector One once Pastak had secured her base and had moved into the triumvirate's area.

With 147 snatched by Quillat and Nasa, and seemingly happy to be so, Pastak's troops had no difficulty with taking over the whole of the administration area. The functioning triumvirate just seemed to have evaporated, much as the previous administrations had done when a superior force confronted them. In this case it was armed women rather than other men.

I can't believe that it was so easy.

Pastak was concerned. The triumvirate, like the other male administration before them, had always fought hard to maintain their position; now they weren't doing so. Capturing 147 was just too easy, as if the larger triumvirate were handing him over to them. But why? And why had they evacuated the administration even without a fight?

Sitting in what was 147's place in the administration communal room, Pastak was beginning to feel that events had moved too quickly, and that she was somehow not really in control in Sector One. Lacking anything other than military experience, she couldn't grasp that the administration and therefore control of the city could be taken over with so little effort and with the involvement of so few people. In reality in the case of the city as few as ten people was all that was necessary to give a particular character to any administration. The rest of the bodies, of activities, of requirements were common to whatever administration was in place. And also in reality the administration could be run from almost anywhere in the city where the leaders could gather.

It was not certain that the triumvirate administration had collapsed, only that it had escaped the administration area.

As Risak finally arrived at the wall-side hut and had reconnoitred it and its surroundings another runner had arrived to report to Kragar that the administration buildings were now in the women's hands. Quickly discovering that there was no Kragar and that the capan seemed incapable of coherent thought, the soldier sought out Meenak and the other tenants to deliver her message.

Reflecting the spectrum of views still apparent amongst the soldiers, the news was received with mixed feelings. It was recognised that holding the buildings wasn't controlling the administration, but at least the administration was in disarray.

As the women soldiers gathered for their meal in the communal area they gravitated naturally into small groups representing the shades of opinion. Kragar's pale-skinned deputy, Senak, was excited. Sharing Kragar's desire to put the clock back to before the original rebellion, she and her small caucus of colleagues began to make plans to return to Sector One. But first Senak wanted to hear what Sorak had to say. She was aware now that without Sorak's endorsement her actions would have no validity, yet she was loath to seek Sorak's approval.

"We must get Sorak to come and tell us what we should do now. If there is to be no attack on the administration area, how do we come to an understanding with the men?"

Meenak, the newly appointed young tenant, made her statement tentatively. Not all of the women were as clear thinking as she was, especially the older soldiers, who in any uncertain situation always looked for guidance from past experience. Having only lived in the post-rebellion world Meenak found this attitude hard to understand. For her you either fought with the men or you did a deal with them. Expecting to dominate without resistance was unthinkable.

Like Risak, Meenak knew where to find Sorak, and she knew that she had remained at the hut despite Leben and Nasa having gone back to Sector One. She knew this because she had recruited one of the civilians who used to work in the animal husbandry unit, to keep an eye on Sorak.

"The attack didn't happen," Sorak told Risak. "Kragar was killed by Marwek in the closed arena."

Risak was incredulous, but her disbelief was overcome by sadness and regret over the death of Leben. Although Leben had been something of an enigma to straightforward people like Risak, she was respected, and her death was a loss.

"Nasa will be sad," Risak said, knowing that Leben and Nasa were on good terms, but not knowing their true relationship.

Having talked through the confrontation between Kragar and Marwek, Risak sensed a new excitement in Sorak. She knew that people like Kragar's deputy Senak were equally against any accommodation with the men, but her sense was that there might now be a majority in favour amongst the troops in Sector Four. She was sure that this was what was exciting Sorak. They had a chance to bring an end to the animosity between the men and the women and to give the city a future again. What had happened to Marwek and where she might be attracted no comment.

"We must get the women together and get their agreement," said Sorak.

Her excitement was certainly rising, almost despite herself. She wished that Nasa was with her to give her strength, and she wished that she knew that Lenar was safe, but, having mentally accepted a role in bringing an end to the gender confrontation, all she wanted to do was get on with it.

She knew that she and Leben had done the groundwork, but they needed to force the issue and work out a plan of action to deal with anyone who might want to try and obstruct an accommodation. Sorak hoped that there wouldn't be many.

What Sorak still didn't yet know was that Pastak was in control of the administration area and that 147 was on his way to Sector Four with Nasa and a group of auxiliary fighters under Quillat. But Meenak and the other tenants in Sector Four did know this.

Meenak wanted Sorak to come and take charge, and Sorak wanted to persuade the women to support a peace initiative.

The scene was set.

40

Meenak's spy alerted her to the fact that Sorak and another soldier had left the herdsmen's hut and were heading for the sewage area. Since this was considered the safest way to Sector Four barracks, Meenak had no doubt that that was where they were headed. Her civilian had no idea who the other soldier was, only that she had been to the hut before and was clearly on good terms with Sorak. After consulting the other tenants, Meenak called all of the available women together to the communal area of the barracks. For form's sake, the old capan was sitting on the small dais that Meenak had had set up so that Sorak, when she arrived, could be seen by everybody.

The women were in a ferment of anticipation. They all knew what they had been called together for. After all the activity of the last few circuits of the distant star, they knew that it had to be decision time. The shades of opinion still existed but the women also knew that some sort of common position had to be achieved. How was the situation to be resolved otherwise? And all the women wanted the situation resolved.

Senak, Kragar's follower, and her small group of discontents, the main opponents of compromise, hovered at the edge of the main gathering.

Although the body of soldiers gathered was only a small proportion of the women of the city, many of whom had disappeared from view over the cycles of the distant star, they were armed, organised and had recognised leaders. Very few civilians would have challenged their right to decide how to deal with the male administration since they were perceived to have the power to enforce any accommodation agreed should that be necessary.

There was a roar and a great stamping of feet as Sorak entered the room accompanied by Meenak, Risak and three of the other tenants. The bemused capan rose to her feet and waved for silence. Her mental faculties much diminished and her hold on reality suspect, she nonetheless was conscious of her seniority. When silence was finally achieved, the capan sat down again, clearly with no idea what was happening or was about to happen.

The dais had been set up at the end of the room with entrances to the communal area at each side, one of which Sorak had just used. The whole area was not secure but, within the heart of the barracks, no one had seen any need for security.

The silence held.

Sorak climbed onto the dais with Meenak. The women surged forward to get the best view possible, but the other tenants were careful to hold them back from coming within weapons' range of Sorak, as every woman present was armed with a sword. Conscious that not all of the women were in support of what it was supposed that Sorak was going to say, the atmosphere was excitable, and unpredictable.

Sorak held up her arms in much the same way as the capan had done to ensure silence. It was a gesture of communication, of establishing contact.

"Pastak's troops have taken control of the administration area." Meenak had hurriedly updated Sorak as they walked to the communal area. "There was no fighting."

Sorak didn't say that there was no one to fight! "As you all know there was a confrontation with the male soldiers in Sector Six but again there was no fighting."

This was code for what had happened outside the closed arena. For Sorak, there was no need to say more, but the rumble of noise that greeted this statement told her that Kragar's death was still an issue. And there were still those who were angry and disappointed that there had been no battle with the male soldiers, irrespective of the clash between Kragar and Marwek.

Sorak continued.

"Only one member of the triumvirate is still alive. We will negotiate with him on a form of administration that recognises men as of equal status as women, that gives control of the administration jointly to men and women, and that punishes any violence between men and women."

Sorak hurried on before there was any reaction to her statement.

"Men and women will be free to breed with whoever they like, but they, and not the city, will be responsible for the care and training of their children."

But Sorak got no further.

A figure suddenly erupted onto the dais, sword in hand, and swung wildly at Sorak. A surge of noise followed.

Meenak moved to grapple with the assailant as Sorak instinctively ducked below the flailing sword arm. Carried forward by the momentum of her swing the sword struck the capan across the neck and almost decapitated her. Sorak had no space to draw her own sword so she rose up and grasped the woman's sword arm trying to force her off balance. Conscious as she bore down on the woman's sword arm that she was preparing to strike down at her with her free hand, Sorak threw her whole body weight against the woman's chest. But, as she did so, her assailant's body went limp and collapsed onto her.

Unseen by Sorak, but not by the gathered women, another figure emerged from the side entrance to the communal room and leapt onto the dais swinging a crossbow like a club. Struck down, the assailant collapsed onto the dais.

There was a moment of total silence then a great surge of noise.

As a scuffle broke out in the front of the crowd between what appeared to be the supporters of the assailant and the women around them, Meenak and one of the other tenants, forcing a passage, dragged the body of the woman from the dais and tossed it face up onto the floor.

"Senak," said Meenak in a surprised voice.

The pale-skinned young woman wasn't dead. Clubbed down with the butt of a crossbow as she tried to resist Sorak's attack, Senak had let out a strangled scream as she collapsed.

In the immediate chaos of the action to stop Senak, no one noticed the expiration of breath as the capan slid to the floor of the dais, blood briefly streaming from a massive neck wound. Sorak, painfully pulling herself to her feet, just had time to register the capan's demise before she was conscious of the figure who moved to stand beside her.

"Marwek!" she said in even greater surprise as she recognised her saviour.

Another surge of noise and the swirling mass of women trying to get a better view of what was happening at the front of the audience quickly subsided when it became known what had transpired. The news of the encounter quickly spread throughout the communal area and to every woman in the building.

Kragar's deputy, known to have been increasingly angry at the way things were turning out, had decided that the best way to halt the momentum gathering was to kill Sorak. Those opposed to integration with the men would then get another chance to force their views on the other women. But Senak could not have known how her murderous intention would be received by the great mass of the women.

Finally, the silence of horror descended as the women at last realised that their capan had been killed in Senak's wild attempt to reach Sorak. The whole communal area was stunned. And to many of the women a sense of reality after all the wild rhetoric and posturing began to set in. There simply had to be an end to the violence, the uncertainties, and a future agreed. The aging capan might not have died in vain.

But they seemed to have lost the moment. Sorak stood on the dais now uncertain how to bring the gathered women back to both reality and to the frame of mind necessary to make long-term decisions.

Angrily tossing aside her crossbow, Marwek stood beside Meenak and studied the seething mass of women with something more like amusement than fear. Sorak moved to stand with them. As a confusion of noise returned as the women began to share their thoughts and fears, none of the three knew how to get the control of the gathering again.

But once again events rushed past the debating women.

Something was happening at the back of the room where there was another entrance to the communal area. Isolated from the action close to the dais, the women at the back of the crowd became aware that they had been joined by a mixed group of strangers. The presence of men in the group was enough to create an outcry that quickly attracted attention from the dais.

Marwek, standing beside Meenak and Sorak, immediately focused on the new upheaval.

"147!"

"Nasa!"

Recognition came to both Marwek and Sorak at the same time.

How can this be?

It was also a common thought.

Quillat and Nasa had hurried 147 through the back streets of Sectors One and Six and then to Sector Four. Quillat was contemptuous of the lack of security but, after so many cycles of the distant star being a fugitive, it was the first time that she had found herself in a safe place for some time. How safe a place, she was maybe about to find out.

The group finally entered the Sector Four barracks area and paused. 147, who was both aged and intermittently fearful, needed to rest. Nasa needed to be sure that they would find Sorak at the communal meeting. As the others settled in a derelict barracks building, he hurriedly reconnoitred the nearby public areas. The noise confirmed a meeting; Sorak's presence was going to have to be an assumption.

But knowing how Sorak thought and being conscious of her determination, Nasa correctly assumed that once the news that Pastak had secured the administration area had arrived Sorak would act.

"They are all gathered in the communal area," Nasa told Quillat and 147 after his scouting expedition. "It's very noisy. Something important has happened, the place is seething."

147's black face was a fleeting picture of uncertainty, of concern, of confidence, and finally of concern again. Turmoil would not be good news for him. Unless the women were united and agreed there was no guarantee of his safety. But there was only one way to know.

"We must confront them," said the ever-practical Quillat.

At first no one took any notice of them as they had entered the communal area via a back entrance. The crowd of women seemed to be entirely focused on what was happening at the front near the dais. It was only when they saw Marwek and Sorak along with a young tenant on the dais that Nasa relaxed a little. But Marwek's presence was a confusion to both him and Quillat.

Very quickly, the women at the back of the crowd, detached from what was going on at the front, noticed them. And then the group on the dais did too.

The young tenant Meenak frantically waved her arms for silence. Eventually it was achieved, but there was tension and uncertainty all round.

What was happening now?

Quillat, followed by 147 flanked by two of her fighters, moved forward. With the rest of her troopers forming a phalanx around Nasa she forced a path through the excited women. Arriving at the dais she gestured 147 onto it, and formed her fighters into a guard in front of it along with the Sector Four tenants.

Nasa moved into the background at the side of the dais and watched with his usual pride as Sorak took command of the situation. Forcing a gap in the wall of fighters so that the general body of women could see 147 she signalled for silence again.

"147, you are welcome."

The rumble that followed Sorak's greeting was quelled by an angry gesture from Meenak, suggesting that Sorak's greeting and its implication was still not universally supported.

Sorak continued.

"We are all agreed that we cannot continue the warfare between the men and women of the city."

Being Sorak, she came straight to the point. This time the rumble was muted and overtaken by a surge of stamping of feet that quickly died away. Increasingly, the mass of women was beginning to agree that things had to change.

"We wish there to be an accommodation between us. We here represent the women of the city. Not all of us agree completely with men and women being equal. Not all men will want to share with the women. But we must agree between us. There has been too much killing, and if the killing continues it will be the city that is eventually killed."

This time the silence was absolute. No one now doubted the gravity of the situation and the imperative to deal with it.

147 was much shorter than Sorak, Marwek or Meenak, but he had a presence that everybody recognised. His anxieties largely banished as he walked through the gathered mass of women, many of whom had never seen a black man before, he knew that he could do a deal with Sorak. But he was conscious that he no longer represented the triumvirate or the administration.

But then, in reality, Sorak only represented the women who supported an accommodation, and who were in the room. Both protagonists had a very limited constituency and the success of any deal was not guaranteed.

"We wish to agree an accommodation also," 147 said simply.

More feet stamping was again quelled by a gesture from Meenak.

"I will need to address the administration senior officials. If they agree, we will have an accommodation."

They will agree!

It was a piece of game-playing on 147's part. He had no idea what the latest state of things was in the administrative area, he just needed to make it appear that there still was a coherent administration.

Quillat, who had the best knowledge of the status of the administration buildings, knew that if they were there, with Pastak and her troops camped around them, disagreement by the triumvirate officials wasn't an option. She also knew that there were many men who yearned for an end to the friction between men and women and who would be only too happy to work with the women, even in their former roles, if only they were guaranteed their personal freedom and independence. But what she didn't know for certain, but suspected, was that the senior triumvirate officials had dispersed. There was no coherent administration any more, whatever 147 might have supposed.

Sorak moved to address the women.

"We will talk with 147 and agree exactly how we want the accommodation to work. Quillat and Marwek will return to the administration buildings in Sector One with him and gain agreement there. I know that we don't all agree with this, but we have to make it work."

Sorak moved off the dais with 147, Marwek, Meenak and Quillat. Suddenly what had been a huge and deadly issue seemed to have resolved into something almost mundane. It was only when the scuffles that broke out after they had left the communal area were reported did Sorak realise that there were still those not reconciled.

And again, Marwek had the feeling that it had all been too easy.

"Nasa?"

When the talking was done, Sorak looked for her partner, but he wasn't anywhere to be seen.

"I will come with you."

Risak had found Sorak and prepared to accompany her back to the hut under the city wall. Risak seemed still to be excited by what had happened.

There were noises coming from the hut, but Risak showed no signs of suspicion.

"Lenar!"

Desak looked on with an expression of amused affection as Lenar disappeared into his mother's arms.

Epilogue

An accommodation between the women of the city represented by the soldiers in Sector Four and the male administration represented by 147 had eventually been agreed.

However, there had still been women and men who didn't support the accommodation. The body of women soldiers led by Pastak had taken over the administrative buildings and living quarters, but it was more as a result of a tactical withdrawal by triumvirate forces than a female victory. The women had subsequently been harassed by small groups of male soldiers led by their commander, until Pastak had responded and had begun to successfully capture and neutralise these groups. During the next circuit of the distant star after the meeting in Sector Four, in a rather desperate bid to bring the men to battle, Pastak had finally been able to capture most of the remaining troopers. But five or six of the triumvirate's senior officials had still been unaccounted for.

Having completed the negotiations, Sorak had been reunited with Nasa and their son, and with a Desak whom she almost didn't recognise, so animated was she. After a further long conversation with 147 and Quillat before they had returned to Sector One to engage with the other leaders of the triumvirate, Sorak had expressed a wish to at last retreat to the hut under the city wall.

But even the youthful Meenak had known that this would not be possible.

After Sorak had addressed them the excited crowd of women had milled around the communal area reluctant to return to their individual quarters. Anger and confusion had still been very much in evidence, and the tenants had had to break up several fights between those happy with the outcome of the meeting and those who had felt betrayed.

"It will take time!"

Marwek had been the most confident that the accommodation would work, but she had also been the only one who had had any intimate dealings with the triumvirate officials and knew their quality.

Risak and Quillat and her body of armed civilians had taken 147 back to the administration buildings only to find an angry Pastak and no senior officials.

Angry, disappointed and weary, 147 offered what insights that he could into where the officials might have been hiding. Pastak instituted a search, but she had also called together as many of the lesser administration officials as she had been able to locate and ordered them to work under the new joint regime. There had been very little dissent.

It had taken time. Sorak had not been allowed to retire from the city. There had been a strong feeling that without her to oversee things, progress might be slow, might be obstructed, and with the prospect of this new joint regime being in place everybody wanted it to have happened as quickly as possible. No one had wanted a return to the uncertainties of the last seventeen cycles of the distant star.

A new Senate had been agreed. With only the experience of the past to draw on, and no Senate library to which to refer, the new administration, in concept, had looked superficially very much like all the other administrations since the rebellion.

But there had been real differences.

"The people must choose the senators. We must have a way of allowing them to do that."

No one had disagreed with Sorak. A small Senate with equal numbers of men and women had been established. With great reluctance, Sorak had agreed to be the chairwoman.

The process of choosing the senators had not been perfect, but new ones were to be chosen every three cycles of the distant star. There were to be no permanent senators and no permanent officials.

Immediately after the agreement on the accommodation had been made, a small body of women who hadn't been able to accept the situation decamped to the forest the other side of the Edge. But, unlike the resistance groups, they had no unifying cause, and one by one they had returned to the city and made their peace with Sorak and the Senate.

Similarly noted, but unremarked upon, a number of elderly men, whom 147 would have readily recognised, had emerged from the damaged regions of the city and made their peace too.

With an administration in place it had taken much more time for the new society that Sorak had so wanted to be established and developed than she had hoped for. But with the introduction of family life, and a reward system that favoured achievement rather than gender, a good start had been made.